Widurok

Widurok

by

C. R. Osborne

THE KING'S ENGLAND PRESS
2016

ISBN 978 1 909548 55 8
WIDUROK
is typeset in Book Antiqua and Hergest,
and published by
The King's England Press
111 Meltham Road
Lockwood
HUDDERSFIELD
West Riding of Yorkshire

2nd impression, 2016

Printed and bound in Great Britain by

4Edge Ltd
Hockley, Essex

To my father,
and all those who daydream
of time-travel.

PART ONE

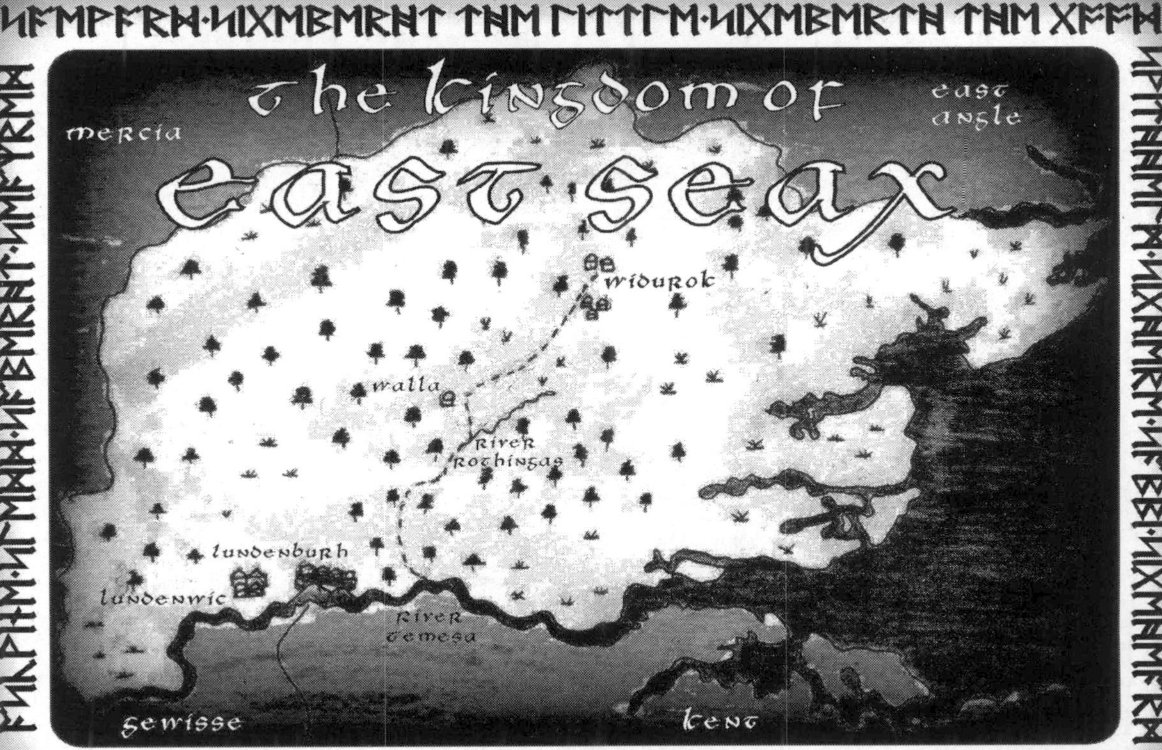

the kingdom of
east seax
mercia
east angle
widurok
walla
river rothingas
lundenburh
lundenwic
river temesa
gewisse
kent

Chapter One: The Pocket Watch

"Hey Millie?" George whispered, "Millie! Are you awake?"

"I am now," his sister grumbled and turned over to face him. Twilight shone through a gap in the thick curtains onto her brother. He was sitting fully awake and clothed on the edge of his bed.

"I think I've lost Grandad's watch."

"What watch?"

"The funny pocket one that he gave to me today, before we went out."

"Umm, he loves that old thing," Millie replied sleepily, wondering why George was bothering her with this now.

"I woke up dreaming about it. I've checked my jeans and it's not there." George rose to his feet. "I'm going to go out and find it."

"*What?* It's the middle of the night! Don't be stupid. Just go back to sleep."

"I can't sleep. Anyway, it's not even that dark. I'm pretty sure it dropped out of my pocket when we were sitting by the skateboard ramp."

Millie pulled the duvet over her head. The power of sleep was commanding her to block George out and sink back into unconsciousness. With no more protests from his sister, George quietly opened their bedroom door and slipped down the stairs of their grandfather's old house.

Chapter Two: Lost

George jogged lightly down the lane with his hands in the pockets of his hoodie and his thick hair bouncing over his face. He headed towards the village churchyard. If he cut straight through the graves he would get to the footpath that led directly to the playing field.

At the churchyard gate George paused. He was slightly reluctant to be alone in the night with the dead, but surely at thirteen you shouldn't believe in ghosts? He took a deep breath and tried hard to consciously put any dark thoughts to the back of his mind. He was *just* taking a short cut.

He lifted the heavy old gate open, willing the rusty hinges to remain silent as they grated against each other. Then with his hands back in his pockets, he headed to the far corner of the churchyard that led down towards the playing field.

Somewhere, the eerie hoot of an owl made George quicken his pace back into a gentle jog. Away from the streetlight the graves stood like dark shadows rising up from the ground. George felt his heart rate quicken and set his eye to the closest source of light as comfort, a brightly lit window of a house. But now, not looking where he was going, George suddenly tripped on the edge of a protruding tree stump and fell hard onto the ground. His hands were still tucked into his pockets and it was his head that took the full force of the fall. George lay on the grassy ground dazed and winded.

Rising onto his knees, he cupped his head in his hands, wincing in pain.

"Ahhh!"

As he started getting his breath back and regaining his full senses, he looked up. The night seemed to have got darker. Something had changed. There was no light coming from any of the houses and the clouds no longer had the orangey glow they normally reflected from the cities. In fact, from the small amount of moonlight, George could only make out trees surrounding the church and the graves. George stood up and squinted his eyes into the dark. Now he felt even more dazed and confused: the churchyard was surrounded by forest! That wasn't right. He turned around to check he was still facing the direction he had been heading in and almost jumped out of his skin. Directly behind him was an enormous ash tree. George was certain he had not seen it here before and he definitely had not just walked past it. He slowly edged his way around the tree to check the church was still in sight. But confirming his worst fears, the church was not there!

"Maybe it's just too dark and I can't see it," George muttered, seeking some logic. "It *is* the middle of the night."

But no, he should be able to make out a grand building such as a church, especially as he could still see the outline of gravestones ... although ... they too were different. There weren't as many stones, and the ones he could distinguish seemed to be very spaced out, although still quite orderly.

George stood next to the tree for several moments not knowing what to do. In the stillness of the night, noises from the forest seemed to grow louder and George became more afraid. The rustling of leaves, the scurrying of some creature, the flapping of wings and then, from further away, the shouting of men!

George remained still, trying to hear which direction the men were coming from as the sound of their voices grew closer. He felt vulnerable standing out in the open ground and quickly ran towards the trees. As he did so a dark grey riderless horse trotted past him and towards the ash tree. George crouched down next to a bush and looked back out to the churchyard. It could no longer be rightfully described as a churchyard, now it was more an open space with a tree in the middle, surrounded by two rings of gravestones.

Through the woodland that surrounded this open space George could make out beacons of light flashing through the trees, which corresponded to the sound of voices. The men were close now. George heard running feet approaching where he crouched, followed by the beating of horse hooves.

"Prince Saeward!" shouted the owner of the footsteps in a thick, slightly Germanic, accent. "Over this way, I can see him in the clearing!"

George crouched down even lower in the bushes. Were they talking about him? The footsteps, followed by hooves, abruptly stopped at the edge of the open space, a few metres away from where George was. He cautiously peered through the leaves.

"There he is, do you see him sir?"

The man talking was standing next to a horse mounted by a young man he had addressed as Prince Saeward. He was pointing towards the huge ash tree. By the light of the torch flame the man was holding, George could guess he was in his early twenties. He was dressed in a cloak and in the same hand as the torch, held a full-faced bronze-coloured helmet. Beneath his cloak, lengths of woollen cloth were bound around his calves and on his feet was a pair of simple leather sandals. The young man on the horse was almost still a boy. He was dressed in much the same attire, although he wore a fine cloak that draped itself luxuriously over the horse's buttocks and thighs. Attached to the saddle was a heavy-looking sword with a hilt of bone.

Maybe they were participating in some kind of travelling show, or returning from a fancy dress party, George tried to reason to himself.

The young prince pivoted in his saddle, keeping a firm grip on the horse's reins. He looked eagerly into the clearing.

"Yes, yes!" Saeward whispered in great excitement.

George followed their line of vision and saw an unsaddled horse standing next to the ash tree that he had fallen beside a few minutes ago. From his viewpoint the horse appeared to have eight legs, instead of four. But surely that must be shadows caused by the light of the moon, which shone onto the dark beast.

Saeward reached for his bow.

"Pass me an arrow Aldwyn," he softly commanded down to the man on foot, his eyes sparking with the thirst of a hunter about to catch his prey. Aldwyn swung down the leather quiver that had been resting on his shoulder. But as he was selecting the finest arrow for his master, another rider approached on the other side of Saeward, concealed from George's viewpoint.

"Sir ... would it not be unwise to kill here?" the rider stammered anxiously. "You know what place this is!"

"Of course I know! The local villagers come here to worship the old gods," Saeward snapped. "What of it?"

"They're not that old. What of the consequences? It's sacrilege!" The panic in the rider's voice overshadowed his reasoning.

"Quiet! You're going to disturb the kill." Saeward reached down and took the arrow from Aldwyn. He felt angry that the magic of this moment now seemed slightly tainted. There *was* a part of him that knew it would be wrong to shoot the grey stallion here. But it was such a unique animal and such a magnificent prize. This was his chance, his moment of recognition. He could prove himself to his father, the King, and bring home one of the greatest of all gifts.

"The old gods are dead," Saeward replied coldly in answer to the rider. "It's time the East Saxon people learnt that."

George watched spellbound as Saeward rested the arrow against the curve of the wood. He pulled back on the flight until the string would stretch no more and then released the arrow.

George heard an unworldly noise from where the animal had stood. With his heart pounding he turned to look. The stallion lay on its side wildly kicking its eight legs, still silhouetted by the moon, but now with the arrow protruding from its side.

Saeward shouted loudly to his men and other shouts responded from around the clearing. He dug his feet into his horse and rode towards his fallen prey.

The animal stopped kicking and rested its head on the ground. To George it seemed as though the fallen horse had turned his head to look directly at him – as though he knew he was hiding here in the bush. A shiver ran down his spine. What was this creature? What had it been doing here, staring up at the ash tree? Who were these men? But now was not a good time to answer such questions. Now was a good time to creep from the bush and put some space between him and the men.

Chapter Three: Where's George?

Later on that night Millie woke again. This time to the screeching noise of a cat through the sash window, which had a tendency to fall slightly ajar. She rubbed her eyes and looked over to George's bed. It was still empty! She wondered what hour it was and how long George had been gone now. She stumbled out of bed and went over to the window to lift it shut. As she pushed the clasp across, a movement at the end of the garden caught her eye. Was that George coming back? Millie went to pull the window back down, in order to shout to him. But as she looked closer she saw that it was somebody wearing a long coat, certainly not George. The moon began to emerge from behind a cloud and Millie saw that it was an elderly woman dressed in a dark shawl, with long silvery hair. The woman appeared to be staring straight up at the house, directly back at Millie. The window suddenly slammed down again! Millie screamed and leapt back into the room.

At once the sound of movement could be heard in the room next door, followed by approaching footsteps. Oh no, she had woken Grandad!

"Millie," called a concerned voice. "Are you okay?"

"Grandad! Sorry, I didn't mean to wake you!"

The room danced with shadows as her grandfather emerged, holding an old saucer with a candle on it. In the light of the flame his white beard and thin hair were illuminated and didn't seem real. Millie frowned, despite her fright, wishing he would just be normal and use the light switches.

"I thought I heard you scream, my love."

"Yes. There's a strange woman outside, she's staring at me."

"Don't be so ridiculous, child," Grandad said. He walked over and peered out into the empty night.

"There's no one there, you probably dreamt it." He said turning back to her. "You know what you youngsters are like, with too much TV and video games. It makes your imagination go haywire." Millie was about to dispute this when Grandad noticed George's empty bed. He frowned.

"Where's George? Is he in the bathroom?"

Millie froze. How could she cover for him?

"He, er, couldn't sleep. I think he went downstairs to read," she stammered, hoping that George would suddenly walk in.

"Downstairs? I didn't notice any light on," Grandad said, now sounding alarmed and walking back onto the landing with his candle and saucer.

"He's probably got the little lamp on," she replied uncomfortably, sensing his disbelief.

"George? George?" Grandad called down to the empty lounge.

Millie gave a guilty sigh as he went downstairs to check, aware he would return in a moment demanding answers from her.

"Right," he said, standing at the bottom of the stairs with his hands on hips. "Where is he?" From his tone Millie could sense that Grandad would tolerate no nonsense. She bit her lip. She couldn't very easily hide the truth from him.

"He lost something when we were out earlier. He just went to look for it."

"No!" Grandad cried. "I specifically warned you both that you must *not* go out in Wybrook after dark, not tonight! Any other night but not *this* night. How long has he been gone?"

"I'm not sure, maybe a couple of hours."

"Right, we'll go and have a look for him. Put your coat on," he commanded. He put his own on over his pyjamas and reached for his walking stick.

Millie looked at her Grandfather in surprise. As well as annoyance, there was fear in his eyes, a look of real vexation. And yes, he had told them both that afternoon that they were to be home before it was dark - drummed it into them, in fact. "But we're *always* home before dark," Millie had appealed to him, as confused then at the extent of his concern as she was now.

Millie grabbed her coat and put it on.

"Tell me exactly where George was going," Grandad demanded, passing her a large black torch. "This is no time for childish games, there still might be time to find him."

"He was going back to the playing field. We'll probably bump into him walking home."

"Right," Grandad said to himself again. "It's two o'clock in the morning. What was he thinking? We've only got a couple of hours before dawn." Grandad headed out of the door. "We'll walk towards the playing field first. Do you usually take any short cuts? Which way do you normally go?"

Millie led the way down the lane. She was often frightened by the dark and the thought of being out walking in the middle of the night was something she would ordinarily find terrifying, but tonight her fears were driven away by Grandad's sense of urgency.

Wybrook was a small village built on higher ground, surrounded by fields which were now full of wheat, golden-yellow rape and potatoes. It was quietly tucked away from the main roads, with a cluster of old timbered-framed buildings scattered amongst more modern dwellings. The village housed a mixture of commuters from the city and generations of local-born villagers, like her grandfather.

Millie stopped at the churchyard. Would George have crossed the graveyard on his own at night? No, he probably would have walked past the church and then down Rosemary Close to the footpath at the bottom. Grandad kept up with her pace, all the time looking around and shining his torch into the shadows.

"George," he whispered coarsely, not wanting to wake up the slumbering villagers. "George! George!"

Millie thought he was over-reacting and tried her best to reassure him. How was it any more dangerous being out at night than it was in the day time? What harm could really come to George in this sleepy little village? He was sensible enough.

They reached the playing field and Grandad sat down by the skateboard ramp to catch his breath.

"Sorry, not quite so young anymore," he wheezed. "But let's not rest too long, time is against us."

Millie wasn't sure what he meant - surely it would be light soon. Probably George was already back at Grandad's. They hadn't passed him on the way and he wasn't here. Maybe he did walk through the churchyard?

Millie had had enough, but at Grandad's insistence they stayed out searching for George until they had looked down every street in Wybrook and shone the torch into every hedge. As it started to grow light Grandad grew wearier and began to rely on his walking stick to prop himself up. He agreed to return to the house but still he remained anxious, despite Millie's constant assurances that George would be in his bed and probably wondering where she was!

Millie ran up the path to the house. Grandad hobbled behind her. He had left the door unlocked and Millie flung it open and rushed upstairs into the bedroom. She was expecting to see George asleep in bed. But the bed was empty and exactly how it had been left.

Downstairs Grandad was slowly taking off his ancient tweed jacket and hanging it back on the old wooden hat stand next to the front door. He didn't even look up at Millie as she came back down the stairs. Instead he shuffled down the hall into the kitchen to switch the kettle on.

"Grandad," Millie followed him into the kitchen, feeling unnerved by his silence. "What are we going to do? Where do you think he's got to?"

Grandad paused as he shakily picked up the kettle and then snapped a reply. "Oh, I expect he's around here somewhere."

Millie was surprised by his tone. He had been so anxious and worried, yet now he was home and the dawn was breaking it was as though he had given up and had decided there was nothing more that could be done or said.

Unable to get any more response from the old man, Millie left him drinking his tea and went back upstairs. She felt a combination of panic and exhaustion. Perhaps if she went back to sleep for a while, George would be here when she woke up. She climbed back into bed and closed her eyes.

Chapter Four: In the Woods

In the woodland there was no moonlight, just darkness. George peered through the trees with the now slightly ridiculous hope of finding the footpath down to the playing field that he had originally been heading for. But even if it had been there, he wouldn't have been able to see it. He would just have to make his own path.

George staggered blindly along through the brambles and rough undergrowth with his arms outstretched to protect his face from the low branches. There was a gentle but constant rustling of tree leaves all around him and a cool breeze blowing through his unkempt hair. A creature, maybe a dog or a fox, howled in the distance just as George felt the flapping of wings pass right in front of his face.

He seemed to be following a narrow animal track, maybe the regular route of some deer. He stumbled and winced as foliage whipped his sides. All the time a constant feeling of unease was upon him. He was alone, he was lost and he had no plan.

The image of George's mother flashed into his mind. He wondered what she would say if she knew where he was now. She would probably be pretty angry with him for going out without permission, but it didn't stop him longing for her. He hadn't seen her for a whole week. Their mother and father had gone off to some idiotic conference in South Africa and had left him and Millie in Wybrook with Grandad.

"You're still close enough to get to your schools from Grandad's house, you're not far from your own home," they'd said, as if to reassure them.

George had been excited at the prospect of some time without his parents ... until he had heard that! Stan was a lovely Grandad but he lived an alternative lifestyle that took a lot of getting used to. Now George wished more than anything to be back in his own home, safe and sound in his own bed, listening to the noise of his parents watching TV downstairs and pottering about. George felt his eyes start to well up.

"That stupid blinking watch," George cursed to himself and wiped his tears away on the back of his sleeve. He had *never* been out this late. In fact, he had sworn to his grandfather that afternoon that he and his sister wouldn't be out after dusk, which was how he had ended up having the ancient timepiece in the first place. Grandad had seemed particularly anxious that they shouldn't be back late and had insisted George take the watch with him so that they wouldn't lose track of time.

George had pointed out that, as it was nearly the end of June, it wouldn't be dark for ages; even if they weren't back until ten it would still be light. But Grandad wanted to give George his watch anyway and George had taken it and slipped it into his jeans pockets to reassure him. He and Millie had laughed about it as they had walked off down the lane to meet Sam, Becky and Lee by the den.

"What do I want a pocket watch for? As if anyone still uses them! My mobile does actually have the time on it."

Their Grandad was an eccentric old man and had turned his back on modern technology long ago.

George suddenly saw a glowing object on the forest floor and was immediately drawn towards it. It was one of the torches the men had been carrying, only now just the embers glowed. He picked it up and turned it over in his hands.

"Hey, can you help me out? I'm over here!"

George jumped out of his skin. He span around in fright but struggled to see anyone.

"Who ... who said that?" he stuttered, trying to hold his guard.

"Down here, lad."

George looked down to see a man lying on the ground with his foot wedged under a tree root.

"I'm one of the King's huntsmen. I tripped over this damn root chasing along with that stupid son of his," the man explained, again with a thick accent.

"Prince Saeward?" George asked.

"That's right. I don't mean to speak out against their new god or nothing but ..."

"What?"

"Well, you know..." the man said, waiting for George to agree with him. "Leave the old ones alone, I say."

George frowned, completely oblivious to what he was talking about.

"Don't just stand there, look around for my hunting knife, would you? It went flying out of my hand when I fell. I need it to cut this cursed tree off me foot, before I get eaten by a pack of wolves."

George swept the torch light over the floor around them and soon the blade glinted back at him. He handed it over to the huntsman, who at once started attacking the tree root whilst continuing to grumble.

"Who wants to be riding in the night, anyway? Damn job being a huntsman. I much preferred it when I was a soldier. We would go into battle then and fight off the Gewisse Saxons in the west - real work, that, giving them everything we'd got, instead of following around some prince all night."

His words reminded George how ludicrous the events of this night had been. Someone *must* be playing a vast and elaborate practical joke on him. Either that or he had walked onto the set of a film production. George looked into the darkness around him, expecting to see a film crew or group of his friends peeking out from behind a tree and laughing. But it was just him and the King's huntsman.

"Is this still England?" George asked.

"England?" the man frowned at him. "This is East Seax, lad. Land of the Saxon descendants of the god Seaxneat and ruled by the mighty King Saberht." George noted a tone of sarcasm on "mighty".

"King? East Seax? Okay," George said, slowly trying to digest this information. He didn't know much about the Saxons but was pretty sure that they ruled in England sometime between the Romans and the Normans. Amazed to even be phrasing such a question he asked, "Who is King Saberht? Are you saying this is a different time?"

The man laughed and broke his leg free from the root. He stood up and gave George a strange look. "You been drinking too much mead! It's the same time as always!"

"Where are you going now?"

"Going to find the rest of the group. They'll be easy to catch up, now they're pulling that creature with them." The man took the glowing torch from George's clasp.

"So this isn't Britain?" George asked again, trying to recap.

"No! I just told you. This is the land of the Saxons. We pushed the Britons into the western hills and lands a hundred years ago. Most of those that stayed work on our farms." He shook his head at George. "Don't you know anything?"

"No, I'm a bit lost."

The man bent down and picked up a large shield that was lying across the path. It was nearly a metre in length and covered with leather from which a sharp conical boss protruded from the centre. When he rose again, the man's expression had eased into an odd, thoughtful stare.

"You didn't come through the world-tree did you?"

"What tree?" George replied.

"Oh, it's nothing. Sorry, forget it. I hope you find where you're heading for," the man said. He held his shield out in front of him and started to run down the narrow path, desperate to catch up with his comrades. "Thanks for your help!" he called back.

George was also desperate - he didn't want to lose his only companion in this strange place. He ran behind him, trying hard to keep up.

"What's ... the ... date ...?" George called out between pants.

But in the dark the huntsman quickly disappeared.

George felt a swell of emotion at the prospect of being left by himself again and flopped down under a tree. He leant his head against the bark of the trunk, overwhelmed with everything he had experienced in the last few hours. He needed time to rest, and time to try and digest what he had been told.

George knew he was lost. What he didn't know was how he had become lost. He was in a place he didn't recognise, yet he hadn't travelled far from Grandad's. Therefore he was either in the same place in a different time or in a different place in the same time. These were the only two options and both were impossible.

He felt something digging into his groin. Of course! His mobile phone, why didn't he think of that before! He excitedly yanked it out of his pocket and turned it on. The screen flashed up "2.07am" and underneath "No signal". He had always had a good signal in Wybrook.

Now he felt even more disheartened. This couldn't be happening! If he had to decide, then men dressed in Saxon cloaks and breeches, plus the huntsman's revelation, suggested he was in a different time. But time travel was impossible! It put into question his entire view of the world, not to mention his own sanity. Could the man have spoken the truth? What George had seen was so out of place from normal life that he could think of no other explanation.

Chapter Five: At the Den

The sound of Millie's alarm clock trilled through the bedroom. She groaned as she blindly hit the off switch and then snuggled back into her pillow, as she did every school morning. Normally this lasted at least twenty minutes or until hunger forced her to get up for breakfast. Today, though, she lay with a strong, physical sense of dread that rose up from the pit of her stomach. She didn't immediately recall the root of it, just knew that something bad had happened. Then Millie rolled over and looked across to Georges' empty bed and remembered last night's drama. She closed her eyes and wished she was still blissfully asleep and that her alarm hadn't gone off.

Millie would have preferred to have stayed hidden in bed for the rest of the day. Instead she solemnly changed out of her night clothes into her school uniform. She stood in front of the mirror that hung on the back of the bedroom door and brushed her long brown hair in long, slow strokes. She was tall for her age and was getting close to catching up with George, although their mother had warned her that he would probably have a growth spurt soon and grow a foot overnight. Millie opened the door and went downstairs to find her grandfather.

Grandad was asleep in his armchair and Millie suspected from his attire that he had been there since they had arrived back, a few hours ago. She didn't want to disturb him so she went back upstairs to find her mobile phone. She plugged it into the socket and waited for it to charge. She wished she had thought of the simple idea to call George last night, but she had been too distracted by her grandfather's behaviour. The first bar lit up and she rang George's number. It went straight to voicemail. She left a message and decided to try again later.

Millie had some cornflakes for her breakfast and then packed her school bag and headed out to wait at the bus stop. What she wanted desperately was to stay at home and continue the search for George. She dreaded to think what her parents would say if he wasn't here when they flew back from South Africa. Grandad was their mother's father and as he lived so close he had been the perfect choice for Millie and George to stay with. They were used to Wybrook and had a small circle of friends here that they had known most of their lives. Her grandfather had not been too keen on the idea but there was no real alternative, not for three weeks.

On the way to the bus stop Millie decided to check George wasn't in the den. Together with a few friends from the village, they had discovered the den a few years ago when she was just seven and George was ten. It was down one of the many village footpaths that ran alongside the fields.

The path was bordered on one side by overgrown hedgerow and trees. Behind that ran a dried-up ditch. On the other side of the ditch were more overgrown hedges, marking the end of a row of back gardens. At a certain point along the footpath was a small stone boulder which was easily distinguishable by the fact that it had several circles etched into it. It was behind this stone that the ditch secretly swelled out, as though it had once been a pond. "Secretly" because over this cavern a large branch of a bent old alder tree formed a roof, blocking out most of the sky and creating a hidden cave. This was the den.

Millie sat down by the stone and peered down into the cave. She couldn't see any sign of George. She dropped her school bag and scrambled down to make sure, but it was clear he had not been here. She sat down on a log that they had put there for a bench and tried to make sense of what had happened. Where was George? And why had Grandad been so frantic? It was as though he knew they wouldn't find him. He had acted so strangely, it almost felt like he was keeping something from her, and what was that odd woman doing behind the house? Had she taken George? Millie felt a wave of panic again - they needed to phone the police immediately.

"Hey, Millie!"

The voice caught her by surprise.

"Becky, hi! Hi Sam!" Millie greeted her friends warmly.

A girl a year or two older than Millie had appeared from behind the hedge. Becky, renowned for her odd dress sense, had spruced up her school uniform by adding a bright red sailor's hat which helped to flatten her mass of wavy blonde hair. Sam followed behind her, grinning. He was closer to Millie's age, very tall and lean, with short dark hair and glasses. Millie had known them both for years, having spent many school holidays in Wybrook biking around the lanes and hanging out at the playing field.

Becky was just as surprised to see Millie.

"Millie! What are you doing down there? You're going to miss the school bus."

Sam held out his hand and helped Millie climb back up the bank of the ditch. She had forgotten that Becky and Sam walked this way in the mornings.

"Well ... I was looking for George. Have you seen him?" Millie asked cautiously as they continued on.

Sam and Becky exchanged a glance.

"Well, not since yesterday, when we were together up the field. Why would he be down in the den at half past eight in the morning?"

"Yes, I know, you're right." Millie replied glumly. "It's just that we checked everywhere for him last night and I wanted to make sure he hadn't come here and fallen asleep or something."

"Do you mean that George is *proper* missing?"

Millie looked down, wringing her fingers as she tried to keep her emotions together. "George went out really late last night and hasn't come back yet."

"What?" gasped Becky.

"Grandad's acting weird too. He made us go out in the middle of the night to search for George but he was nowhere."

"Have you called the police yet?"

"No. I guess Grandad will if he's not back today. He probably doesn't want to make a fuss unnecessarily."

"My Mum would call the police if I was missing for five minutes!" exclaimed Becky.

"Mine too," Sam agreed.

There was an awkward silence. Millie had hoped her friends would set her mind at rest, but instead they made her fears seem all the more real and worrying. They reached the end of the path and turned onto the main road, towards their stop.

"Where was George going?" Sam asked.

"He had lost Grandad's pocket watch. You know, the one he showed you yesterday."

Sam nodded.

"I don't know what time it was, maybe eleven or twelve I suppose. He thought he'd lost it down by the skate ramps."

"I remember. George said your Grandad really didn't want you going out around the midsummer. Lots of parents are funny about it around here. My mum and dad are too, always telling us not to go off on our own and to stay with friends."

"Midsummer? What's that?"

"Don't you know?" Sam mocked. "It's the longest day of the year, when it doesn't really get dark. Solstice it's called."

"Oh right, yeah, I know about the solstice. But why isn't anyone allowed out late?"

"Oh, some stupid village thing," Sam rolled his eyes. "Anyway, George has most likely gone to see a friend somewhere and forgotten to tell you."

"Yeah, Sam's right. He probably just ran out of credit or he would have called you," Becky agreed.

Millie frowned, "What about Lee?" Lee also lived in Wybrook and was in George's year at school. Maybe they had gone off somewhere together.

"He went to his Dad's last night, but George has other mates."

Although Millie appreciated her friends' assurances, their words did little to settle her thoughts. She knew George wouldn't have gone anywhere without telling anyone, especially her.

They approached the bus stop. Unlike the others Millie was still at primary school, although now in her final weeks. Her bus was already there waiting.

"Look, I've really got to go," she said, starting to run. "I'll come round some time, maybe tomorrow?"

"Yeah, make sure you do! We'll both be in," Becky called.

"It's not like there's anywhere to go around here," Sam added. His words echoed in Millie's thoughts as she stared out of the bus window.

Chapter Six: Leof and the Black Wolf

George opened his eyes to daylight and blinked as he made out his surroundings. Confused, he sat up and looked around. This certainty wasn't his bedroom at his grandfather's!

The memories of the previous night came flooding back. He ran his fingers hard through his thick mousy hair and over his scalp, as though trying to brush them from his mind. He didn't yet feel able to face the new day.

His mobile phone was digging into his groin and he pulled it out of his pocket. Twenty past ten. He'd been asleep for hours. George frowned and put it back: there was still no signal.

If this was a dream, it was certainly the clearest dream he'd ever had. But when did you ever go to sleep *and* wake up in a dream? Everything was so real and yet everything seemed slightly different. Even the air smelt unfamiliar.

He couldn't help thinking about what Grandad had said to him yesterday afternoon. He had been rambling on about the solstice and the danger of being out late. Was *this* what the old man had been talking about? That he would be plummeted back into another time? George wished he had paid more attention. Perhaps his grandfather was wiser and more knowledgeable than he had ever given him credit for.

Poor Grandad, George didn't want to imagine how worried he must be. Although ... maybe if he had known something might happen then he might also know where George was and therefore send for help. George felt slightly more confident with this thought in mind and contemplated what to do next. He really needed to get some food and water and find someone who could help him.

He started walking in what he hoped was the direction he had come, careful to avoid the brambles and holly, and listening diligently for any strange noises. Despite the fact that it was now light, George was still very much on his guard and was paying a great deal of attention to everything about him. He noticed how tall the trees were and the thickness of their great trunks. They seemed different too and they were all indigenous to England: enormous oaks, ashes, thorns, hornbeams and beech trees. And the sound of birds! It was almost deafening.

After a half hour or so George saw a deer darting through the trees just to his left. It seemed to be moving along a much more established track than the one he was on, so he clambered through the brambles to follow it. The deer had shot out of sight and was gone but George decided to stick to the new track.

Almost immediately he realised he had made a grave mistake. He had merely walked a few metres when he heard a menacing growl. The deer had been running from something. George slowly turned around. A black wolf stood behind him, its dark soulless eyes fixed upon him. George froze to the spot in terror. He had never seen a wolf before and was completely unprepared for its size.

The creature edged its way closer to him, baring its sharp teeth. Fearing the wolf would pounce at any movement, George remained riveted to the spot. He closed his eyes and tried to carry on believing that this was all a bad dream. The wolf lowered his back legs ready for the kill and was about to leap when a whizzing noise came through the trees and an arrow struck the creature deep in its side. The wolf fell to the ground with a deathly moan. George gasped, his heart rushing with adrenaline as he tried to take in this change of fate. To his surprise a boy about his own age appeared from the thicket of the forest carrying a bow. He acknowledged George with a slight nod of the head and went over to check the wolf was truly slain. After poking the creature with the tip of his bow he established that it most definitely was. The boy pulled the arrow from the wolf's side and wiped it clean on some weeds, before putting it into a leather pack he was carrying.

He looked at George. "Wes Hal," he said.

"Hi," George replied shakily as he recovered from the near-death encounter.

The boy had somewhat matted hair that was blonde and a couple of inches longer than George's, falling almost to his shoulders. On his top half he wore a long-sleeved linen tunic that had been dyed a bright red and was girdled around the waist by a leather belt tied in a loop. From this dangled a knife sheath, a small pouch and what George guessed was a water container. On his legs he wore tight-fitting brown trousers secured around his shins by woven fabric. These reached down to a pair of rounded sandals made from laced leather. Similar in attire to the men George had seen the night before.

The boy eyed George with equal curiosity, no doubt observing George's unusual jeans, patterned T-shirt and hoodie. He noted George's lack of any weaponry and approached him confidently.

"Are you trying to kill yourself walking alone? You haven't even got a spear. Where have you come from?"

George thought he sounded slightly Germanic, like the huntsman, and decided it was better to avoid the boy's questions until he knew more about him.

"Thank you so much. I thought I was definitely dead then. Wow! That was an excellent shot, you got him with a single arrow."

"That's all right," the boy said, coolly taking in the praise. "I've been following you for a while. There's been a couple of wolves frightening the village recently. Really, you did us a favour by luring him as bait. So are you a Briton, then?"

"Er, yes." George said and then added quickly, "but only on my mother's side," unsure if it was the best thing to admit to.

"Oh? There's not many Britons left in these parts, except the farm workers of course. Where's your mother from?"

George gave a nod to the right to indicate the direction.

"The Walasden settlement on the northern border?" George nodded again. "I've never been up there but I've heard there's a whole tribe of Britons that live there. Haven't they got some kind of agreement with the King?"

"Yes, something like that." George hoped the boy would stop asking him questions he didn't know the answers to.

"So is your dad Saxon, then? You look fair enough to be one of us."

The boy bent over the wolf and yanked its hind legs straight.

"Here, do you want to give me a hand carrying this to the village? I'll fix you some grub when we get there if you like."

George's stomach ached with hunger and he was only too pleased to assist.

"My name's George."

"George! What sort of a name is that? I'm Leofwine."

"Leofwine?"

"Call me Leof."

Leof dragged a long branch from the forest and tied the front legs of the wolf to one end with hemp rope, while George tied the hind legs to the other. Lifting up the wolf they heaved the branch over their shoulders and headed off.

The wolf was heavy and the weight bore down on George's shoulder. He realised he wasn't as fit as Leof and was soon breathing deeply as he tried to keep up the pace.

The path meandered through the woodland until it opened up into a large meadow. George felt an immense relief to be finally free from the darkness of the trees. Out here he had a wider depth of vision and felt safer and more at home. The path now skirted alongside the meadow and adjacent to a large stream. A few small brown sheep were drinking from its water. As they passed by, they stared at the two of them then quickly darted back towards the rest of their flock, grazing in the meadow.

"Look what we got for you," Leof shouted after them, "the beast that stole your babes."

"Baaaa," they answered back.

“Right, let's put him down by that road marker,” Leof suggested, pointing to a stone boulder beside a pond that had formed from the stream.

They carefully lowered the wolf to the ground. George felt light-footed as the weight left him and stooped to rub some feeling back into his shoulder.

“How far is your village from here?” he asked, looking around him and assuming the sheep belonged to somebody.

“Widurok's just around the corner, the other side of the stone circle.”

“Widurok!” George was dumbfounded, he was sure that Grandad had told him Wybrook was once called something like that.

“Do you know it?”

“No, it’s just my village is called Wybrook, quite similar, that's all.” George replied, still cautious about revealing his true identity.

“Oh, I've not heard of it. I thought you came from Walasden?”

“I moved there when I was young. It's far from here.” George could have kicked himself.

Fortunately though, Leof was more interested in boasting to George about his hunting experiences, and the fear that the wolves had been inflicting on the villagers, than in probing George any further on his own past.

As George stood next to the pond listening to Leof, he had a sudden feeling of déjà vu. He knew this place. The stone the wolf lay next to was the exact same stone that was at the top of the den in Wybrook. A stone boulder, about a foot high with a group of small circles etched into its surface. He was at the den! There was no other stone like it.

George was stunned. So it hadn't always been a dried-out ditch; it used to be a stream and a pond, and the stone was an old road marker that had been used for hundreds of years to guide travellers. The huntsman man had been right, George was no longer in his own time. He was in the Dark Ages of the Anglo-Saxons.

Chapter Seven: Still no George

All day Millie thought about George. Even when the teacher stood in front of the class talking about the new topic and work she had set for them, Millie could not concentrate and failed to catch a single word. The teacher had finished explaining the task and everyone hurriedly opened their work books and sat busily writing, but Millie stayed in her chair staring into space, unaware and indifferent to those around her. She let the school day pass her by in a daze and at three o'clock she felt relieved to be going home to Wybrook.

Millie jumped off the school bus and ran through the high street to reach the small lane that led to her grandad's house. As she turned the corner she saw Mrs Gordon's car was parked outside the front gate and Mrs Gordon was climbing back into it, about to leave. Mrs Gordon was often very temperamental towards her and George, but since their grandmother had died five years ago, she had kindly taken on Grandad's welfare as her personal duty. She was fit for her seventy-odd years, despite being a plump woman who enjoyed baking. She carried herself in a way that revealed her personality, always looking around in a prying manner, and often walking with her elbows out like a hen trying to get first peckings at feeding time. But in her charitable nature Mrs Gordon had come around to check on Grandad, as she usually did on a Thursday. She drove towards Millie and stopped the car, beckoning her over as she wound down the window.

"Your grandfather's in a bit of a state, Millie. Make sure you look after him. I'll come by later."

Before Millie could make any reply Mrs Gordon pressed on the accelerator and was gone.

Millie carried on to the house and went in through the back gate, knowing the French windows that led into the back room would be wide open.

Grandad's home was very old. The structure of the building was so bent and warped with time it could only be considered a miracle that it still stood. It consisted of four storeys including the loft room, where most of the space was taken up by a model train track Grandad had spent years building, and the damp old cellar, which their Gran had used to keep rabbits in and which was now full of empty cages.

In the main living area, the walls were covered with fading wallpaper of various designs, all a couple of decades old and pasted between blackened old beams. The floors were carpeted in worn psychedelic orange and brown patterns that had been popular in the Seventies and the stuffy air smelt to Millie like a combination of an old musty bookshop and a tool shed. It was a house that was now too big for its single occupier and its many rooms reflected this with a sad silence.

Millie glanced around the back room at the endless books piled upon numerous shelves and the general bric-à-brac accumulated by her grandparents over the years. The only real furniture in the room was the dining table and the old oak cabinet that housed the "best" crockery and cutlery.

Afternoon tea was laid out and she could hear her grandfather busying himself in the kitchen. She noticed that the table was only laid for two. So Grandad wasn't expecting George back for tea. She didn't feel hungry but she sat down with her grandfather to eat anyway.

"Have you called the police yet, Grandad? I'm really worried."

"Oh my dear, you know I don't do all that."

By "all that" Grandad was referring to the fact that he lived very simply without a phone or a television, let alone the internet. He said they interfered with his thinking.

"I'll call them on my mobile then, shall I?"

"Well there's no need to cause a big panic. Wait until you've finished your tea."

Grandad's discouraging replies ended the conversation and he changed the subject by smiling affectionately at his granddaughter.

"So how are your mum and dad doing? Have you heard from them this week?"

They made small talk over the ham sandwiches and Jaffa Cakes, Grandad chatting about the locals in the village and the new pavilion that was being built by the cricket ground. George wasn't mentioned again.

As soon as the meal was over Millie went upstairs to try and contact her parents while her grandfather cleared away the tea. Grandad must surely be in denial about what had happened, or maybe he felt so responsible for George's welfare that he couldn't cope with the notion that anything bad had occurred. Millie opened up her parents' contact details and pressed the green phone symbol. She wasn't sure of the time difference so it didn't surprise her that the call was answered by voicemail. Millie left a message asking her mother to call back urgently and lay down on her bed. She was still exhausted from being awake most of the night and her eyes felt heavy in her head. Without meaning to she soon dozed off.

Millie woke a couple of hours later. The bedroom door was ajar and she could hear a woman's stern voice downstairs in the hallway. She crept to the top of the stairs. It sounded like Mrs Gordon had returned.

"This is getting ridiculous! You're going to have to tell them, Stan. You can't just keep this a secret," Mrs Gordon was saying. Then she lowered her voice and Millie had to strain her ears to hear. "I know he's not the first boy to go missing but you mustn't let superstitions get the better of you."

Millie's grandfather was mumbling apologetically in agreement. He seemed very distressed.

"Stan! I don't think you're really listening to me. This is serious. You have to face the fact that George has not just taken off for the night. You won't be able to make excuses to the school or his family. A thirteen-year old child is missing. I'm going to call the police this instant."

Millie felt a chill run down her spine.

Despite her suspicions, she had almost convinced herself that everything was going to be okay. After all, Mum always told her that most of what she worried about would never happen. No longer caring about being seen, Millie flew down the stairs.

Her grandfather looked up at her with weary eyes.

"We have to call the police! George is truly missing, isn't he?" she cried.

The old man was silent and then nodded.

"Yes. He seems to be gone." His words carried with them a slow, sorrowful shrug.

"Do … do you think he's been abducted? He will be alive, won't he?" Millie dreaded the reply.

Grandad's eyes filled with tears and he shrugged again. "I can't really answer, my love. We can only pray that he is safe."

Millie's stomach tightened as her muscles and nerves knotted inside her. She didn't want to add to her grandfather's distress, but she couldn't control herself.

"But you must have some idea where he is, you must! You kept saying last night that it was dangerous for him to be out, so you must know something!"

A tear rolled down the old man's cheek. "I was ... being foolish. I hoped we would find him. Maybe we still will."

"Why don't you tell me the truth?" Millie demanded.

"Millie dear, I know little more than you do," he pleaded with her.

Distraught, Millie turned and ran through the hall, into the back room and through the French windows.

"You don't understand," he called after her, "it's happened before!" But Millie was already out of earshot.

Millie ran until she was out of breath and her sobs forced her to stop. She wasn't really upset with Grandad, but the stress and lack of sleep had got to her. In all her young years she had never had to cope with such a serious matter.

Millie had run in no particular direction, but now she realised she was actually quite close to the playing field. On reaching the empty children's area, she sat down on one of the swings. The gentle motion rocked her as the tears dried on her cheeks. Millie's sobs had released some of the tension that had built up in her throughout the day and she now felt calmer and more in control of herself.

She wondered if George had made it here last night and found the watch, or if he had disappeared before he got here. The grass and weeds around the two benches by the skateboard ramp was long and overgrown: could it be lost somewhere in their foliage? She went over to them and got down on her knees, running her fingers through the grass. The watch was quite a large object, she should be able to find it fairly easily. Her search was fruitless. She moved over to the other bench. The same. Not willing to give up so easily she lifted up one end of the bench and put it down at a different angle. Straightaway Millie saw the shiny glint of metal. The watch!

"So George never even found it," she muttered to herself as she turned it over in her hands. Somehow, finding it made her feel a little closer to him and gave her some encouragement. She had found the watch, so maybe she would find him.

Out of the corner of her eye Millie saw a flashing light go by on the far side of the playground. Was it a police car? Her question was immediately answered by another police car that followed behind it. She felt suddenly ashamed of fleeing from the house. Her grandfather needed her support right now, not the strain of worrying about her as well.

*

When Millie returned, the two police cars were parked outside the house. She found Grandad sitting at the dining room table with a young officer taking notes and asking questions, while a policeman and woman hovered over them. In the background Mrs Gordon clattered about in the kitchen, presumably making tea.

Grandad seemed happy to see her and at once introduced her to the police.

"We'll be keen to speak to you next, Millie, if that's okay? Any little details you might remember could be really useful to us." The policewoman smiled kindly at her.

"Well, actually ..." Millie turned to her grandfather, "I just found your pocket watch. It's what George went out to look for last night."

Grandad took the watch in surprise. "George went out to look for my watch! I gave it to him to ensure he *wasn't* out late!" He smiled sadly at the irony of it.

The police looked at her inquisitively and Millie tried to elaborate in as much detail as she could the events of the previous night. The young policeman continued to take notes and gently prompted her for any extra details.

"What about the clothes your brother was wearing when he left the house? Do you remember what brand they are? Do you have a photo of him wearing the same clothes? Would you have noticed if he had taken a bag with him? Did you actually see him leave the house? Has he ever done this before? Do you think he may have tried to go back to your normal residence? Can we have the address and we'll send someone there to check? Does he have any older friends who drive?"

The image of George sitting on the bed last night fully-clothed was clear in Millie's mind, but it had been dark in the room and she had been half asleep. She was pretty sure he had been wearing his jeans and his red jumper with the hood and pockets but she couldn't say for definite. At the police woman's request she went up to the bedroom to check they weren't in the room. She was right and the pale blue patterned T-shirt that he had been wearing yesterday afternoon was also missing.

The young policeman continued to ask her lots of questions, whilst the other two officers left the dining room to glance around the house and mutter quietly to themselves. At length Millie felt that she had given as much information as she possibly could about George's school life and friends and the things he enjoyed doing, although she wasn't sure how any of her replies would help to find him.

The police finally left, promising to keep in direct contact through Mrs Gordon's and Millie's mobile numbers. Their next lines of action were to check George wasn't at his usual home and then to question everyone involved in George's life. They told Millie, Mrs Gordon and her grandfather to sit tight in the meantime and to continue to try and get through to Millie and George's parents.

The three of them sat in the lounge holding their mugs of tea, trying to recover from the intense questioning.

"Oh no!" Millie exclaimed, "I completely forgot to tell them about the lady that was outside last night!"

"What lady?" Mrs Gordon asked.

"I was trying to shut the window in the night and I saw a woman at the bottom of the garden." Millie described her appearance to Mrs Gordon.

"Why didn't you mention this to me, Stan?" she said turning her back on Millie and addressing Grandad, who shrugged back a reply. "Sounds like one of the old Wirde sisters. Probably out collecting herbs, knowing them, or doing some weird pagan solstice thing," she said disapprovingly. "They've got some funny old ideas."

"They're harmless, though, and they've lived in the village quite happily for countless generations," Grandad said defensively.

"Should I call the police and tell them about her?" Millie asked.

"No, let it go," Grandad replied stiffly. "It wouldn't be fair on them to be bothered by the police. It'll just complicate matters. It's highly unlikely that any of them have got George with them."

Millie heard her phone ringing in the next room and rushed to answer it. It was her mother. She took a deep breath and for the final time that day she began to retell the events of the previous night.

"Mum" she began, "please don't get too upset ... Something's happened to George..."

Chapter Eight: The Path to Widurok

George and Leof continued down the path with the weight of the wolf over their shoulders. Underneath the soft moss George could feel paved stones through his shoes. The path had once been carefully constructed although it no longer appeared to be maintained.

"This road was laid down by the Romans, you know," Leof said as if reading his mind. "That's why it's got all that stonework."

George kicked repeatedly at an area of the moss. "Don't you make roads like this anymore, then?"

"No, we don't like to live like they did."

"What do you mean?"

"Well, we've got different ways. We use the same roads that they did, but we don't make things in the same way."

"Do you mean that your houses are different?"

"Yes, we use wood mainly. The Romans used to make tiles and bricks for their houses and live all close together. It's not natural. We prefer to live as part of our land - you know, amongst the tree spirits and drinking water which comes straight from the springs of Hel, not …"

"Hel? Like heaven and hell?"

"No, we're not Christian, even if King Saberht says that we are now. I mean the Hel that our ancestors have talked about since before they came across the sea," Leof replied. "Nah, it's not natural to be cooped up in brick like those Romans were. Still, the ruins are good fun to mess about in. When we were younger we used to pretend we were soldiers fighting in Bodica's army. Have you ever been to Colneceastre?"

"No, where's that?"

"It's an old town north-east of here. People pillage it for building materials and stuff now. The old folk say it was the chief city over the whole of Roman Britain, which is lucky for us cos they built loads of good roads in the kingdom."

"Oh yes, I think I have been there. It's got a wall round it," George said, thinking of Colchester.

"Yeah, that's right. The older villagers are always telling stories of how it was built by the Ettins but I think they're just worried that it's dangerous us going there."

"What's an Ettin?"

"You know, a very big person."

"You mean a giant?"

"Yeah," Leof answered dismissively, unfamiliar with the word.

They had only been walking a few minutes when Leof led them right, off the main path, and headed down a track into an area where the trees thinned out. George could see they were approaching a clearing.

"Oh my goodness!" he exclaimed.

The clearing was dotted with upright stones two or three feet high. They were in a formation of two circles, one inside the other, and in the centre was a huge ash tree. It was the graveyard in Wybrook that he had been in last night, except ... they weren't really graves at all, they were part of two stone circles.

"What is this place?" he said, staring around in wonder.

"This is our Hearg. It's one of the most sacred sites in the north of the kingdom," Leof said proudly. "We come here to worship the gods, mainly Seaxneat, and in return they give us protection and a good harvest. There is a winter festival here on the Modraniht - Mothers' Night, that means - when it's the shortest day of the year and the start of the twelve days of Yule. But there was a fire here yesterday cos it's the Litha, you know, the longest day."

George noticed that Leof seemed to have grown accustomed to his lack of cultural knowledge and he was grateful for the information. He walked around the stones in awe. They reminded him of a smaller version of Stonehenge. He wondered how long they had stood here and who had erected them. He ran his hand over the rough stone and noticed that several of them bore strange markings in some sort of dark paint, which appeared quite recent.

"What are these symbols on the stones?" George asked, walking over to Leof who was poking at the remains of a fire with a stick.

"They're probably part of a magic spell that the Druids used last night. There's different spells for different festivals and days and stuff." Leof reached down and pulled out a charred remain from the ashes.

"Here, there's a bit of chicken left."

Leof tore the charred meat in half and George saw that inside it was still white. It tasted good too, despite being tough. He hadn't realised how hungry he was. George's hands were left blackened with charcoal and he knelt down to wipe them on the grass.

Lying on the ground next to him George noticed a piece of thick half-burnt parchment that must have blown loose from the fire. Curious, he picked it up. On it were written the same symbols that he had just been studying on the stones. Although blackened, they were clearly legible and were laid out on the page in the formation of circles.

"Do you use these symbols as your letters, then?" George asked showing Leof the parchment.

"Yes, those are rune letters. Only the wise use them. They're a gift from Woden."

George guessed that Woden was another god.

"It's probably the rune spell they put on the stones last night. We should leave it alone." Leof took it from him with a slight flinch of fear and threw it into the dead fire and then walked away towards the branches of the great ash.

With Leof's back to him, George retrieved it again. He remembered the huntsman's strange comment about coming "through the world-tree". He had a feeling that the symbols might be important. There must have been some kind of magic or weird science taking place to have got him here. George checked that Leof was still occupied and seized the opportunity to use his mobile phone. Trying to be as discreet as possible, George quickly opened the camera lens and took a photo of the old script, then he focused on the stones within the lens' field of view and captured them too. A second later the phone was back in his jeans pocket, well concealed.

The ash tree in the centre was the largest George had ever seen. He noticed there were idols carved out of wood hanging from some of its lower branches.

"Are these your gods?" he asked Leof.

"Yes, that's right. This is Woden here, the chief of the gods." Leof pointed to a bearded figure carved in wood. "And this one with the curved sword is Seaxneat, the founder of the East Saxon tribes. This one carrying the new-born child is Eostre, the goddess of new life, and this one is Thunor, the god of sky and thunder" Leof pointed to a god holding a hammer, which George recognised as Thor. "Over here is Tiw, god of war and this is Frige, goddess of love."

George wondered what Leof thought of his ignorance; surely he must think it strange.

"This tree," Leof continued "is our world-tree. They say," Leof lowered his voice, "that the gods travel between the seven worlds through the world-tree."

"Is that why you come here? To worship them?" George whispered back.

"Yes, here they can enter our world."

"I think this is where I was last night when I was lost." George could see no harm in telling Leof this much. "There were some men shooting arrows at a horse. Actually, this must have been where it fell," he said, looking down at the ground around them. "See here! The grass is all patchy, like blood."

Leof frowned and knelt down on the ground close to the tree, running his fingertips over the dark area.

"Yes, it does seem like blood. I don't know anything about a hunt in the night, though," he said, somewhat bewildered. "Wasn't anyone from our village else I would have heard about it."

They heaved the wolf and branch back onto their shoulders and left the clearing. Smoke rose from above the treetops and George could hear the clucking of livestock nearby. They emerged through the trees that surrounded the north side of the Hearg into the village where they were greeted almost at once by a huge dog that came barking and bounding towards them. The English mastiff circled the pair, wagging its tail, and then jumped up at Leof and licked his face, happy that its master had returned.

"Get off, Fen." Leof tried to maintain his balance as he pushed the dog down.

The dog leapt up at George instead, with its small black ears perked and his broad face almost touching George's.

"Fen! Get down. Sorry, George."

But George had hardly noticed the dog. He was staring at the scene before him. A large group of buildings inhabited roughly the same vicinity as the lower part of Wybrook where Sam lived and where most of the old houses were. He recognised the contours of the landscape and the track that ran through the village, which followed the same course as the now tarmacked road that went through Wybrook. Yet it was totally different. Instead of being surrounded by large fields, crops were being grown in much smaller divisions and he could see men were busily working in them, tending to their yields. A tall hedge of thorny brambles surrounded most of the village, giving the effect of barbed wire and protecting the inhabitants from wild animals and other unwanted guests. Open meadows filled the spaces between the fields and trees, and poultry seemed to wander about freely.

George walked closer, still gaping in amazement. The houses were all built from wood, as Leof had said, with thatched roofs and looking rather basic. None of them had windows, although some had shutters. Maybe glass was rare? The houses seemed to be divided into three groups, which Leof told him belonged to different extended families. It was more of a settlement than a village.

"Come on, stop staring. Anyone would think you'd never seen a village before." Leof pulled at his end of the branch, eager to get home and show off their quarry. Then he remembered George's attire and reconsidered. "Maybe I should try and sneak you some better clothes first. No offence, but if anyone sees you looking like that they might wonder where you're from or what you're after. People around here can't afford to be too friendly to strangers. Stay here, I won't be long."

They lowered the wolf and George crouched down out of sight whilst Leof raced along to one of the buildings and disappeared.

It was strange being alone again. It made him feel uneasy and he didn't like it. He wondered if Millie and his friends were out looking for him. They would have called the police by now; everyone would be fussing and searching for him. George felt a wave of guilt, imagining his panic-stricken parents flying half-way around the world from their important conference on his account.

"Hey, try these. They should fit you." Leof returned, throwing George a brown tunic and a belt made of lamb skin, some woollen leggings and a pair of old leather sandals.

George couldn't help turning his nose up as he took them - they smelt strongly of body odour. Obviously washing powder hadn't been invented yet and he hoped there was nothing living in the fabric. He reluctantly slipped off his T-shirt and tied the tunic around him with the belt. Then, as he took his jeans off, he made a big mistake. He forgot about the contents of his pockets and he forgot to be careful that nothing fell out. George's mobile phone landed in full view, right at Leof's feet. He closed his eyes in dread.

"What's that?" Leof picked it up immediately.

"It's a device for writing things," George said, simplifying a part truth.

"Wow! Do you know how to write?" He looked wide-eyed with respect at George and pressed down on the screen. "How does it work, then?"

Taking it from him, George turned it on. A message flicked up on the screen, "Low battery", and then disappeared. Leof's mouth dropped open.

"It must have come from the gods! How did you get it?"

"My ... brother was given it by the King ... as a reward for fighting in battle." George spluttered out a lie.

"You'd better hide it. They've got pretty vivid imaginations in the village."

"Yeah, you're probably right."

George put the phone in the pouch that hung from his belt and stepped into the tight-fitting trousers and the leather sandals. He wrapped his modern clothes into a bundle and hid them under a bush.

"Where's your horn?" Leof asked.

"My what?"

"Your horn. You can't be travelling without one! You have to blow a horn when you approach a settlement to let the villagers know you come in peace, else they'll think you've come to take their livestock and you'll end up with a spear through you." Leof shook his head in disbelief. "It's lucky that you met me, George."

George was very much inclined to agree.

"Right, let's take this wolf to the mead hall."

A small following of villagers gathered around Leof and George as they heaved the wolf down into the settlement and through a gap in the thorny hedge. The arrival of a stranger along with the wolf was causing a buzz of excitement and curiosity.

"Wes Hal," Leof said in greeting, drawing "Wes Hal" in reply.

"That's the wolf that been after the livestock."

"...and nearly took Aethelwold's arm off."

"Do you reckon it was Leof or that lad that caught it?"

"Must be a mighty good huntsman."

"Wonder where he's from?"

"Don't have much hair on him."

George could feel the hands of small children tugging on his tunic and could hear the whisperings of village girls, eager to know who he was. For a moment he felt like a great knight who had just ridden into town and he couldn't help proudly puffing up his chest and grinning.

Leof led George towards the mead hall which stood central to the village. It was built similarly to the other huts with wood-panelled sides and a straw roof, but its length of forty feet made it by far the grandest building in the village. They went through its tall oak doors, carved with strange symbols and patterns, and into its dark interior. With no windows, the main source of light shone from the open doorway now behind them. Once George's eyes had adjusted he saw that the room was furnished with trestle tables lining the edge of the room on which stood beeswax candles and lamps waiting to be lit. The walls were plastered a dirty white and decorated with long woven wall-hangings that depicted colourful scenes of soldiers fighting in battle, grand social feasts and animals grazing in woodlands. In the centre of the hall were two great pit fires; over one a black cauldron hung from an iron stand and over the other a spit roast was being prepared. George looked above him for a chimney but could only see the enormous oak beams that supported the roof.

The crowd surrounded Leof as he flamboyantly retold the story of slaying the wolf, with a few extra, rather exaggerated, details. He had just begun to tell it again when he was silenced by a hush. George turned around to see a large man with a long bushy beard had entered the room. He could tell the man was important from his attire. He wore a long cloak fastened to his tunic by a very elaborate gold buckle and on his waist another gold buckle adorned his belt.

"What's the uproar in here?" the man boomed.

The crowd moved back to reveal the wolf lying on the wooden floor. He went over to examine it and then, looking more jovial, addressed the crowd again.

"Whoever has slain this creature will sit and feast at my family's table today."

Hands pushed George and Leof into the centre of the hall.

"Well Leofwine! And who's this young hunter?"

"This is George. He's from the north. His brother's been fighting for our King. I wouldn't have caught the wolf without him."

"We are all very grateful to you, Orge. I am Freodheric, the headman of this village and this is my wife Ceolburh and daughter Aelfaed." He gestured to the two women standing beside him. "You are welcome to stay in Widurok for as long as you wish. We are always in need of good hunters and healthy young men are of great use in the fields. Now please excuse me, there is much preparation to be done for the feast and celebrations today, as there is for the rest of you. Oh, and call in the harp player and have him write some music to this story. We shall have it retold as a poem after the feastings." With that the headman turned and left the hall.

There was a scurry as everyone followed him out to return to their work.

"What's happening today?" George whispered to Leof.

"The Litha, remember? They're continuing the celebrations today. There's going to be a huge feast here later with music and storytelling and fires will be lit."

"It sounds like fun."

"I have to help with the food but if you like I can show you around the village first."

"Actually Leof, I don't mean to be rude at all, only I've been awake for most of the night. Is there somewhere I could sleep for a few hours?"

"Of course, come with me I'll show you our family's houses. There's a spare bed in the hut I sleep in, you can use that."

George followed Leof out of the hall and over to a smaller rectangular building. Along either side of the room were four wooden beds, almost like large cots and low to the ground.

"I'll come and get you when the horns start to sound. You've got a few hours yet, you can sleep on that bed over there." He pointed to one in the corner of the hut.

"Okay, thanks Leof. See you in a bit."

George climbed onto the straw mattress and lay on his back, staring up at the exposed rafters and beams.

It seemed that the day had been put aside to continue celebrating what Leof had called the Litha and the slaying of the wolf had heightened the villagers' spirits. But despite the warm welcome George had received, the strangeness of the customs and people, and his familiar yet unfamiliar surroundings, were overwhelming. He felt mentally and physically exhausted. In the last twelve hours he had experienced more than he ever had in his lifetime. Now all he needed was to sleep and allow his mind some time to absorb and adjust to this new world.

Chapter Nine: The Police Search

Early the next morning the police made their base at the village hall. Initially the main focus of the investigation was to interview anyone else who might have seen George and to carry out an extensive search between the playing field and Grandad's front door.

The first search was to be carried out solely by two police dogs and their handlers. There was concern that George's scent would become indistinguishable if the area was contaminated by the perfumes and odours of a horde of locals eager to help.

It was just before Millie was leaving to catch the school bus that the dogs arrived at the house. Grandad brought down the school shirt that George had worn two days before and the dog handlers gave it to the canines to sniff. They immediately set off in the direction that Grandad and Millie had taken on the night George went missing, down the lane towards the heart of the village. When the dogs got to the graveyard, they went straight through the church gates, unlike the route Grandad and Millie had taken past the church and down Rosemary Close. Millie followed at a distance, knowing that George would have been heading for the little gate in the corner of the graveyard, using it as a short cut. However, the dogs suddenly stopped in the middle of the graves and started circling round and going back on themselves. It appeared that George's trail had suddenly gone cold.

The dog handlers gave them the shirt to sniff again but the dogs seemed unable to pick up the trail.

"Well, the boy couldn't have vanished into thin air. Why can't the dogs find any more of his scent?" one of the police officers said, frowning.

"I'm not sure, it's a bit unusual. But it has been quite dry lately and you need moisture in the air for the scent to stick to the ground and vegetation," the handlers explained. "It was also a bit windy last night, which can push the scent in a different direction."

The police and their dogs returned to the base at the village hall to discuss their findings. A couple of hours later a search took place with many of the local villagers volunteering to join in with the police effort. The inspector in charge led the group as they retraced all of the possible routes to the playing field. The few empty houses in the village were checked and a helicopter did a search by air, but there was no sign of anything that could relate to George. The ground being quite dry, not even a footprint was discovered.

The police visited George's school and spoke to his form class and teachers, but no one had any new information for them despite everyone's willingness to assist.

Throughout the afternoon and evening, Millie's parents phoned her continuously but she had nothing reassuring to tell them. Sick with worry they arranged to fly back immediately from South Africa and promised to be in Wybrook by Sunday.

The search was called off for the evening. Millie went straight up to her bedroom knowing there would be no more news to hang around for. She was emotionally drained and yet she was sure she would hardly sleep. Her grandfather came in with some hot chocolate he had made for her. He looked exhausted.

"It's Saturday tomorrow, dear. Make sure you have a good lie-in and catch up on your sleep. Goodnight."

"Goodnight, Grandad."

Millie drank her hot chocolate and closed her eyes.

During the weekend the police expanded their hunt. The village reservoir, which was half a mile from the playing field, was searched by divers, while volunteers walked through nearby woods and the helicopter also continued to skim the village and surrounding fields. All of George's closest school friends were spoken to and questioned.

Sunday morning finally arrived. An airport taxi drew up outside Grandad's cottage and a woman of medium height and build with a short blonde bob stepped out. She was followed closely by a tall man, who was smartly dressed and looked like he took pride in his appearance. Millie rushed to the door and ran into her mother's arms, overjoyed to see her. She felt so relieved she didn't even notice how haggard and distraught both her parents looked. But Grandad did, and the sight of his daughter in such an overwrought state brought tears to his eyes. He must have been nervous about her arrival because now he let out a string of sentences that didn't make much sense to Millie.

"Ann, dear, I'm so sorry. I told him not to go out in the night. Everything has been done to find him, but it's happened again, Ann dear. They've taken away one of our boys. I told him not to go out on the solstice! I told him! I tried to find him that night, I searched till I couldn't walk, but then it started to get light and I knew it was too late. I wish I'd locked the door. I should have stayed awake through the night and made sure they were both safe."

"Dad, please, I'm not interested in those stupid stories." Ann gently took the old man's hand in shared sympathy. "He'll come back, Dad. He has to be somewhere." Ann let go of Grandad's hand and the tears in her eyes reflected her true fears.

Millie's father, Tim, approached from behind and put a protective arm around his wife. He was a man who had followed the life expected of him. He had worked hard at his A-levels, gone to university, began his career, married his girlfriend and then later started a family with the average two children. This seemingly uninteresting path had made him a very reliable father figure, even if he was often too busy to spend time with Millie and George. Unfortunately, he could also be a very unforgiving and unreasonable man when he was upset, as he was now on seeing Grandad.

"If you were so worried, why the hell didn't you call the police the second you found George was gone? Or at least contacted us!"

"It's not Grandad's fault," Millie said stepping between them.

"He was left in your care!" her father continued.

"I never asked to have him here," Grandad replied softly. "I was only trying to help you out."

"Come on, not in front of Millie," her mother said, giving both Grandad and her husband an adult stare.

After a shower and meal, her parents went to the village hall to talk to those in charge of the investigation and spent the remaining day there; but with no good news and no new information, they returned to the house dispirited and quiet.

For some reason Millie had thought everything would be okay once her parents were here, that they would know what to do. Instead things felt worse because now it all felt more real. During the night Millie kept waking to the sound of their voices. Sometimes in hushed tones, sometimes lively and angry, but always with desperation.

The next morning it had been decided that Millie and her parents would go back to their own home and Mrs Gordon would look after Grandad while everything was up in the air. Millie went up to the room to pack her bags. She wasn't sure what to do with George's things, so she folded and collected everything up neatly and put it away in the spare drawers they had been using, out of sight but not gone. Like George was, she hoped.

*

In the months that followed, Millie's parents changed. During the first few weeks they drove around the surrounding towns and villages putting up posters of George. They called newspapers and TV stations to keep him in the public eye. They stayed in constant contact with the police, pestering them for more to be done and jumping to answer the phone or a knock at the door. But no news came.

After a week or so the police stopped actively searching. Officially George's disappearance was an ongoing investigation but the police had as little idea as to his whereabouts as anyone else did. Even the media lost interest and the locals gossiped that George must have run away. George was gone and nothing could be done to change that.

With a lack of community support, a hopelessness took its hold on Ann and Tim. Few words were spoken in the house and Millie often walked into a room to find them sitting alone and simply staring into space, stricken with grief.

Chapter Ten: George's new life

Later in the day George woke with an uncomfortable sensation in his side and thigh. He looked down and pulled back the woollen blanket he was lying on. He had been sleeping on a mattress of straw and horsehair, bits of which were poking through and prodding various parts of his body.

"Cluck! Cluck!"

A noise in the hut startled him. He leaned over the wooden bed and saw two chickens pecking at his clothes on the floor next to the bed. More surprisingly, a goat stood in the open doorway, staring at him motionlessly. George flung off his blanket and climbed out of bed. He shooed the chickens off his clothes and got dressed. His mouth felt dry and he was desperately in need of a drink. He looked around, half expecting to see a sink and tap. Instead he spotted a jug and an empty cup on a table in the corner. He poured himself a drink and took a large gulp. Urgh! It tasted like his father's beer, mixed with warm water. It was disgusting, but in order to quench his thirst he drank it nonetheless.

George had no idea what the time was and hoped to find Leof. He straightened his tunic and pushed past the goat, who obstinately blocked the only exit.

The day was still bright and sunny. The village seemed emptier than it had done when he arrived. He could only guess that the villagers were in their various huts busily preparing for the Litha feast or out hunting. George wandered over to the closest hut and looked in through the open door. Inside, the gloomy space was dominated by a large board with a cloth of red and brown thread stretched upon it.

The huts were not all sleeping areas. Rather, the village as a whole was like the rooms of a modern home split up into separate buildings. Although several of the huts were for sleeping, the mead hall was the dining room and other buildings were used for cooking and storing food; metal and woodwork; keeping livestock; or weaving and sewing clothes. Several different extended families each occupied a group of these huts, although there was only one headman of the village. George was sure he remembered Leof saying that three of the families were free and one wasn't, although he was unsure quite what that meant.

A young girl of about eight was sitting next to the loom, untangling a ball of mustard coloured yarn. She looked up at George.

"Are you looking for Leof?" she asked, recognising George as his new friend.

George nodded.

"He's helping to milk the cows in the field back there," she said, pointing behind her.

George left the room and saw she was directing him to an animal enclosure where there were a dozen cattle and a few horses. In front of the enclosure was a small hut. He walked towards it and peered through the doorway. Inside three boys were attempting to milk a cow that didn't seem to want to be milked. Leof and one of the boys were trying to hold her steady, whilst the other boy was squeezing the milk into a large wooden pail that was almost full.

Leof nodded at George acknowledging him. "Almost done here. This one's a bit frisky when it comes to milking."

The cow suddenly kicked out with her leg and George instinctively rushed to prevent the pail from being knocked over.

"That was close!" one of the boys said, relieved.

Leof came over and took the other side of the pail whilst the boys moved the cow out.

"I need to take this to the women to make into cheese. Come if you want."

Holding the pail between them George and Leof walked back through the village. In the cheese hut a group of women were taking it in turns to churn milk into butter in a barrel while they gossiped.

"Talking about us, ladies?" Leof grinned cheekily. "Where do you want your milk put for curdling, Freya?"

"On the table at the back," the eldest of the women answered. "Is it sheep or goats?

"It's cow's milk this time."

"We were just wondering where your friend is from," said a younger woman with long blonde plaited hair.

"He's from a village north of here. Did you hear about our wolf-slaying?" Leof asked.

"Can't he talk by himself?"

"Yeah, you tell us what happened, Wolf-slayer."

George began to retell the story, carefully leaving out the true reason he was wandering alone in the woods unarmed, and exaggerating his bravery the moment the wolf attacked.

The women and girls listened, hanging on his every word. It wasn't often they had visitors in the village.

"You know you really look and sound like Bordley did when he came here all those summers ago," Freya commented.

"Who's Bordley?"

"He came to the village one summer when he was a young boy and I was just a girl. He married when he reached manhood and set up his own homestead south of here, down past the Hrothingas. I've heard they've got a great brood of children. You're not one of his, are you?"

"No, I'm afraid not." George replied. He was starting to grow accustomed to their curiosity.

They left the women and walked through the village. A group of young, inquisitive children followed them at a distance, giggling and pointing. It seemed to George that whilst he slept, Leof had been busy making his way round the village retelling his wolf-slaying story as much as possible. However, despite all the attention, which Leof obviously enjoyed, he seemed to George a little distant and strange.

"What was that disgusting drink left in the hut I slept in? It was okay to drink, right?" George said jovially.

"It was weak ale. Water isn't always safe to drink," Leof answered flatly.

"Are you okay, Leof?" George asked, taken aback by his tone.

"I'm just wondering when you're going to tell me where you're really from. Because you obviously don't come from any place around here."

"Why would you say that? Where else could I be from?"

"George, your clothes weren't like any I've ever seen, and that magical box you had! You were in the woods alone without any weapons, you've never drunk ale before, you acted like you've never been in a village, let alone seen a simple thing like a cow being milked. What do you imagine I'm thinking?"

"I don't really know what to tell you, Leof."

"Ever since we met I've been trying to decide whether you are a god or some kind of elf. I've just never met anyone as different as you before."

"I swear I'm just a normal boy, not a god, and certainly *not* an elf!" George sighed, "But you're right, I haven't been very honest. I'm ... a bit lost. Well, no, really lost. I have no idea how I got here and absolutely no idea how to get home. I don't *mean* to lie to you, really I don't." George didn't want to lose his only friend and certainly didn't want to be left alone again. "I don't know your kind of people. I'm worried I'll end being sacrificed or burnt for magic."

"Who are you, then?"

George hesitated, unsure if he was able to completely trust Leof yet. But seeing as he *already* didn't believe him, there seemed no harm in confiding in him.

"I'm from the future ... I think. I was walking through my Grandad's village last night in the twenty-first century, which is very different from this one, and then I fell over and hurt my head. Then I was here, in this time, lost in the woods. I know it doesn't sound as if it makes any sense, which is why I couldn't have possibly told you this when we met. You would have thought I was mad ... Well, you probably do now."

George looked at Leof, who was frowning thoughtfully.

"When I met you," he went on "I was just wandering around, hoping to find somebody who would help me. I feel like I'm in a dream, but I guess this is all real, isn't it?"

"Yes it's real. But how can you be from the future if you're not a god?"

"I wish I knew, but I really don't. You will swear not to tell anyone else, won't you?"

"No, I won't tell a soul. I promise," Leof assured him. "They'd probably cut my head off first for bringing you here!" he joked. "Hey, have you still got that box that lights up?"

"Yes, it's in my pouch here."

"We should find a better place for that. Come on, there's a loose floorboard under the bed you slept in, you can hide it in there for now. Who knows what they'll make of it if it ever gets discovered?"

George felt so lucky to have found Leof and so grateful to him for being open-minded.

Before George hid the phone he wrote a short text with the little remaining battery power and sent it to Millie. He knew there was no signal but maybe, somehow, the message would float around in time and would eventually be read. More impossible things had happened to him in the last twenty-four hours. He saved the message in "Drafts" and turned off the phone. Then he took Leof's advice and stashed away the only thing that remained of his old life.

*

George's first day in Widurok soon turned into his first week and then his first month, as he began to adjust to his new way of life. There was always something in the village to keep him occupied and plenty of new skills to learn: farming techniques, carpentry, pottery, new customs and a whole new culture. Leof taught him the Saxon beliefs in the gods and the seven worlds of the cosmos, including their own world, Middangeard. In return for Leof's continuing patience with him, George started to teach him how to write in the modern alphabet. It was a very slow process, but they began every day to have a lesson in private, somewhere they could mark out words in the dust, or mud, without being seen or queried.

One of the hardest changes George had to adjust to was the food, and coping with the cravings he suffered from. There were no sweets, crisps, oranges, bananas, no yoghurts, no chocolate. No coke or lemonade, no tomatoes, no sweetcorn, no fried chips or even potatoes. The food the Saxons ate was very different. It was extremely wholesome and they certainly made the most of the ingredients that nature had provided them with. Plants that George could never have imagined were edible, were gathered and added to dishes. But the variety of cuisine was minuscule compared to what he was used to.

Some days George found harder than others. He missed so much from his old life, even going to school and having books to read! The longing for absent friends and family was the most difficult emotion to deal with. Sometimes it felt so intense that it was like a physical pain stabbing at George, deep inside. At such times he would wander down to the stone marker by the den, where he would sit and stare over to the land where he knew Grandad's house would be built in the future, and he would try to imagine what his friends and family were doing in their time.

As those weeks and months turned into years, the hope he would ever return home began to fade into reverie. George's only consolation was in remaining close to the stone circles, certain that they held the key to his journey through time.

Chapter Eleven: Return to Wybrook

Time passed by slowly. In September, Millie began at the same secondary school that George had been attending when he went missing. She made new friends and discovered new subjects she was passionate to learn about and some she was a little less enthusiastic about. Sometimes she would pass Becky, or Sam and Lee in the school corridor and would acknowledge them, but she avoided conversation which, inevitably, would involve George and never-ending condolences.

Months passed as Millie grew used to George's absence, and then, without her realising, it became years. He always remained in her thoughts, a shadow that she followed out of the house when she walked to school, an empty place that was always at the dinner table, the missing presents for him under the Christmas tree and the extra seat in the family car. Sometimes it was too much. She would bump into a group of his old friends and turn, expecting to see him. Or a certain song or a scene in a film would remind her of him and she would have to sneak away somewhere to cry quietly to herself. Christmas and birthdays were the hardest and, of course, the solstice, when their lives had been changed forever.

Nowadays the family rarely spoke of that summer. Her parents were burdened with the guilt that they had been abroad when George went missing and had been too occupied with their work and careers. Now her mother worked part-time and was home more often, and although her father was out of the house for long hours, they both made an effort to be more involved in Millie's life, almost to the point of annoyance.

Millie hadn't seen her grandfather since the time of George's disappearance, now almost three years ago. The family no longer visited or spoke to Stan, and Millie often wondered how he was and worried if he was coping all right on his own. Millie's father had held him partially accountable as he had taken so long to contact the police and her mother found it too emotional to go back to Wybrook. Most of the time Millie felt it was inappropriate to even mention Grandad's name.

Then one afternoon in May the mood between her parents regarding Grandad began to change. Millie overheard her mother talking in the kitchen on her phone. Her father had called from the office where her parents both worked.

"Why have they decided to change it back to South Africa? I thought they had agreed that the annual conferences will be held in the UK now ... Who are we going to leave Millie with for three weeks? ... No Tim, I don't think so! ... No! It's an absolute no! ... It will not help me come to terms with anything! ... I really don't think my father would actually be willing to have her, anyway ... Trust? I thought you were the one that didn't want her to go there? ... Okay, I'll think about it ... We'll talk when you get back ...Okay ... Okay ... Maybe I'll write him a letter ... I have *not* said yes ... Right ... Bye ... Bye."

Ann put the phone down and turned round to see her daughter staring at her inquisitively.

"Well, I suppose you heard most of that."

"You're going to South Africa again?"

"Maybe, but it's next month, which is too soon to arrange things properly."

"I'm happy to stay with Grandad if you do go: I want to."

"It's not that simple."

"Yes it is."

Her mother sighed irritably in reply and left the room.

Millie didn't hear any more discussion on the matter until a couple of weeks later when she was sitting in her room doing her homework and her parents knocked on the door. To Millie's alarm they entered looking very serious. But they had come to tell her they would be going away and that arrangements had been made for her to stay with Grandad. Millie was overjoyed.

"Well, you've lost your brother, it's not fair on you to lose your grandfather as well," her mother explained.

"It's going to be hard for us and you too, Millie. But I think this will be a good step towards moving on from the past and I hope it will bring some closure." Her father's tone was deep and serious. "Your mother and I both went to see your grandfather last week and we've talked things through. I think it is important that families do stick together and like your mother said, we've already lost one close member and I was wrong to have cut Stan out of our lives. But losing George was the worst thing that has ever happened to me, to all of us, and I hope you understand that."

Of course Millie understood, but she didn't agree that it would bring acceptance. To her, George could never be lost forever, he had to be somewhere in this world.

*

On the first Saturday in June, Millie sat eating her cornflakes while her father faffed around checking that passports and boarding cards had been packed. Her mother was busy preparing Millie's lunch box.

"Our taxi is arriving a few minutes after you leave. So don't forget when you finish school that you are getting on the bus going to Wybrook and the other villages, and not walking home. Are you sure you know exactly where to get off?"

"Yes, Mum. I'm not going to forget. I'm thirteen, not five." Millie rolled her eyes, "I know where Wybrook is."

"And you're sure you're okay with that backpack?"

"Yes Mum, I'm going to leave it in my form-room cupboard, I already told you."

"Ok, well I worry about you. And Grandad for that matter. Make sure you do all your own washing and tidying up. He's not a young man you know."

"Yes Mum, don't worry. We'll both be fine."

Her parents waved to her from the doorstep as she left laden with her backpack. Turning the corner Millie saw a taxi slow down into their road. She felt a sudden exhilarated rush of freedom - no more parents for three weeks!

*

After school Millie sat alone downstairs on the double-decker bus next to the window. She had avoided the other pupils she knew from Wybrook; she wanted to be alone.

The town quickly disappeared and was replaced with wide open green and yellow fields. Millie twirled the strands of her straight, chestnut brown hair. It had recently been cut into a straight bob with a styled fringe and a few blonde highlights. She found herself thinking about George and grinned to herself at the thought of his stupid jokes and their playful fights. It had been lonely at home without him.

The sun shone brightly through the smeared glass, making Millie sleepy. She closed her eyes and rested her head against the window. She dozed off and woke a little later, panicking that they had passed her stop. An elderly lady now sat opposite her. She was clutching an old hessian sack to her chest and was looking directly at Millie.

"Excuse me," Millie asked her shyly, "have we gone through Wybrook yet?"

"Not yet," the woman replied with a rough and crackly voice.

The woman had long, white hair woven into a plait that hung down from a brown scarf and over the shoulder of her long dark coat. Her face was ingrained with deep wrinkles but her eyes were a very bright blue, although looking into them Millie couldn't tell if the woman was looking at her or straight past her. Feeling unnerved, Millie tried to avoid the woman's gaze by watching the moving clouds through the window instead. She sensed the woman's stare still upon her, and wanted to tell her that staring was rude when the woman spoke again.

"What is it you see?"

"Excuse me?" Millie responded in surprise.

"In the clouds, what is it you see?"

Confused, Millie looked back to the sky. The clouds had formed into a shape similar to a curved dagger.

"Seaxneat is sending a warning." The woman spoke slowly. "The path ahead of you will be testing." She leaned forward and shook a long, bony finger in Millie's direction. "Beware of those that hide the truths."

Millie wondered if she was slightly mad, or drunk, and shifted uneasily in her seat. She glanced across at her fellow passengers to see if they were listening but it appeared not. She wished now she had sat upstairs next to Becky.

"Are you a fortune teller?" she asked.

The woman made no reply and returned to staring out of the window.

There was a general rustling as the other passengers gathered their belongings; the bus was approaching Wybrook. Millie heaved her backpack over her shoulders and then picked up her school satchel with her free hand and climbed down from the bus.

A large lady swung her heavy shopping into Millie as she barged by, knocking the bag out of her hand. The flap fell open and the contents were strewn untidily across the pavement. Millie hastily bent down to stop her books being trampled on but it was too late. She let out a "tut" of annoyance as her English book was stepped on by a man wearing shiny brown shoes.

"My goodness, what on earth are you doing?" the owner of the shoes joked.

Millie looked up to see a familiar face.

"Grandad!"

"Don't worry, my love, I'll take care of this." Stan carefully bent down and scooped everything back up into the satchel. "Why have you brought so much stuff? Are you planning on staying for good?" He chuckled warmly and put his arm around his granddaughter and her backpack. "Well, you know you're always welcome."

"It's not all mine. I've got some things for you, from Mum." Millie was pleased to see her grandfather. Despite the three-year gap, he was immediately the same with her.

They walked slowly along the high street and down the lane to Grandad's house. Millie took her bags up to the room she had always shared here with George. She unpacked some of her clothes and folded them away into one of the drawers. It was good to be back. In the bottom drawers were George's things. She recalled putting them away on the night she was last here. She took out a pair of his trousers and held them up against herself. They were probably too small for her now, let alone George.

She could hear the loud volume of Radio 4's "PM" programme coming up from the back room and went downstairs to find her grandfather. He was in his old armchair with an unlit pipe in his mouth and dressed in a smoking jacket that was as faded as the décor of the room.

"Millie, my love. Have you found everything you need up there?"

"Yes, it's great. Thank you," Millie replied.

"Oh, by the way, it's meant to get stormy at the end of the week and I must confess that I have never managed to get around to fixing that latch on your window."

"Okay, I'll let you know if it keeps falling open."

"Well, I can always nail it shut if need be. Now, I don't suppose you have the time on you, dear?"

"It's five to six."

"Morning or evening?"

"Erm, evening ..." Millie replied, catching the twinkle in his eye.

"That must mean it's time for supper, then."

Grandad got up and shuffled to the kitchen to prepare some sandwiches. Millie followed, remembering her promise to help out.

Chapter Twelve: Under the Alder Tree

The weather was extremely warm for June and Millie spent the next few days making the most of the long evenings and catching up with Sam, Lee and Becky. They were either on their bikes or up at the playing field and skate ramp. However, towards the end of the week the sky became overcast, as predicted, and the wind grew steadily stronger. The air felt electrically charged with the brewing of a summer storm.

Millie lay on her bed reading as the rain began to patter against the window panes. From her room she could hear the church bell-ringers practising. Every Thursday the noise of the bells rang down the village streets and through the houses. Tonight the wind and rain were joining in, like one big celestial orchestra.

Millie yawned and closed her book. It had been a long day and although it wasn't quite dark yet, she was ready to sleep. As she got under the covers the whistling wind began to howl and the rain became heavier and now pelted against the window, drowning out the sound of the bell-ringers. Millie did her best to ignore the outside world and managed to drift off to sleep.

The power of the storm increased as darkness fell. Sometime in the night, as the wind threw itself repeatedly against the house, the top pane of Millie's sash window dropped to the window sill with a crash. Millie woke with a start as the gale swept freely into the room and the floral curtains flapped about madly. She was instantly reminded of when the window had slid down on the night George had gone missing, and she had seen the old woman in the garden.

The wind and shadows created strange shapes that moved around the room and Millie couldn't help but feel afraid; she clung to the safety of her duvet.

"I'm being ridiculous!" she told herself and bravely crept out of bed. Her hair was swept from her face by the gale as she tried to push the window back up. Trying not to look through the glass into the shadowy world of the garden she managed to get it back in place and firmly pushed the latch across to hold it there. The room was still once more. Millie breathed a sigh of relief and climbed back into bed.

She tried to remember the strange dream she'd been having. Yes, the old woman on the bus had been trying to tell her something, something about old stones and a prince on a horse - or was it a unicorn? She dropped back to sleep, imagining that the animal was chasing George and that someone behind was waving a sword.

"Bang!" Within a few minutes the window had fallen open and woken her again. But this time there was a scratching noise from somewhere above her: something was sliding its way down from the top of the roof. She held her breath. The slithering noise paused just above her open window and then turned into a crash as it smashed onto the patio below. Millie reached over to turn on the lamp but nothing happened. She pressed the switch again, but still nothing.

"Millie, are you okay?" her grandfather anxiously called out to her.

"Grandad!"

"Isn't it windy?" Stan exclaimed as he entered the room and rushed over to shut the window. "Well! They said there was going to be a storm, but they didn't say anything about a hurricane. The whole roof's going to come off if it carries on like this!"

Millie hoped he was exaggerating. "Is that what that noise was? I heard something coming off the roof."

"Yes, we've lost a few tiles from the front of the house, too. Never mind, there's nothing that can be done about it now. But I *can* do something about that window. Give me a couple of minutes, the power seems to have gone off, too."

He returned with a hammer and a few nails which he drove into the wooden frame while Millie shone a torch for him. Feeling satisfied with his handiwork he bade Millie goodnight and went back to his bed.

*

The gale continued through the night but by the morning it had passed and the village was calm again. From her bedroom Millie could see a fallen tree at the end of the garden and debris was littering the lawn. She quickly got dressed and ran down stairs. Her grandfather was in the hall taking off his hat and hanging up his walking stick.

"Grandad," she called, "have you seen the garden?"

"Yes, isn't it a mess? I've just walked down the road and according to Teddy Butcher, there are trees blocking every exit out of the village. I hope the fête won't be cancelled."

"The fête's not till next week."

"Yes, that's true. Well, there won't be any school buses today. They're saying it's the worst gale here in fifteen years. Oh, and I saw Becky, who had been waiting at the bus stop. She was asking after you. I said you were still asleep - that I hadn't wanted to wake you after your disturbed night."

"No school!" Millie grinned with joy: hurricanes were almost as good as snow!

After breakfast Millie went out to look for her friends. She saw Lee on the corner of the street clearing some fallen branches with a neighbour.

"Hey, Mills!" he shouted, calling her over.

"Lee, I can't believe the storm last night. There are tiles from our roof all over the street!"

"Yeah, I know. Next door had a tree land on their car roof. It's all dented."

"Oh no, that's terrible. It's pretty good there's no school, though! I'm going over to Becky's if you want to come."

"All right, let's take the short cut, then."

Becky's house was just outside the village; a footpath led them through the fields and halved the journey. On the way Millie spotted the den. It had been devastated. The big alder tree that had created the den's roof had been entirely uprooted and was now lying on its trunk across the ditch and into the unkempt garden of one of the bungalows behind.

They clambered down into the ditch, amazed at how different and open it was. No one had been down here in three years. They had all outgrown the excitement of having a den, but now she felt almost guilty for having abandoned it. It had been sacred to them as young children, a secret place that they had discovered that no one else knew about. Now it was destroyed.

"What's that?" Millie knelt down. Something was protruding from amongst the uplifted earth. It looked like the underside of a clay bowl. She began to dig out the earth and roots around it. Lee joined her and together they excavated what appeared to be a completely intact clay urn. Careful not to damage it, Millie picked it up with both hands. It was about five inches high and a rough cylinder shape, sealed with a rounded top.

"Is it hollow?" Lee asked.

She turned it over in her hands and there was a knock as an object moved inside.

"There's something in it!" Millie cried excitedly.

"Here, let me have a look." Lee reached out and snatched it from her.

"Oy! Give it back!" She argued with him as he held it up high, at arm's length.

"Someone must have made the pot around it. Let's smash it open."

"No, leave it. It's probably really ancient."

Millie tried to grab it but Lee quickly spun around. Then as she yanked at his arm, the urn fell from his grasp. It hit the flat stone rock and immediately cracked into five pieces. They both gasped in disbelief. Between the broken clay lay a very un-ancient mobile phone.

It was a fairly large phone of an earlier model and was protected by a crumbling green camouflage case. It lay in its bed of clay pieces with its LCD screen looking up at them. They stared at it for a second in confusion before both diving down to grab it.

"Mine!" shouted Lee wrapping a hand around it.

"It's George's!" Millie yelled.

"What?" Lee thought she must be joking.

"Give it here." She reached out an open palm.

"Wait a minute." He shoved her away with his elbow and held the phone up. "I remember George did have a mobile like this. We used to make fun of it because it only had a camera on it, no games or internet. And he definitely had a camouflage case, cos we made fun of that as well."

Millie snatched at the phone. Some of the plastic flaked off into her hands.

"Our parents got us both one of these phones ages ago. I wonder if it still works." She pressed down on the green button but nothing happened.

"Might just be the battery. Have you still got yours?"

"It probably got thrown away, unless it's somewhere in my room. I don't suppose they make them any more."

"Are you sure it's George's?"

"I don't know, it looks like it and you recognised it too. It would be a bit of a coincidence otherwise wouldn't it? I mean, it has to be somebody's and he did use to come here."

"I suppose. Unless it was put there by someone else ... but no one else knows this place."

"Yeah, and who would bother to put it in a clay jar like that?"

"No one I know. But it got there somehow."

Millie was as baffled as Lee. She put the phone in her coat pocket and made sure it was zipped up.

"We should take it to the police."

"Yes, we should, but not right now - they'll just take it straight off me. I'd rather keep it for a bit. I'll be going back home in a couple of weeks, I might be able to get it working again."

"Okay, I won't tell anyone. Come on, let's get to Becky's."

Where was her old phone? It must be back at her parents' home in the box under her bed. Millie had a spare key for an emergency; she wondered if she could make an excuse to go back there next weekend.

Chapter Thirteen: The Urn

After seeing Becky, Millie spent the rest of the day helping Grandad clear the garden and fix the roof. Her grandfather's garden was overgrown with tall weeds that her family had offered to cut in the past, but her grandfather had refused, saying that nature grows as nature intends. Lying across the high grass were loose branches, leaves and tiny hard apples that had been ripped from the garden trees in the storm. A collection of old newspapers that had been kept in a black bin-liner had also been tipped up and paper was strewn everywhere. As the nettles repeatedly stung Millie's hands she didn't feel that she quite agreed with Grandad's philosophy of gardening. But he seemed very jolly as he whistled to himself whilst he loaded the debris she gathered into the wheelbarrow.

"Are you enjoying your day off from school?" he called out to her.

"Of course. I always enjoy any days off school," she lied.

"Oh, well that's good. Back on Monday, though."

"Grandad?"

"What, dear?"

Millie hesitated. They hadn't really spoken of George since she had been back. "That night George went missing ... Where do you think he went?"

Grandad dropped the branch he was holding and sighed as though he was about to say something, but then shook his head instead.

"What, Grandad? Will you *please* tell me? He is my brother!"

"I really don't know, Millie." The look on Millie's face showed that this was *not* an acceptable answer. Grandad reached over and patted her on the arm. "In the first few months I thought he would somehow find his way back to us, but all these years ... I just don't know now. Maybe we will never find out what happened to him."

"But Grandad, you can't give up on him!" Millie exclaimed. "You're one of the only people that truly believed he didn't run away. You *do* believe that, don't you?"

Stan only shrugged his shoulders sympathetically.

Millie pictured in her mind what George had looked like when they had last seen him. A thirteen-year-old with scruffy hair, usually hidden under a hood or a cap, and always dressed in the same blue jeans. She thought of them playing out here in the garden and the time she had beaten him scoring goals after he had teased her all day for being a girl. He would be sixteen now. Millie fought back the tears that swelled in her eyes. Why did it always have to be so hard to talk about? She turned the mobile over in her pocket. Perhaps it was time to put the past behind them; being embroiled in grief had only worn them all down. Maybe it was better to give up than be forever waiting and hoping for George's return. What difference did it make that she had his phone now?

"I found something of George's." There was no point in keeping it a secret from Grandad. And besides, she wanted to see his reaction.

"What do you mean? What is it?"

"Down by the field over there," she said pointing across the garden, "we used to have a den we would meet in. An old tree next to it was uprooted in the storm and I found a clay pot in its roots. Me and Lee argued over it and it broke and inside was something of George's."

"A clay pot?"

"Yes, like an urn."

"Do you have it with you now?"

"No it broke, like I said." Millie hadn't thought to take it with her. They had been too concerned about the phone. "It's still in the den, though. I could go now and collect the pieces."

"Yes, I think you should. I would be very interested in seeing them."

*

Millie ran back to the den and climbed down its muddy bank again. The clay pieces were lying where they had fallen. She picked up a piece and turned it over in her hand. It was covered in a layer of soil. She spat on the sleeve of her jumper and rubbed away at it until her sleeve turned dark brown. An image of her mother's scowling face on washing day flickered in her mind. She smiled and put the five broken pieces into a large sandwich bag and took them back to the house. Grandad helped her to lay them out on the dining table.

"What do you make of it, Grandad?"

He rolled a piece over in his hands.

"Hmm, looks like they need a bit of cleaning up." He walked out of the room and came back with an old toothbrush. "Here," he said handing it to her, "you can use the sink."

Millie carefully submerged the broken urn in warm water and then used the brush to gently scrub at one of the pieces. The dirt began to fall away and she noticed what looked like scratches. The more she cleaned it, the more deliberate they started to look. It appeared to be some form of writing going across the clay in a banner. She scrubbed at another two pieces and held them together. The strange inscription ran right around the circumference of the urn.

Once the bits of clay had all been cleaned, Millie dried them with some kitchen towel and took them back through to the dining room. Her grandfather had returned to his work in the garden and she was alone. Opening the bureau she searched for some super-glue and carefully ran it along each edge of the clay before holding the pieces together in a firm grip. She left the glue to set for a couple of minutes, then took out some thin paper and, putting it over the markings, gently pencilled a rubbing of the inscription. As she did so the writing became clearer. She wasn't sure if it *was* an inscription. The letters weren't like any others she had seen before and each one was different. Millie counted them, there were twenty-nine in total. Some looked similar to the alphabet - she could make out what seemed like an F, an R, an M, an I and an X - but they were all written using straight lines. There was also a pattern of intertwining swirls surrounded by a circle of chevrons on the top. Finally Millie turned the urn over to see if there was anything on the bottom. She stopped dead. Emblazoned in the urn as clear as day was her name "Millie" and the word "Saberht" written below.

Grandad appeared behind Millie and patted her on the head, making her jump. He softly said, "Only once did anyone ever come back."

"Come back from where?" Millie was busy recovering from the shock of seeing her name.

"From the time when civilisation was young and nature was respected."

"What? What do you mean, Grandad?"

"Over a thousand years ago, Wybrook was surrounded by ancient woodland further than the eye could see, a place anyone could get lost in. Unfortunately the ancient sometimes gets mixed up with the modern, or the other way round."

Millie sighed. Grandad frequently went off on a tangent and talked in riddles.

"I don't know what you are talking about, Grandad. This is just an old pot, not a magical lamp with a genie inside."

Grandad gave a strange knowing look. "You'd be surprised. Your generation will never understand the realness of things. For you lot, all the magic in the world is just sold to you as make-believe films for you to watch and games for you to play on your X-stations."

"Play-stations and X-boxes," Millie mumbled under her breath.

"You know, my dear, being old doesn't mean being stupid. There's a lot of things your generation has forgotten about, things you've never been told and didn't know existed. Look around you, Millie: everything you see, everything you do or touch. Where do you think it came from?"

"Someone made it?"

"Yes, they did. Everything in your life has come from those before you, knowledge passed on and built upon. Some things change, some things remain and some things are forgotten. But everything is linked to ways of the past. That cup sitting next to you on the table. The form of it was designed by people thousands of years ago. The cars that we build, the shape of the wheel that makes it able to move forward was invented in the fifth millennium BC. And so it is with everything."

"But that's got nothing to do with George!"

"Everything is connected to the past. Everything. And maybe everything is not as strictly linear as we think."

"Linear?"

"Yes, dear. Time as we know it goes forward in a straight direction - 2014, then 2015 and 2016. It's not 2016 one year then 2205 the next then back to 1998."

"But you just said everything's not linear."

"I said *maybe* everything's not always as *strictly* linear as we think. You need to decide that for yourself."

"So you're saying that George disappeared back in time?"

Whatever the point Grandad was trying to make, it seemed long-winded and didn't make much sense. But he did know something, Millie was sure of it. What was it that odd woman had said? "Beware of those that hide the truths."

It was up to Millie to discover what had happened. She only had two weeks left in Wybrook. This was her best - maybe her only - chance of solving the mystery.

She knew it didn't add up. How could a piece of modern technology get entwined in the roots of an old tree? The broken urn lay on the bureau in front of her as testimony to something for which there was no logical explanation. After listening to Grandad talking about time, Millie wondered whether the world was as simple as most adults pretended it was. Perhaps if she could prove the age of the urn she could begin to make some sense of it all.

Millie remembered that Sam's dad worked in a museum and that he had something to do with archaeology: he would be the best person to ask. It was getting late now but she could go there tomorrow. It would be the weekend so there was a good chance that Mr Reynolds would be home.

*

The next morning Millie slipped out of the house carrying her satchel bag with the urn and rubbing safely inside. Sam's family lived in one of the new houses built at the opposite end of Wybrook. She decided not to tell Mr Reynolds about the phone. It wasn't always a good idea to tell people everything, especially when "everything" included theories that were barely credible.

"Hello, Millie. I'm afraid Sam's gone out with his mother."

Mr Reynolds was a tall slender man in his late fifties. Millie had only ever seen him dressed in a suit, and even now he answered the door in neatly pressed trousers and a smart shirt under a woollen waistcoat, a style that Sam certainly hadn't inherited.

"Hello, Mr Reynolds. Actually I was wondering if I could speak to you."

Mr Reynolds looked surprised. He rarely had much to do with the younger generation, although he was always very friendly and happy to help.

"It's about history," she added.

"Oh, of course. My favourite subject! Please come in and I'll do my best to assist."

Millie stepped into the hall and showed him the contents of the plastic bag.

"I found this in a ditch near my grandad's house. The storm blew over a tree and uncovered it. I thought it looked very old and I wanted to get your opinion as to when it might have been left there."

"Mm, let's get it under some light."

Millie followed him through to his study where he took the urn from her and held it under a magnifying glass that was attached to a bright lamp.

"I see you've glued it together." He turned the clay over in his hands. "It certainly looks as if it could be very old. I would say it is an urn but it's rather unusual not having an opening. Maybe a vessel designed to keep something safe, or even a decoration of some kind. I'm only able to speculate, of course."

Millie leant over the microscope in wonder; Mr Reynolds was reminded of what it was like to be young and curious about the past.

"OK, I'll tell you what. We're currently researching a new method of pinpointing the age of pottery at the museum. It's called rehydroxylation dating. Unfortunately you can't use carbon dating on pottery because it doesn't contain any carbon, so it's all been a bit complicated in the past with ceramics, but hopefully this method will revolutionise things. It basically tells us the date of a piece by how much its weight has changed. Pottery reacts with moisture from the environment as soon as it leaves the kiln and so it starts to regain weight - only a little bit, but we can measure how much. And by following a precise kinetic law, we can work out how long it took to regain that much moisture and so figure out its age, roughly. Clever stuff, eh? I can take your urn in with me on Monday and include it in the research programme. Does that sound good?"

Millie beamed, although most of what he'd said had gone over her head. "Really? That's fantastic! Thank you so much. I am desperate to know more about it. There's also that mark at the top there and the writing around the edge."

"Oh yes, well that pattern is probably the printer's seal. It might give us an idea of what era it's from and I'll have a look at the inscription."

"Thank you, Mr Reynolds."

"It's a pleasure. I'll see you again next week, bye now."

Millie walked home feeling excited. Although she was unsure what she wanted the results to prove.

Chapter Fourteen: Mrs Gordon

"Mum?" Millie's mother had called her from South Africa on Sunday afternoon and had been talking non-stop about their trip. Her parents had been to a safari park for the first time. They had stroked a zebra and come within a few yards of a lion.

"Mum?" Millie was finding it hard to get a word in edgeways.

"What is it, dear?"

"Do you know where my old phone and charger are? The phone you got me when I was ten?"

"That old thing? What do you want it for? I thought the screen was cracked?"

"I just wanted to find out Jenny's number. I haven't spoken to her since primary school. We always said we would stay in contact

"Sorry dear, I think it was thrown out. I'll check next time I'm in the loft. That's the only place it could be ... unless it's with all that junk under your bed."

"All right. Thanks, Mum." Millie paused for a moment. She desperately wanted to speak to her mother about George. "Mum?"

"Yes, Millie?"

"Has Grandad ever spoken to you about time travel? Have you ever thought that George went back in time?"

"Please don't do this to me when I'm the other side of the world, Millie," her mother replied, irritated. Millie heard her draw in a long breath and could picture her rubbing her temples to compose herself. When her mother finally spoke again it was with a soft tone. "Yes, Grandad use to talk about it a lot when I was a child and I probably did believe him then. And sometimes, when I needed an answer as to what had happened to my little boy, I imagined that George was having a great adventure sometime in the past. But these are just dreams and vivid imaginings. Sometimes you have to confront the truth. Like I've said for the past year, it's time to move on."

Millie bit her lip and didn't reply.

"Have you been speaking to that Mrs Gordon?" her mother said with a change of tone. "You know her husband was half mad. Whatever she's said to you, you shouldn't go believing it."

"I haven't spoken to her at all! Why? Does *she* know something about George?"

"No. She doesn't know anything, that's my point."

The conversation ended shortly. But her mother's remarks about Mrs Gordon left Millie thoughtful.

*

That night Millie dreamed again. She found herself standing outside in the dark. She wasn't sure what she was doing there but it didn't seem to matter. A figure was shuffling towards her; it got within a few metres of her and then stopped. From the person's attire Millie recognised it as the elderly woman she had seen on the night George had left. The woman lifted up her head and pushed back the hood of the cloak that shadowed her face. Now Millie saw it was the lady who had sat opposite her on the bus last week. The woman was mouthing something Millie couldn't make out. With a slow movement she stretched out her left arm and turned to point to something behind her. In the background was the village church.

"Runes in the stones."

Millie opened her eyes and sat up in bed gasping, relieved that it was only a dream. She dressed in her school uniform and went downstairs. The kitchen clock told her it was only seven o'clock. Millie finished a bowl of cornflakes and grabbed her school bag and front door key. She shouted goodbye up the stairs to Grandad and took the route to Becky's house.

Millie was feeling a growing sense of obligation to George. She was becoming increasingly convinced that there was more to his disappearance than she was aware of and who was ever going to solve this mystery if she didn't? It was up to her and time was running out. She needed answers and she needed help.

"Millie," Becky's mother greeted her at the door, "you're up early!"

Pat Hockley was a big woman with the same bird's-nest hair as Becky, plus a heavy touch of peroxide.

"Come in. Becky is just ironing her school shirt so I'm afraid you're going to have wait for her. I'll make you a cup of tea."

Millie followed her through to the kitchen with their golden retriever, Perkins, running through her legs. Millie sat down at the table and watched Becky bending over the ironing board.

"Are you alright, Mills? You look a bit stressed." Becky was still clothed in her zebra onesie pyjamas.

Millie told them both about recent events: finding the pot with George's phone; what Grandad had said about time travel; Mr Reynolds' confirmation that the urn was very old; and now her mother's odd remark about Mrs Gordon. Mrs Hockley had lived in Wybrook all her life and harboured a love for gossiping. If anyone knew anything about what was going on in the village, it was her.

"Well to be honest, I don't believe in all that magic and stuff, but I do think it's rather odd that George went missing like that on Midsummer Eve. People here are always going on about it - well mostly the older locals, especially with Mrs Gordon's son going missing on the solstice all those years ago. That's why they reckon her husband died, never got over it."

"He went missing on the *same day*?" A shiver crept down Millie's spine.

"Well, yes. Same day, but well over thirty years ago. That's probably what your mother was talking about. I would imagine it's also why the police have still kept the case open, although nobody could piece together any connection. Bit embarrassing for them I reckon. That's why they decided he was a runaway. And not just that," Mrs Hockley went on, "for generations there's been talk of people going missing every now and then from Wybrook, and always on the solstice. But nothing has ever been proven and so it's just become hearsay. Poor Mr Gordon was the only one whoever really knew anything. The search for his son consumed him, took over his whole life. He gave up his shop-keeping to find out what had happened to little

Bobby and turned the shop into his study. 'Course he's been dead … erm … must be ten years now, but he told his wife never to touch anything in there and so she hasn't. As well as which, in his will he left all the shop's contents to his son, convinced he was alive, which can't be proven otherwise, and so legally speaking they're not even Mrs Gordon's to touch."

Mrs Hockley leaned closer to Millie and lowered her voice. "But you know, Mr Gordon was my mum's cousin so we used to go round there sometimes …"

"Did you ever go in the old shop?" Millie asked.

"Only once, just before Mr Gordon died. My mum and Mrs Gordon left me alone in the dining room while they went to make tea and chat in the kitchen. I noticed that the door that leads through to the old shop had been left slightly open. Naturally, curiosity got the better of me and I went inside. All the old shop shelves were still there, even the counter. I'm sure there were even old cans of food still waiting to be sold. But most of all there were books. They filled every corner. I had a peep at some of the titles. All about history and time travel and ancient forests and old myths they were. Loads of books, like a library. Then Mrs Gordon saw me and ushered me out. I think she was a bit embarrassed about her husband being so obsessed by it all. Poor little Bobby. He was a few years older than me but I still remember him."

"Maybe I should ask her about it."

"Oh no, I wouldn't recommend you do that, dear. She won't want to bring it all up and she's ever so funny around kids anyway, you should know that."

"Perhaps we remind her of Bobby."

"You're probably right, but it doesn't make any difference."

"But I'll be leaving in a couple of weeks and I really have to find out what happened to George!" Millie argued.

"I'll go round to her house with you, Millie, after school," Becky offered, not wanting to see her friend upset. "But don't be surprised if she doesn't want to talk to us."

It seemed to Millie that there was a lot of hidden mysteries amongst the older generation of Wybrook. Things that were talked about in whispers or discussed after doors had been closed.

*

Mrs Gordon lived in the middle of the village on the high street. The section that had been the old shop always had the blinds pulled right down over the windows, although the rest of the house looked very respectable and well kept. There were two entrances to the house - the opening to the old shop, that hadn't been in use for decades, and the side entrance to which Millie and Becky approached to ring the bell. Mrs Gordon opened the door. She frowned, recognising the girls and their school uniforms.

"Can I help you with something?"

Neither of the girls were sure of the best approach. After a cold silence, during which Mrs Gordon looked from one girl to the other, Becky spoke.

"Mrs Gordon, I've been telling Millie about my Gran's cousin, Mr Gordon, and your son Bobby."

Mrs Gordon turned bright red. "Oh, have you?" she said in a haughty tone, "That's what you like to talk about, is it?"

"We heard he went missing on the same day as George and we thought you might ..."

"You thought I might what?" Mrs Gordon interrupted. "Want to discuss the ghosts of the past with two little girls! I trust you don't go sticking your nose into everyone's business!"

Mrs Gordon went to shut the door but Millie instinctively wedged her foot in the way.

"Please, Mrs Gordon, if you know anything about George, please help us."

"There's nothing for you to know," she replied from behind the door, "and would you kindly remove your foot!"

Millie did so and the door slammed shut. She sighed and looked at Becky.

"Well that went well," Millie said sarcastically.

"We'll just have to go in there when she goes out."
"What! We can't do that!"

"What do you mean? You're the one that just stuck your foot in her door! Listen we're won't be taking anything, just looking at stuff. And anyway it's not hers, is it? Its Mr Gordon's and Bobby's and we'd be helping them if we could find out what had happened to George. What do you say?"

"I suppose. But what if we get caught?" Millie wasn't convinced by Becky's reasoning. It still amounted to breaking into someone's home.

"Sometimes you've just got to do things that seem wrong, in order to make things better. You heard what my mum said. Mr Gordon might have found out something really important."

Millie was always wary of being led astray by friends and felt uncomfortable with the idea, but the shop was the only lead she had for getting information and time *was* of the essence.

"She usually goes with my grandad to the Monday Club at the village hall. It'll be on this evening at about seven. Look, Becky, are you sure this is going to work? I mean how are we going to get in for a start? Someone is bound to see us and call the police or tell our parents."

"It'll be fine. Oldies here never lock their houses and if they do they usually leave a spare key under the door mat, so it won't exactly be breaking in. Come on, we'll go home, then meet here at seven." Becky enjoyed being in charge. "I'll get Sam and Lee to help us - they can keep look out."

The boys were always a bit restless living in a small village and Becky was confident that they wouldn't need much persuasion.

At seven o'clock the four of them were crouching below a hedge behind Mrs Gordon's property. Her car came to life and sputtered out of the driveway to fetch Grandad.

"Come on, then!"

Sam took the lead and crawled through a gap in the hedge into the back yard. Lee and the two girls followed him. He reached the side entrance and turned the door knob.

"At least try knocking first, just in case," Millie whispered nervously.

Sam rapped his knuckles briefly at the door. There was no reply,

"Best just go in."

It was an old cottage like Millie's grandfather's, with exposed beams lining the wall and ceiling. The hall looked like it had recently been decorated and the carpet was immaculate. Millie wondered if they should take their shoes off; she had never invited herself into someone else's house before.

"Come on, it's this way," motioned Becky. She led Millie through the lounge to a door. It was locked. "This is it! This is Mr Gordon's shop."

"Where do you think she keeps the key?" Sam asked. He and Lee had followed the girls in, too curious to be left outside.

"Why don't you have a quick look in the kitchen and I'll check the hall."

Millie looked around the dining room and checked the dresser, but found nothing. She spotted a pot on the mantelpiece and lifting it up she heard the noise of metal against china. Inside was a long key. She took it out and tried it in the door. After a bit of resistance it gave a sudden click and turned. The door opened.

Chapter Fifteen: The Old Shop, and a History Lesson

The room was very dark but Millie could immediately see that this was the old shop. She looked around, gawking in disbelief. She had walked from an immaculately clean and tidy house into a large room piled with more objects and clutter and dust than she had ever seen. The shelves next to her still housed glass sweet jars, now empty and ageing, and on the counter was the rusty old-fashioned till. Odd items were strewn amongst the aisles: china dolls, a bread bin, a bicycle wheel. Everything was at least thirty years old. In between this bric-à-brac, where there had once been packets of food, were rows of books, just like Mrs Hockley had said: old, ancient, new, thick, thin, big and small.

"Wow!" The others entered behind her. "Why does she keep all this stuff? It's amazing, it's like going back in time."

Millie echoed Stan's words under her breath: "Everything is connected to the past."

The area in which she stood had once served as the serving counter. It was now stacked with paperwork, on top of which lay an open book covered in dust. Millie picked it up and looked at the cover. Pressed into old leather was the title *The Anglo-Saxon Chronicles*[1]. She turned back to the page where it had been left open.

"Oh my goodness, this is ancient! It's written in Old English or something. I can't understand it. Look, this bit's been underlined."

604: Mellitum he sende to bodiende East-Seaxum fulluht. ðar was se cing gehaten Sæbyrht.

"There's some modern English in the margin," observed Lee, leaning over her shoulder. "Perhaps it's a translation."

Millie wiped away the dust and read the faintly pencilled text: "Six Hundred and Four AD: Mellitus he sent to preach baptism to the East Saxons. There the king was called Saberht."

"The East Saxons? That's us, that's what Essex is short for," Sam told them.

"Saberht?" Millie said, repeating the King's name. "That was written on the urn we found."

If Saberht was the King in 604AD, did that mean the urn was from the same time? But if George wanted to tell her the time he was in, why hadn't he written the year instead of the King's name? Millie put the book down, her heart beating rapidly. Maybe George hadn't known the year, so had used the King's name instead, hoping she would research it.

"Hey, what about this, then?" Becky was standing in front of a map of seventh century East Saxony that was pinned onto the wall. "Essex is loads bigger than it is now. Look, it includes Middlesex and London, and Epping Forest goes all the way to Colchester! It covers two-thirds of the whole county!"

"Wow! That would have been brilliant for mountain biking and single track," Lee exclaimed.

"Or motocross!" Sam added.

The friends wandered around the aisles, marvelling at all the antiques. Millie watched as they played around with an old peasant girl costume and then sat on the cashier's counter to read through the titles of some of the books. *British Mythology, Spells from the Dark Ages, History of Essex, Saxons in England.* Her eyes scanned the spread of clutter for something more specific and she noticed the edge of a folder tucked under the till. She pulled it out and saw that it had "Important - Bobby" scrawled on its cover. Inside was a wad of various papers, on top of which was a photograph of a very old painting. It was extremely faded but it appeared to be a young girl standing at the edge of a lake, breathing yellow smoke into a boy's mouth. Millie turned it over and saw "St Mary" scrawled on the back.

"Is the church here called St Mary's?" Millie called out to them.

Becky came over and took the photo from her. "Yes, that's the name of Wybrook church. I wonder if this is one of the wall paintings that they uncovered there." Beckys' father was church warden and she often wandered about the building whilst he was locking up. Millie made a mental note to quiz her about the painting later.

Underneath the photo was an article that had been torn from the *Essex Chronicle.*

"Village boy still missing" announced the headline. "Bobby Gordon is still missing a month after he was last seen on the 21 June. Locals are preparing for the worst."

Click. Bang!

"What was that?" whispered Becky.

"She's back!"

"Already?"

"Quick, over here," Sam called. "The shop door looks like it's just bolted!"

But the bolt was stiff with age and lack of use and had almost rusted into the cleats.

"There must be some oil in here," said Becky. "There's just about everything else."

"Give me your lip balm," Sam said.

Becky rummaged in her pocket and gave him a small tub.

"Don't use it all, it's chocolate flavour," she whispered as he smeared it generously over the bolt and cleats.

With a wiggle they were free and with a sharp tug the door opened. They ran off but Millie, remembering the folder, dashed back in to grab it from the counter. As she picked it up there was an exclamation from the dining room next door and she saw the door handle begin to turn. She hurried towards the shop entrance and out onto the street, running as fast as she could. Millie passed a row of fir trees and heard a whistle to her right. Ducking into a driveway she found Becky, Lee and Sam hiding in the hedge.

When the four of them were sure that they hadn't been followed they crept back out onto the path.

Becky breathed a sigh of relief, "Oh my goodness, that was so close."

"I thought she was going to catch you in there, Millie!" Sam said. "What did you go back for?"

"I had to get this folder. But I think she saw me - only from behind, but she's bound to know it was me. She sees me every time I'm at my grandad's."

"What did you take it for, you idiot?" Lee said.

"It looks really important."

"Then she's definitely going to want it back."

"Yeah," Becky agreed "you're going to have to return it to her."

"Or sneak it back in."

"Look, we've got a photocopier. I can copy some of it for you first," Sam offered, guessing that Stan didn't own one.

"Thanks Sam. That would be great." Millie handed him the folder.

They parted company and headed to their separate homes.

*

"Millie, dear, back from school already. Gosh the day flies by." Stan was in his usual chair in the back room. "The Monday Club was cancelled yesterday. Apparently a fallen tree smashed one of the windows in the village hall and it still hasn't been fixed yet."

Millie eyed him suspiciously, wondering why he had felt the need to tell her that.

"Why don't you put the kettle on and make us a lovely pot of tea?"

Millie went into the kitchen and took some tea bags out of a jar with "Coffee" inscribed on it and a few moments later carried back a tray with cups and a teapot.

"Sorry I took the urn before you had really examined it," Millie began.

"That's all right, my love. Did you find anything interesting on it?"

"Well, yes. But I've left it with Mr Reynolds."

"And?"

"I don't know yet. He's going to try and prove how old it is."

"How's he going to do that?"

"He said he would take it to the museum for dating. They can work out how old ceramics are by how much water they've lost over the years."

"Very smart. Good thinking, girl. I can tell we're related." He paused and then looked at Millie with a more serious expression. "Has anything else happened?"

Millie fidgeted in her seat. "Mrs Gordon's spoken to you, hasn't she?"

"Yes she has, and she'll be on her way round shortly, so you'd better get me on your side quickly."

Millie related the events of the previous evening. It was hard for her to explain herself when she knew she was in the wrong. She waited for Stan to be cross and interrupt her but he let her talk.

"We didn't want to upset Mrs Gordon at all and I'm so worried Mum will find out and know I've been looking for George."

Grandad patted her hand in reassurance.

"Well, you did what you thought was best, you were only thinking of your brother. However, I don't think Mrs Gordon will be seeing it that way. It's not very social behaviour, Millie - in fact it is breaking and entering, which puts me in a difficult position, as I'm sure you realise."

The doorbell rang. Millie got up to answer it and was relieved to see it was Sam and Becky with the original folder and the photocopies.

"There's some really interesting stuff in there," Sam whispered as he handed her the two folders.

Millie quickly hid the copy behind the hat stand.

"Come through," she said, leading the way into the back room.

"Ah, who's this you've brought to see me?" Stan looked at Sam. "Is this your new husband?" Sam opened his mouth to say something but instead blushed.

"I'm Sam Reynolds, Mr Reynolds' son."

"Ah, Sam Reynolds. Here, let me put on my other glasses and have a look at you."

Grandad took off the glasses he was wearing and fumbled around for another pair. Becky saw them on the table and handed them to him.

"And you're Becky, aren't you? Well, you'd better help yourselves to a biscuit and a drink, then."

Stan noticed the folder Sam was carrying. "I hear you've been doing some investigating in other people's houses?"

Becky and Sam shifted uncomfortably and mumbled their apologies.

"I was about to say to Millie that I've been waiting to be asked about all this for quite some time," he turned to his granddaughter, "but your mother kept us apart and she wouldn't tolerate any talk of such matters. But seeing as you're doing your own investigation now, well it's a bit different. I'm not as stupid as I am old and I've seen a few things in my time. And yes, I do have my own notions as to where George went."

With that, Grandad picked up his tea and carried on drinking. Millie felt a surge of embarrassment. Did he have to make these dramatic speeches in front of her friends? She glanced at Sam who looked back and shrugged.

"Are you going to go on about magic again and ancient woodland that hasn't been here for hundreds of years, Grandad?"

"And you would do well to listen! I'm talking about *before* the forest started to be chopped down and killed." Stan leaned forward, wide-eyed and excited. "When Essex was rich with all the great myths and legends that they talk about in stories. When Christianity hadn't yet reached our shores and it was a place filled with the great deities and elves and wolves and magical beasts. When it was a free land that hadn't yet been divided up by gate-posts and fences and by greed and dominance."

"You don't honestly think those kind of creatures really existed, do you?"

Stan turned to Sam fiercely. "Of course they existed. Don't you think your Dad looks a bit like an elf, Sam?"

"What!"

Becky giggled as Grandad continued. "Do you think that the idea of magic came from nowhere? Why would it be, then, that in cultures all over the world they talk about it? From China and Africa to South America and Europe. It's about time you stopped listening to that jabbering science teacher at your school and started listening to some truths about the world!"

Millie sensed Grandad had become agitated and butted in. "It's not that we don't believe you, Grandad, it's just that we've never had any reason to. What happened to it all?"

"Well, children, I'll try and start from the beginning. There are tales and stories that have been written down and passed on through generations, despite the efforts of many to stop it." The three of them were silent as Stan succeeded in holding their attention.

"Now, before the world started to get full of people, there wasn't so much need to turn every part of this land into ugly brown fields for crops. Instead the county was still covered with ancient woodland and forests that had been there since the dawn of time. Lush green trees, taller than any buildings, wild animals, like elks and wolves, people and beings of all kinds lived in those forests, living harmoniously with nature - although not always harmoniously with each other!" He chuckled. "And through the forests ran little streams and great rivers, where people would fish and bathe and sail boats along, carrying furs and pottery and yarns from all over Europe."

"But why did it change?" Becky asked.

"Well, over time all things change. It says in history books that the East Saxon king gave up the old ways of the ancestors in favour of the new religion, although he was probably bullied into it by Athelberht, the King of Kent." Stan paused to build up the suspense. "Now myth has it that during the reign of the Essex King a curse was put upon the land by the East Saxon god Seaxneat, and after that the end of their era drew closer."

"Was the king's name King Saberht?" interrupted Millie.

"Ah yes, Cyning Saberht. But there is a story ..." Stan stood up now. "This King had three sons and one of them wanted to please his father and his new religion so much that he committed a great sacrilege in the forest that brought a curse to the kingdom in the form of an epidemic. They say hundreds died. As soon as the three sons came into power they immediately renounced their father's beliefs and turned back to the old ways. But it was too late, the old gods had abandoned their people.

"Over the centuries the forests gradually got smaller and smaller. All the wild creatures were hunted or captured, and with no one to protect them, many of the magical peoples of the forest died or were slaughtered. Some tried to escape across the sea to Norway. Others, well, they tried to live with human-folk in disguise, but many were found out in later years and burnt alive or worse. Sadly most of that knowledge is gone now: the medicines have been lost, magical plants destroyed before they could be categorised, species slain to extinction." Stan stopped for a moment and gazed into the distance. He looked as though he was reminiscing, or maybe just imagining what may have been. "Our precious bond with nature has been severed beyond repair. Just look at us nowadays, people don't even notice the harvest."

He hobbled over to one of the many shelves of books that lined the room, pulled out one with the inscription *Secrets of the Dark Ages* and passed it to Millie.

"Here, have this to add to your collection of findings. Maybe it'll offer you some insight."

"Thanks, Grandad, I'll start reading it tonight," Millie said cheerfully to brighten the mood.

However the mood was stifled by the ringing of the doorbell and the sound of Mrs Gordon letting herself in (an act which Millie later reflected upon as being slightly hypocritical). She came into the room and looked fiercely at the three teenagers.

"I'll have my husband's folder back, if it's not too much to ask," she snapped.

Sam handed it to her immediately.

"Is it all there?" Mrs Gordon flicked through the contents. "Hmm. I'm sure this was a tracing of the church, it looks more like a photocopy! Oh well I suppose everything is here."

"We're really sorry, Mrs Gordon," they apologised.

"Sorry? Well I hope you realise that it is a criminal offence to enter someone's house without permission! You should all be locked up. Have you any idea how frightening it was for a woman of my age to hear uninvited guests wandering about in my own home. It's outrageous!"

"I've given them a good telling off," Stan interrupted, "and they're eager to make it up to you."

"I see," she huffed. "Well then," (another huff) "the three of you, and Lee, can look after the tombola stall at the village fête on Saturday, if you can be trusted."

"Yes, of course we can. We really are sorry, Mrs Gordon."

"Right. Well that's settled then," said Stan.

Mrs Gordon headed back to the front door. She said a stiff goodbye to them all and left.

"Now Becky and Samuel, I'm afraid I'm going to have to ask you to leave, although it's been very nice seeing you all. I need my rest."

"But you said you knew what had happened to George!" Sam exclaimed.

"I said I had my own notions. However, seeing as none of you would believe me if I told you, you'll have to find out for yourselves."

"Grandad, this is important! It's George. We need to know everything there is to know." But Stan had sat back down in his armchair and closed his eyes to signify that it was nap time and that he wasn't to be disturbed.

Chapter Sixteen: Buried Clues

George knew the solstice was drawing near. The village had a sun dial constructed from wooden sticks which cast a shadow from the sun to mark the passing days. This line now drew very close to the mark that denoted the longest day of the year. For George it symbolised another year in the seventh century, hundreds of years from home.

Throughout his time in Widurok George had been waiting for something to happen that would lead him back to the future. Lately though, he had begun to reproach himself for his own idleness. Unless he actually *did* something, then he could be stuck in this time forever with only himself to blame. There were just a couple of days left, but maybe this solstice would be different and something would happen. He had to make it so - but how?

George had promised to help with the pottery this week. With the feast of the Litha approaching, the village was running out of clay bowls and cooking pots for the celebrations. George approached the workshop early one morning. The head potter was busy lighting up the covered fire pit they used as a kiln to heat the pottery.

"Good morning, Wolf Slayer," he said, greeting George with the name he had become known as in the village. "You've come to give me a hand again?"

The potter was an older brother of Leof's, named Wynnstan. He was a large, gentle man with a great bushy beard that covered half his face. He was very experienced with clay and a lot of his goods were sold at market. Some of the detail he managed to mould into the pottery he churned out seemed incredible to George. It had taken George his whole first year in Widurok to make a simple cup that would sit flat and have sides that stayed up! Making Saxon dining ware had proved to be a very different experience from the pottery lesson he had once participated in at school.

While Wynnstan heated the fire pit, George began the task of preparing the clay. This was hard work, although a large amount of clay had already been unearthed and steeped in water. Now George's job was to beat it with a large wooden spatula until it was well mixed and to remove any gravel and stones from it. Next, he added body to it using sand, pounded pottery and some chaff, which had to be kneaded into the clay to help bind it together.

When the mixture was ready Wyn took a generous handful of it and, using a large pebble, skilfully shaped it over a circular wooden mould into the form of a serving plate. With wet hands and a bone, Wyn burnished the surface smooth by smearing the clay particles over each other to help it become watertight. Around the edge, he used a very small animal bone to cut a pattern of tiny little rune letters into the surface.

"What are you writing?" George asked.

"Oh, I don't know how to spell much. I've just put what I always write in runes, which is to ask the gods for a fruitful summer and a good harvest. Not much else you can ask for in life, is there? I've got all the runes written out on that wooden marker over there to remind me," he said, nodding to his tool basket.

Wynn proudly marked the bottom of the plate with his own potter's stamp of chevrons and swirls. Now the clay was shaped into crockery it was ready to be placed into the pit to be fired. This raised the finer grains to the surface and again, ensured it would be watertight. Normally it would be in there for a while and then left for several hours to cool. But this time Wynn wanted to decorate the pieces, so they were given an initial firing until the clay was as hard as leather, then taken out and glazed, and then returned to the pit a second time.

Wynn and George continued to work together until late morning when the smell of cooking began to drift through the air. As well as the serving plate they had managed to craft two fine serving bowls, an urn for keeping salt and a large drinking jug, which was still firing.

"Come on, Wolf Slayer, it's time we got ourselves a feed," Wynn announced and began to wash the clay from his hands in a bowl of water.

"I think I'll stay here for a bit longer. I want to try and make a pot like that urn over there. Besides, someone needs to keep an eye on the jug while it's heating."

"All right then, I'll get someone to bring you some stew and bread over." Wynn went off humming happily to himself.

Although George's stomach was rumbling, a plan had been formulating in his mind. He began to work quickly. Ever since he had watched Wynn mould the urn, George had been thinking about making a sealed pot to hide his mobile phone in. An urn shape would be perfect: watertight and sealed, it would last centuries. If he buried it somewhere in Widurok there was a chance that it might be found one day - maybe by Grandad or Millie. He knew that it was a long shot, almost ridiculous in fact, but he couldn't risk having such technology hidden under his bed forever. And at least he would have done something proactive towards his goal of getting home.

George took a ball of clay and shaped it as he had seen Wynn do, coiling and pinching it around in rings as he built up the sides, then smoothing the rings together with wet hands to make the urn shape. There was already a lid that Wynn had discarded from earlier; he shaped his urn so the lid fitted it perfectly, although it had Wynn's potter's stamp on the top. The stamp gave George an idea. He looked in the tool basket for the marker with the runes scratched on it and marked each one around the circumference of the urn as a message to whoever found it. But it still wasn't ready, he needed to make it more personal. He scratched on the bottom Millie's name and the name of the King: Saberht. Satisfied, George took the jug out of the pit and replaced it with his urn, for an initial firing.

While it was changing into a leathery consistency, George hurried to his hut and dug out the phone from under the loose floorboard. It was never going to be any use to him now, not with a dead battery. He returned to the pottery to find a bowl of stew had been brought for him while he was gone and he hungrily gobbled it up.

When the urn was ready George took it out of the pit and put the mobile inside. It was a good snug fit. With the clay still soft he was able to seal the lid onto the pot with some wet clay mix. He didn't want to put the phone into the fire so he decided to take the urn to a spot in one of the meadows where it could dry in the sun naturally without anyone questioning it.

The next day George retrieved the urn and rode his horse, a beautiful white mare named Elvina, through the woods to the stone marker by the pond - the place he and Millie had once known as the den. In the corner next to the rock he dug away at the soil with a wooden spatula until he had made a fairly deep grave for his urn.

"Please find this, Millie," he whispered as he covered the pot with soil.

He knew it was unlikely that Millie, or anyone else for that matter, would ever find it, but at least there was a chance that someone might and that gave him a reason to keep on hoping.

Chapter Seventeen: Old Letters, Hidden Stones and a Wall Painting

Millie sat at the open bureau staring absent-mindedly at the long list of sums in front of her, as she had done for the past ten minutes. Her mind couldn't concentrate on numbers or homework, it was too occupied with what lay hidden behind the hat stand. She closed the maths book that urgently needed her attention and retrieved the folder, taking it back to the privacy of her bedroom. This was more important. A tremor of excitement ran through her fingertips as she opened the cover and pulled out a letter. It was addressed to Mr Gordon from an Eric Drayton.

October '87

Dear Mr Gordon,

I was surprised to receive your letter, it's been a long time since I've thought about my childhood in Wybrook although the memory of my brother James has remained vivid throughout my years. The suddenness of his disappearance blotted such a stain across the safe world I lived in that my attitude towards life changed dramatically. I became aware of an uncertainty in everything and was no longer the child I had been.

It was generally believed that having the susceptible mind of a young boy, Jim had perhaps run off to join the army. My mother on the other hand was convinced a German had parachuted down and snatched him away (as you are aware the incident happened during the Second World War). However I have always known neither to be true. We were very close, Jim and I, and it is a fact that he would not have left of his own accord without telling me.

That day we had been working late in the fields after school, there was often a few shillings to be had up at Graham's farm. We came home shattered and fell asleep almost immediately. But later that night we were woken by a knock at the door. It was Mr Peterson from across the road, reporting he had heard one of the Graham cows over the back of the field. Mr Graham was one of the few farmers in the area to keep livestock and Jim's last job that evening had been to round up the cows and put them in the sheds for the night. Jim was convinced he had missed one - either that or he hadn't secured the shed door. Our mother tried to persuade him not to go, said it was bad luck to be alone on the solstice. He went anyway and that was the last we ever saw of him.

Many times I thought back to how casually we said goodbye and how cruelly fate can turn against us without warning. I questioned where he went a million times in my head until I realised that, as unknowing as death, there could be no answer and no proof of any of my theories. If I could have had one wish it would have been to take a time machine back to that moment and follow him to wherever he went. Alas, dreams and wishes are just that and I have accepted that I am to die never knowing.

I am aware from your letter that you refuse to allow your mind to settle and in this I offer you my deepest sympathy and above all my best wishes that you persevere in your search. It is strange to learn that there has been another disappearance as I have heard snippets of gossip as evidence that there were more before my brother.

Good luck, Mr Gordon,

Yours sincerely,

Eric Drayton

P.S. Please understand that having come to a time in my life where I have been able to put the past to rest, I wish to be contacted no further on this matter.

Millie put down the letter and wiped the tears from her cheeks. What had been the last thing she had said to George? She couldn't even remember. Would it be the same for her, would she accept the mystery of it at the end of her life like Eric had, or would she persist like Bobby's Dad and always be hunting for new clues? She looked down at the folder and pulled out another letter written in the same handwriting. This time it was much briefer.

March '88

Dear Mr Gordon,

Although, as I have said before, I have a deep understanding as to your state of mind, I must implore you to respect my wishes and to refrain from writing to me about such matters. I have relayed to you as much as I can recall and to be honest such memories are painful at the best of times.

When I mentioned snippets of gossip, it was something that was only talked about in whispers. It ill behoved the congregation to discuss witchcraft and such-like.

However, amongst some of the older villagers there were memories of other disappearances having occurred on the solstice, the most recent being a Joanna Hockley. She was the postlady in the village at the end of the last century. On the day of the solstice she delivered the post to the Church Warden's cottage, but then disappeared before she got to the next house. However, six months later she reappeared on the winter solstice. She claimed to those close to her that she had been living in the Dark Ages and had travelled through the world-tree of the gods!

When poor Miss Hockley was threatened with a long sojourn in a mental institution, the rumours changed and it was said that she had been pregnant and had run away with her lover to have the baby. Which explanation of events you choose to believe is up to you. Unfortunately she died in childbirth the following year and the truth went with her to the grave.

Once again I wish you luck, but regret that I can be of no further assistance.

Farewell,

E. Dayton

So that was where all the talk about trees and the Anglo-Saxons came from! Millie pulled out a clipping from the *Essex Chronicle* and looked at the date, Thursday 23rd June 1983, the week Bobby Gordon had gone missing. Surely this was proof? Something for the police to look into. But how could the same event occur on the same day over such a long period of time? And what about the other incidences that Eric remembered as village gossip? All gossip had a root.

Millie emptied out everything from the folder and eagerly scanned through it, hoping that Mr Gordon had discovered the answers. Amongst several sprawled pages of handwritten notes on Essex history were some maps of Anglo-Saxon England and East Seax; some poems written in Old English and translated into modern English; and the photograph of the painting. There was also a tracing that someone, perhaps Mr Gordon, had made of an aerial plan of a church and its surrounding grounds and boundaries, which Millie realised was the original, so Mrs Gordon had indeed got the photocopy. She stared at it closely, speculating as to whether it could be the plans and layout of Wybrook church. It would make sense if it were, although most churches do have similar layouts. Finally she pulled out a strange diagram entitled The Stones. The diagram appeared to be a drawing of two stone circles: twenty elongated stones encircling a smaller group of nine slightly larger ones which then encircled a picture of a tree. Twenty-nine stones and a tree? She held the diagram closer. Around the edge of the circle Mr Gordon had sketched some of the stones in detail with their measurements pencilled in. Stones of the outer ring measured around two foot high by a foot wide, and those of the inner circle around three foot by two. It all seemed very mysterious.

Millie's' train of thought was interrupted by her mobile singing out its ringtone.

"Mills?" Becky answered excitedly. "I've got something to tell you. I've just been in the church helping my Dad lock up ..."

"Did you find something?"

"Well, my Dad said that in the late Eighties some old wall paintings in our church were restored, led by some local historians including Mr Gordon and your Grandad! Apparently for hundreds of years it was normal for the inside walls of churches to be covered with loads of colourful paintings. But then after the sixteenth century they were plastered over, which is why you normally only see white walls now in churches."

"So underneath the plaster of any old church are medieval paintings?"

"Most likely. So anyway, in the Eighties some plaster came off in the chancel here and there was part of a painting behind it, so the local parishioners got together and decided to see what else was there and ended up uncovering the walls on all sides of the chancel. You've probably seen it before, if you've been in the church."

Millie couldn't remember. "Did you see the painting Mr Gordon had a photo of?"

"I'm pretty sure it's here, but you should come and look for yourself. I'll ask my Dad if we can help him tomorrow. He normally locks up early on a Wednesday."

"Okay, cool. See you tomorrow."

*

Millie rushed home from school the next day, excited that she was getting closer to the truth.

"Grandad! I'm home." There was no answer. The house appeared empty.

She went upstairs to get changed but when she opened her bedroom door she jumped with fright. Sitting there on her bed, was Mrs Gordon! She was holding the copies of Mr Gordon's papers and looking very angry.

"Mrs Gordon!" Millie cried in shock. She noticed the hoover on the floor and remembered that Mrs Gordon now came to clean on a Wednesday, but Millie hadn't expected her to be cleaning her room. She suspected that it was an excuse on Mrs Gordon's behalf to be nosy.

"I know what these are! These are things I told you to leave well alone, yet when I went to hoover under your bed I find a whole folder of this nonsense!"

Mrs Gordon stood up and threw the papers to the floor.

"I really thought you had a bit more respect for my wishes, Millie!" she said haughtily, then softened her tone slightly to one of exasperation. "I really am so sorry that you lost your brother. I can imagine how much you want him back, but all this ...?" she waved her hand over the pile of papers accusingly. "Pipe dreams! You need to put a stop to it all. There is no magic in the world. If George or Bobby were ever going to come back, then they would have by now. It's past time you came to terms with that, else you'll drive yourself mad."

Millie was taken aback by Mrs Gordon's sudden directness and was rendered speechless. Now more than ever before Millie believed the exact opposite. She desperately wanted Mrs Gordon to tell her everything she knew and to offer to help. But clearly this wasn't going to happen and so instead Millie nodded timidly in agreement at Mrs Gordon who left, dragging the hoover behind her.

Millie sat still for a while, indolently gazing at the mess of papers that were strewn across the floor. Then something caught her attention. The tracing of the church and grounds had landed exactly on top of the picture of the stone circles. She picked them up. They appeared to fit together! Small red marks had been made on the tracing along the boundary walls of the graveyard, where the main church gates were, and also in the church itself. When the tracing was directly placed over the picture of the stone circles these marks fitted exactly over many of the stones in the two rings.

Millie tried to picture Wybrook's church gate in her head. Its wooden posts were fixed on either side to a brick wall. She wasn't completely sure but she seemed to recollect that right next to both gate-posts the bottom of the wall did have a large stone buried into it, as though the wall had been built up to and over it. Yes, they were speckled light-coloured stones, a couple of feet high and about a foot in width! Millie looked back at the position of the inner circle and now vaguely remembered passing a couple of stones on the way to the playing field that didn't have the usual cut of a headstone and bore no inscription. She had assumed they were nothing more than very old and weathered gravestones, but maybe they weren't. Perhaps they could be part of the inner ring. Surely it all tallied too well to be just a coincidence? Could the stone circles be hidden amongst the graves? And so what, if they were? How did this relate to Bobby or George's disappearance?

Millie felt an urge to run to the church now and look for them, but the smell of dinner cooking was drifting up the stairs and she didn't want to upset Grandad by missing it. With the paperwork back in the folder, she carefully put it in her school bag and waited until it was time to meet Becky.

*

A couple of hours later Millie stood at the church gates holding in front of her the two drawings. Yes, there were the speckled stones, right next to the bottom of the gate-posts and exactly the same shape and size as those drawn in the diagram. She followed the churchyard wall as it curved to the left, encompassing the graves. It wasn't long before she spotted another similar stone set into the base of the wall. Then another a little further on, and then another. Millie counted out eight footsteps between each stone. After the sixth stone, the curved wall ended and continued instead in the manner of a hedge, which ran in a straight line to constitute the southern boundary. Guided by the diagrams Millie stopped following the boundary line and instead continued walking the line of the curve. She walked eight steps to a stone that stood by itself, one that had probably been mistaken for a grave marker many times. Then she walked a further eight steps and reached another "weathered headstone", and then a shorter block of stone, set furthest to the east, eight steps later. She continued around the graveyard in a large circle until she had found all the stones of the outer ring. The church walls and porch had been built over three of the stones which were still visible from the outside. There were also a couple which lay flat on the ground with their underbellies protruding from the grass.

Millie stood next to the church entrance, looking up at its towering grandeur and feeling as though she had made a great discovery. But then a cold shiver ran down her spine: she had already dreamt about this, a woman had pointed towards the church and told her about the stones! How was that even slightly possible? She began to feel dizzy like she was in a dream-like state again. Then a noise from inside the church brought her back to reality and reminded her she was meeting Becky. She must already be in the church. Millie heard her friend's voice echoing into the porch as she went through the huge oak doors to find her.

"Hi Millie," Becky called and then projected her voice to the back of the building. "Dad! Millie's here, she's just going to help us close up."

"Okay my love, make sure everything gets locked properly," Mr Hockley called from the tower steps.

"Becky, guess what?" Millie whispered excitedly.

"What?"

"See these diagrams that we got from the old shop." Millie opened the flap of her bag and passed her the drawings one on top of the other. "It's of this church and there's two stone circles in the graveyard! I've just seen them!"

"Oh right," Becky seemed a bit doubtful and not as enthusiastic as Millie had expected.

"Don't you think it's amazing?"

"Well, what does it mean? It's just some stones, Millie," Becky replied.

"Yeah, but it might be really important. Mr Gordon thought it was." Millie felt it hard to explain the conviction she felt that the stones *were* somehow relevant to George.

The only solid link she had was that Mr Gordon had researched them in his quest to find Bobby.

"I suppose. I'm surprised no one else has noticed them before."

"Well, some of them are hidden in the walls and the rest look like gravestones."

"Are they all there?" Becky asked.

"I think so. I haven't checked the ones in the middle but they're probably too heavy to have been moved."

"All right, show me later. We haven't got much time now. Come on," Becky beckoned her, "the chancel is up here, where the altar is."

Millie followed Becky through the pews to the area where the choir normally sat. The walls were decorated with faded and cracked paintings, mostly depicting Biblical scenes. On the back wall of the chancel the twelve apostles were elaborately decorated and bordered by woven patterns; elsewhere figures and animals told the story of the plight and fate of various saints and sinners. Most of the paintings were so faint with age, it was hard to make out all of the artists' elaborate work, but all were fascinating. Millie could only begin to imagine the people who had drawn them and the lives they had led, all those aeons of time ago. She scanned the walls looking for "her" picture. There it was, between two pillars on the left, next to the organ.

The original picture revealed a lot more of the finer detail than the photo had. Being almost twice her height, it was a lot larger than she was expecting. The scene was set with a lake in the background and two small islands in its centre. At the edge of the lake a small gathering of people stood, dressed in tunics as in the pictures from the Dark Ages book. They were hovering over the girl breathing golden breath into the boy. The girl had short brown hair and a fringe with light streaks and standing beside her was a boy with lighter coloured hair. Millie could almost imagine that she was looking at herself and George. But of course that was stupid!

"Look at this, written here in the corner, 610," Millie pointed.

"That can't be the date, there's no way it could be that old!"

"No. But it could have been painted years after 610 and be telling a story or an old legend that happened back then. That's what the other paintings are doing."

"Yes, I suppose ... or it could have been copied from an older painting or a tapestry. Hey, have you seen this writing along the bottom? It's not written in the normal alphabet."

"Your grandad might know what it is. You should ask him."

Millie carefully began to copy the strange letters onto the back of the folder.

ᚷᛟᛞ ᚨᚾᛚᛁᚳᚾᛖᛋ ᚻᛇ ᚠᛖᚱᚨᚾ ᚦᚢᚱ ᛋᛇᚠᚨᚾ ᚹᛟᚱᛚᛞᛋ ᚠᚱᚨᛗ ᚨᛋᚳ

ᚷᛟᛞ ᚨᚾᛚᛁᚳᚾᛖᛋ ᚻᛇ ᛒᚱᚨᚦ ᛚᛁᚠ ᚨᛏ ᚻᚨᛚᛁᚷ ᛚᚨᚷᚢ

"Don't you think that could be the lake up near Bernard's woods," Becky whispered, "you know, behind Sam's house? It's got the same little islands on it."

"Perhaps. If it's in this church it could be local."

Clung!

The noise of the tower door being pulled shut sounded down the church.

"You girls finished up there?" Mr Hockley called.

"Nearly, Dad." Becky replied and quickly rushed into the vestry to lock the side door and turn off the lights whilst Millie finished writing.

As they walked down the nave Becky asked in a lowered voice, "Hey, did you ever get that mobile working that you and Lee found?"

"No," Millie put the folder back in her school bag, "and Sam's dad has still got the clay pot."

The lights went out, leaving only a flickering coloured light that shone from the stained glass windows. Mr Hockley stood in the porch next to the light switches, jingling his keys impatiently and joking that he was going to lock them in.

Chapter Eighteen: The Nature of Time

Millie's immediate thought as she walked out of the churchyard was of Grandad. He was the only adult she could confide in. When she returned to the cottage he was sitting in the back room listening to *The Archers* on the radio. Stan got up as Millie came into the room.

"Millie, how's the research going? No, shhh, wait," he said. "Put the kettle on first and then we can have a good old natter."

A few moments later Millie set two cups of tea down on the table with the biscuit tin. She reached into the folder and pulled out the diagrams.

"Grandad, you know I borrowed Mr Gordon's folder? Well, I realise it was probably wrong but Sam photocopied some of the sheets for me and I found something interesting in these two. This is a picture of some stones

"Ah yes, the mini Stonehenge of Wybrook."

"Do you know about it?"

"A bit, but not much, really. Mr Gordon mentioned it a few times. I think he believed it was connected to Bobby's disappearance but he never found them - or at least if he did, he never told me so. I'm not too sure that they ever existed. You see, there isn't much natural stone in this county, all clay and chalk, which is why the Romans made their buildings out of brick. We do have pudding-stone in Essex, though."

"What's pudding-stone?"

"Stone that looks like plum pudding stuffed with currants, like your grandmother used to make - lovely with custard," Grandad joked. He noted Millie's confused frown and grew serious again. "To be exact it's a conglomerate type of rock, made from pebbles, mainly flint that has been cemented together by river sediment. Here, there's no point in giving a geology lesson without a specimen. I've got a bit in the house somewhere as a door stop. I'll go and find it." He got up and went into the hall, returning with a lump of stone which he handed to her. It was similar to the stone in the churchyard.

"Yes, it's always been rare in this county," Stan said, continuing where their discussion had left off. "So it may well have had a special significance to pagan people. But what a grand task to construct such a monument - a ring of stone! It would probably have been erected way before the Roman age and no doubt have been sacred ever since to whatever people inhabited the land. But if such a circle ever did exist here, where was it?"

"I think it's in the churchyard."

"What - the churchyard?" Grandad was wide-eyed.

"Yes. amongst the graves and in the church walls too. Look, this tracing fits over the stone diagram like this." Millie placed the tracing on top. "See how the stones all match up. I've seen them myself."

"That's very interesting, I never thought of that." Stan rubbed his chin thoughtfully. "I suppose it might add up, though. When Christianity first arrived in Britain, churches were often built on sacred pagan sites to encourage the people to take up the new religion. That way they wouldn't keep going off somewhere else to worship their pagan gods. Yes, it would make sense that if there *was* a stone circle, it would be near the church."

"Do you really think so?" Millie said.

"Yes, but ..." he shook his head in disbelief. "In all these years, I never thought of it. What else have you been finding out?"

"Where the original painting from this photo is." Millie showed Grandad the copy. "We found it in the church chancel. It's of a lake and a girl with the date 610."

"Yes, the wall paintings. This is the one Bettie Cook worked on. We spent years painstakingly uncovering them. They're rather beautiful, don't you think?"

"Yes, they're amazing. What made you get involved with the restoration?"

"Mr Gordon asked for my help. I offered to join in out of compassion for him: seemed like he needed a project to take his mind off things. Besides which, I've always been interested in local history and our church is one of the few surviving in England that was built pre-Conquest. Many of the Saxon churches built before 1066 were made of wood and burnt down in Danish raids, or were rebuilt later using stone and brick. Unfortunately, Mr Gordon's interest in history turned into a bit of an obsession," he sighed in melancholy.

"Well, I guessed he'd kept this photo for a reason. I found some strange writing along the bottom of it. I copied it onto here, look."

Millie showed him the back of the folder where she had scribbled it down. Stan put on his reading glasses and studied the passage.

"Hmm," he looked thoughtful. "Hmm, yes that's right, I remember seeing this now. Yes, it was quite an unusual find. These are rune letters."

"Runes? I think there's a poem in the folder called *The Old English Rune Poem*[2]. What are they?" (Hadn't she dreamt about runes too?)

"What are they?" Grandad repeated, tutting "Are you sure you go to school? They were the system the Anglo-Saxons used to write down Old English for about five hundred years. Sadly by the time the Normans invaded, runes had completely disappeared from use and had been replaced by the Latin alphabet, similar to the one we use today. Each rune had its own phonic sound. This first one I know, it's a 'G' sound." Grandad pointed to the 'X' shape at the beginning of the runic sentence. "And each rune also had a name. This X was known as *Gyfu*, meaning gift."

"Are you able to translate it?" Millie asked, awestruck.

"Maybe, I could give it a go. I could try writing out the sound of each rune into the corresponding alphabet sound, so writing down *Gyfu*'s X as a G, and so on, which would probably give us a translation in Old English. Then *that* could be translated into Modern English. It might take a while, I'm by no means fluent, but there is an Old English to Modern English translation book up there somewhere, with the runes and their names and sounds written in the appendix. Could you have a look for me, dear, and I'll take these cups and things out."

Stan got up and plodded into the kitchen while Millie went over to the bookcase. As she was glancing over the titles she noticed a large, leather-bound book protruding from the shelf as though it hadn't been put back properly. She tried to push it back into place but something was blocking it. She slid the book off the shelf and reaching up, found a small cardboard box was behind it. She took it down and pushed the book back. A hand-written note had been Sellotaped onto the box.

Dear Stan,

I know that you will live longer than I. This being the case I have instructed in my final will that my lawyers be obliged to deliver this letter into your care, or into that of your surviving family.

Best Wishes,

Arthur Gordon

Millie's heart skipped a beat. Why hadn't Grandad told her about this? This was information on George's disappearance! What could Mr Gordon possibly have known? She opened the box and found a ceramic jar about twenty centimetres long. She took off the lid and inside was a very ancient-looking scroll. Unable to contain her curiosity, she carefully pulled it out and unravelled it. She began to read,

Wes Hal Millie and George…

"Put that down!" Grandad was marching towards her, red-faced. He snatched the scroll from her hands and frantically put it back into the jar. *"That is not yours to read!"* He opened the bottom drawer of the desk and threw it in, then locked the drawer shut and put the key into his pocket.

"But Grandad …" Millie was shocked. She had never heard him shout before or seen him so furious; it was totally out of character.

"No, Millie." Stan tried to regain his composure. "That is not for you."

"But it said 'Millie and George'."

"It was a different Millie and George, a coincidence. They were an elderly couple who used to run the church hand-bell group, that's all."

"But the note said …"

"It's was an old party invitation to a Medieval-themed dinner. It's probably about twenty years old." Grandad avoided her eyes. "I don't know why I've kept it, nostalgia I suppose. I just had it in that box to keep it safe."

Millie could think of nothing to say. She couldn't understand why her grandfather would lie to her but she certainly didn't believe he was telling the truth, either, not after such an outburst. Whatever his reason, he clearly wasn't going to reveal anything else.

There was an awkward silence.

"Why don't you finish off your homework and I'll have a look at translating this."

Millie took her school books upstairs feeling like a naughty little child being banished to her room.

*

A couple of hours later Millie had just finished brushing her teeth and was about to get into bed when Grandad knocked at her bedroom door.

"I've finished," he announced proudly as she opened the door. "I can't promise it's completely accurate and I may have used a little guess-work, but it's the best I could do." He handed her a sheet of paper, the tensions from earlier in the day now forgotten.

ᚷ ᛟ ᛞ ᚨ ᚾ ᛚ ᛁ ᚳ ᚾ ᛖ ᛋ ᚻ ᛇ ᚠ ᛖ ᚱ ᚨ ᚾ ᚦ ᚢ ᚱ ᛋ ᛇ ᚠ ᚨ ᚾ ᚹ ᛟ ᚱ ᛚ ᛞ ᛋ ᚠ ᚱ ᚨ ᛗ ᚨ ᛋ ᚳ

God anlicnes heo feran thurh seofan worulds fram asc

Godlike, she travelled across seven worlds by ashtree

ᚷ ᛟ ᛞ ᚨ ᚾ ᛚ ᛁ ᚳ ᚾ ᛖ ᛋ ᚻ ᛇ ᛒ ᚱ ᚨ ᚦ ᛚ ᛁ ᚠ ᚨ ᛏ ᚻ ᚨ ᛚ ᛁ ᚷ ᛚ ᚨ ᚷ ᚢ

God anclicnes heo brath lif at halig lagu

Godlike, she breathed life at the sacred lake

"I'm not sure what this means," Millie said.

"There could be a few different interpretations. It seems to me that they are talking about the Anglo-Saxon belief in there being seven worlds in the cosmos, including Middangeard, the one we're on. Some of their gods, like Woden - the one Wednesday is named after - were able to travel through these worlds via the 'world-tree', which I suppose may have been an ash tree. It would also explain why it was written in runes: the writer probably didn't want any of the Christians, who used the Latin alphabet, to know he was writing about Saxon gods in a Christian church."

"So basically, a girl travelled across the cosmos in a tree and then at a lake she breathed life into the boy in the painting," Millie summarised nonchalantly.

"It's mythology, Millie," Grandad laughed. "It doesn't have to make sense!"

"I suppose," Millie replied. "Do you know anything else about runes?"

"Well, in this little part of northern Europe there were twenty-nine of them. They are all written out in that poem you mentioned. They were used similarly to our alphabet but each one also implied a different meaning, such as wisdom or victory in battle, and each one represented something physical like a horse or the sun."

"Or a gift?" Millie interrupted.

"Yes, a gift, as I mentioned before. Only a few of the more learned peoples could read the runes and so they became associated with mysticism and magic. They could be used to tell a person's future or …" he added with a secretive wink, "they could become a magic code. Do you believe in magic Millie?"

"Not since I left pre-school." Did he really have to ask her that?

"What about time travel?"

"What's that got to do with anything, Grandad?"

"Everything Millie. All of your life you have no doubt thought of time not as some 'thing' but as an unquestionable steady progression through your everyday life," Grandad said dramatically. "Maybe you've imagined it as a simple straight line with various historical dates dotted along it and an arrow pointing forward, or perhaps as the calendar your mother has hanging in her kitchen."

Millie frowned. She wasn't sure she had thought much about the nature of time at all.

"But," he continued, "time could be imagined as a fourth dimension like the other three dimensions we live by." Grandad had now began to slowly pace around the room. "If you were going to meet someone outside your English class you might say 'on the fourth floor, on the left, second door, at three o'clock', using all four dimensions. The only difference is that we don't experience time in the same way as the first three, we can't actually see it," he paused.

"Have you ever wondered why time exists at all? What purpose does time have in the universe? It is only there to allow change, to make change possible. Just like we use a map in the car, time can also be thought of as being mapped, part of which shows the route from here to the time you're trying to find and then the route back."

"So you're saying time travel is basically a journey in a different dimension?"

"More or less. Come on, let's go outside. I want to show you the past."

Millie followed him down the stairs and out into the back garden.

"It's almost the longest day of the year so there aren't too many stars shining above us yet," Stan said and muttered under his breath, "especially not with all the light pollution we've got nowadays."

"Is the solstice this week?"

"Yes, it's on Sunday." Grandad took Millie's hand and with his other hand he pointed up at the stars which were just beginning to show their light.

"When you look up there at the rest of the universe you're actually looking directly into the past, maybe thousands and thousands of years ago. All of those stars are so far away that by the time their light gets to us we are seeing the star how it was in the past. Do you understand?"

"Yes, I think so. Does that mean that if right now somebody was a thousand light years from earth with a massive telescope, something really, really powerful, they could look at earth and see how it was a thousand years ago?"

"Exactly, that's the theory. Even if you look at yourself in the mirror, you're looking at yourself a minute fraction of a second in the past because of the time it takes the light to travel."

Millie was thoughtful for a moment. "Do you reckon it's possible to build a time machine then?"

"Well Millie, the science is there. There are things that do affect time, like movement or gravity. Have you heard of Einstein?"

"Yeah, the old scientist with crazy white hair?"

"Einstein found out that time is relative - in other words, it's elastic. If you travel on an aeroplane, time will actually slow down: although only by fifty-nine nanoseconds, relative to ground time, it is still time-travel. And believe it or not, if you ran around all day time would pass faster than if you spent the day sitting down. What this means is that there is no such time as 'now', because time is different everywhere for everyone even if by an unnoticeable amount. It really is elastic. So then if you decided to travel a lot faster, say at the speed of light for seven years, you would arrive seven years into the future. And then there's gravity, which also slows down time. Which is why in space, time is a fraction of a microsecond faster than our time on earth."

"Do you believe that George went back in time?" Millie was wondering what else her Grandfather could possibly be implying by divulging all this knowledge to her.

"Let's just say I like to keep an open mind about things," Grandad replied, avoiding a direct answer. "I wouldn't want you to think me a mad, demented old man."

He may not have given her a direct answer but he certainly seemed to have a theory about George. It was enough to keep Millie's hope ignited.

"In the Thirties," Grandad carried on, "scientists started to come up with ideas of black holes, which are the direct result of a star collapsing in on itself when it dies and so creating a very powerful gravitational field. Useful for time travel. They realised this wouldn't be enough to create a path to travel in time so they came up with the concept of wormholes effected by space-time that had been curved. Are you still following?"

Millie nodded, trying to digest this information and picturing George falling head first through a wormhole.

"If you could somehow manipulate space to make a wormhole along with a load of anti-gravity matter and negative energy, you could create a closed loop in time. It's the science of magic." He smiled at her affectionately as she yawned. "Come on, I've gone on far too much. That's what happens when you read too many books and spend too much time by yourself! You'd better go up to bed before I send you to sleep out here."

"OK. It's amazing though, all that stuff. I never knew that time was like that," Millie said as they went back inside. "Goodnight, Grandad, see you in the morning."

As she was going up the stairs Stan called out,

"One last thing, do you know what Wybrook means?"

"Isn't it just a place name?"

"It comes from the Anglo-Saxon Widurok. 'Widu' means tree, similar to our word 'wood' and 'rok' means 'fate', like the Norse name for the end of the world, Ragnarok."

A tree that could change your fate …? A gateway through time and the cosmos …? No, it had to be nonsense. She wished that Grandad had the internet, so she could do some more of her own research. The solstice was going to be on Sunday. If the disappearances were somehow linked to that day, it might be her only opportunity to somehow solve this mystery and get George back. But it didn't leave her much time to piece everything together.

Millie looked out of her window to the darkening countryside around her.

"Oh George, where are you? Where are you?" she called, softly.

Chapter Nineteen: Reading the Runes

Saturday turned out to be perfect weather for the village fête. The sky was clear blue without a cloud in sight and was forecast to remain that way all week. Becky, Sam, Lee and Millie arrived at the playing field in the early morning, as they had been instructed to by Mrs Gordon. She was waiting for them next to the bouncy castle with two folding tables, the large tombola drum, a book of raffle tickets and several boxes of prizes, most of which were packs of confectionery or bottles of alcohol and soft drinks.

"Right, Lee and Sam I want these tables put up please. Girls, you can tear off all the raffle tickets that end in five and Sellotape them onto the prizes and then display them on the table. Then boys, I want you to screw up the matching pairs of tickets and those left over and put them into the tombola drum. Okay, if you think you can cope with that I'll be back over in a while with your money boxes and some pens to make a sign with."

"Oh great, I love making signs!" Becky said enthusiastically.

Mrs Gordon gave Becky an odd look, no doubt taking in her blue and gold rah-rah skirt and pink leggings. Then satisfied that her orders were going to be carried out she marched across to the village hall.

"Go on then boys, get them tables up!" Becky joked as they set to work.

The field rapidly became transformed with various stalls and games to play and a stage set up opposite the village hall. The inhabitants of Wybrook and surrounding villages started to arrive as the beautiful weather drew them outside. It wasn't long before the tombola stall had a queue of customers.

In the early afternoon Millie spotted Mr Reynolds and his wife coming towards them.

"Hi!" Sam called out to his parents.

"Sam!" his mother replied. "How's the stall going? Gosh, it looks like you've been busy. I hope we haven't missed out on a chance to win a bottle of wine!"

As Sam's mum chatted to her son Mr Reynolds walked over to Millie.

"Ah Millie, the girl with the artefact. I've got some exciting news for you. Your little pot has been dated as early seventh century, so it is quite a find."

"Seventh century?" Millie repeated, knowing that this was impossible.

"Yes. A couple of the students did some research on it and concluded it to be a type of urn. The sealed top is pretty unusual, very uncommon for that era. Sam said you'd be here so I brought it along with me. Dear," he said turning his back to his wife, "can you reach into my rucksack and get the shoe box out?"

Mrs Reynolds unzipped his bag and passed him a box containing the urn.

"I'd quite like to hold onto it but I thought you'd probably want it back."

"Yes, if you don't mind."

Mr Reynolds put the box down on the table and removed the lid.

"It was definitely made in the six hundreds?" Millie asked, wanting to make sure there was no mistake. "There's no way it could be an old clay pot that someone stuck something in a few years ago and then sealed up?"

"No, of course not! Maybe if you had found it broken and had then glued it back together, but certainly not if you found it whole. Why, was there something else with it?"

"No, that's it," she fibbed.

"It's definitely all of the same clay and the same age. Believe me, Millie, it's a very specialised subject, it would be extremely hard to counterfeit something like this." He lifted the urn from the box. "See this pattern at the top? That's a potter's stamp and it's similar to other stamps found on pottery in North Essex. The chevrons are a typical symbol on urns. Back then there was a strong belief that when a person died the only way to release the soul from the body was through cremation. That way the soul would be carried away by Woden, who was god of the wind, into their otherworld."

"What about the writing?"

"They're the letters of the runic alphabet and actually its not unusual to see them on Saxon crafts. A sword was found in the Thames dating from the seventh century with the same letters engraved down the blade, although I haven't seen them on urns before."

"Yes, I was thinking that they might be runes."

"Well if you want to know more about runes, there's a fortune telling tent over there." Mr Reynolds waved his arm towards the corner of the field. "One of the old Wirde sisters is doing rune readings. She does it here every few years or so, but I wouldn't take it too seriously, though."

Millie looked across the playing field and saw someone going into a tepee-shaped tent. She had heard of the Wirde sisters before when Mrs Gordon had spoken of the lady Millie saw on the night of the disappearance.

"This on the underneath is a rather bizarre coincidence," Mr Reynolds said drawing her attention back to the urn. "I suppose you've noticed it looks like your name written on the bottom? I guess that's what interested you in the first place. And of course the name 'Saberht' which confirms our results. Again, a bit unusual for the era to write the king's name in the Latin alphabet and on the base of an urn."

"Do you know much about King Saberht?" Millie asked, keeping the line of conversation away from topic of her engraved name. "I heard the county changed to Christianity during his rule."

"Yes, so it did. Well Millie, I can see you have a mind for history. Let's hope that we have you on our undergraduate team one day!"

Millie blushed. "I've just been doing a bit of research, that's all."

"Well, after seeing his name on the pot I did some myself. Converting Essex to Christianity is mainly what Saberht is remembered for. However, after his death in 616 his three sons turned the kingdom back to the old religion, so it was pretty short-lived. London was part of Essex then, so that's probably where the King would have had his headquarters. Actually, it is believed his grave was found a few years back in Prittlewell. The tabloids were calling him the King of Bling, although there's still some debate that he's buried in Westminster Abbey. Unfortunately though not much else is known about that time. That's why they call it the Dark Ages. Most of the old writings we've found are about spells and gods and magic; not much fact. But I do hope I've been of some help. Please feel welcome to call round if you have any more questions."

Mr Reynolds left Millie with the shoe box and after briefly chatting to Sam, strolled off to the adjacent stall where his wife was browsing.

Millie felt suddenly overcome by a wave of shock and disbelief as the implications of the dating sank in. Mobile phones had *not* existed in the six hundreds.

"Millie, that's weird, really weird." Lee had been standing next to her, turning the tombola wheel for their customers.

"I know, it's not possible. I think I'm starting to believe in time travel."

"Time travel? What are you talking about? What did Mr Reynolds say?" asked Becky as she came over, leaving Sam as the cashier. Lee filled her in.

"How did George's phone get inside a seventh century urn? What logical reason could there possibly be?" Millie looked at her perplexed.

"You don't believe it, do you? You can't think George went back in time?"

"I don't know, it seems so far-fetched ... and yet all the evidence points to it. Grandad was saying that time can change, like if something could travel near the speed of light or alter its gravity it would end up in a different time."

"Yeah but even if they get the technology to do it in a hundred years it wouldn't make sense, cos when you think about it, we would've already met people from the future visiting us - and we haven't," Becky said.

"I suppose. But if I let myself believe that *is* what happened then everything else I've found out falls into place and makes sense. What do you think, Lee? You're always getting A's in science."

"I'm open-minded. I know what you're saying, Becks, about how we would've already met people but maybe you *have*, or someone has. Or maybe someone went back in time and everything they were going to do was already written in history, so they weren't actually changing it. I don't know," he shook his head slowly, "that urn thing is pretty weird, I'm not sure what to believe. Right now nothing would really surprise me."

"It would be pretty cool to go back and see how everything used to be, but imagine if you got stuck there forever."

"Like George," Millie said quietly. "You would be waiting forever to get home."

Millie decided to take her break and wander around the other stalls to clear her head. She spent most of her money failing to knock down a coconut but was able to redeem herself at the Ladies' Welly-Throwing Corner with the second highest score.

Really though, Millie was avoiding the only pitch she was curious about - the fortune telling tent. It was made from a heavily woven cloth that had been draped over a large tent frame, giving it an Eastern appearance. There was an untidy-looking white horse tied to a peg at its entrance and a thick purple curtain hung over the doorway. Millie kept hoping to catch a glimpse of what was inside when the curtain was pulled back, but it remained closed. By now her break time was nearly over. Feeling apprehensive she took a deep breath and approached the tent. She heard a small cough followed by a "Come in" and realised that her feet were visible under the curtain. Millie had to go in now that she had been spotted.

It was darker inside and Millie's eyes took a moment to adjust. In the centre of the tent was a low table covered in an embroidered cloth that dropped down to the floor. On each side of the table was an old worn armchair. In the chair directly facing Millie was sat a small, very elderly lady and to each side of her sat women Millie presumed were her sisters, equally as ancient: the three Wirde sisters. The woman sitting on the right Millie recognised as being the lady who spoke to her on the bus when she arrived in Wybrook a couple of weeks ago. The woman to the left bore a strong resemblance to the person Millie had seen in her dreams (although that was of course impossible) and the woman facing her with long silver hair poking out in strands from under a black scarf could be the person Millie had seen on the night of George's disappearance. But if any of them recognised Millie they made no indication of it.

"Sit down, then, if you want your fortune told," the woman in the centre said in a thin, breathy voice. "Three pounds in the pot, please."

Millie sat down opposite her in the empty chair and dropped the last of her money into an old jam jar. The woman then spilled out a pile of flat pebbles from a small drawstring bag onto the table. On one side of each stone was painted a rune, a few of which Millie recognised from the wall-painting, whilst the other side was blank. The Wirde sister turned them over with nimble fingers so that only the blank sides were visible.

"What are they?" Millie asked.

"Rune stones."

They were laid out in six rows of five. Millie noticed that this was one more than her grandfather had talked about.

"I thought there were only twenty-nine?"

"And what do you know of the runes, child?" the woman answered.

"I know that they were an old way of writing down language."

"They are touched by fate and blessed with magic. If a rune spell is written in the correct arrangement, its magic contains great power." The woman picked up a stone that was blank on both sides. "This is Wyrd, the last rune. Many don't accept it as being a true rune because it doesn't have a symbol. But we regard it as the mystery rune." The woman's voice was so weak that Millie had to strain to hear her, but she seemed to be the spokesperson for the sisters, whilst the other two remained silent.

"Now first you must pick out nine runes from the rest." She took Millie's hands and placed them over the stones. "Mix them around with your fingers and focus on your inner being. Allow the rest of the world to drift away until you find the runes that you are drawn to. Close your eyes if it helps. And then when you are ready, and only when you are ready, pick up the first stone and place it here." She pointed at a spot on the table.

Millie closed her eyes and tried to empty her thoughts of the outside world. She tried to forget about Sam, Lee and Becky waiting for her at the tombola stall, forget about the fear of never seeing George again, forget about the guilt of being Mrs Gordon's uninvited guest and forget all the unanswered questions that buzzed though her head. With her mind clear Millie chose nine stones and laid them down one by one in a specific order as she was directed. When she had finished the woman pointed at the line closest to Millie.

"These three reveal the past and this first stone in the line represents the hidden influences you have had to deal with." The woman turned it over and Millie could sense the curiosity of the other two women as they leant forward to see. "Ah, the eleventh rune: 'Is'. The rune of ice. Like ice waits for spring to melt, you put your problems on hold hoping that they would solve themselves. Maybe you were influenced by those around you, but a problem we allow ourselves to harbour is only in hibernation, it has not left us. Now this next stone, 'Yr', shows the basic influences in your past. 'Yr' is the yew tree from which bows are made and arrows are fired. Arrows that can seek and pin down the things that we have lost. Perhaps you have lost something?" The woman looked at her enquiringly.

"I ... I lost my brother." Millie stammered.

"I see, missing a sibling," she replied as if taking note and turned over the last stone in the row.

"'Ior', the sea serpent. Your attitude towards these past events was a feeling of unavoidable hardship. There were things which you felt you would never be able to change and so you let them be." Millie flushed as she thought of the years in which she had just accepted that George was gone, instead of searching for him.

"This middle line is the present," the woman continued, "and this stone is your hidden influence. Ah, 'Eolh', the elk and the fifteenth rune. This is a positive sign. It points to success being close at hand and that those with determination in their heart will always prevail. Now let us see the current state of your affairs revealed by this next stone." She paused. "Well, well fancy that ..."

"What is it?" asked Millie.

"'Peord,'" the woman replied showing her a M-shaped rune. "There are many uncertainties in your life. Things are hidden and unexplained and they are causing a conflict within you. You no longer feel in control and your mind ... your mind is troubled by this burden as you try to understand your world." The woman leant closer to her. "Hidden things that only you must unravel," she said in a very slow and deliberate manner.

Millie felt a little scared. Did she know about her notion of George going back in time?

"This is your present attitude," she continued turning over the next stone. "'Rad', the rune of travel. You have become increasingly aware that now is the time to move and make important decisions."

"Yes, I suppose it is," Millie agreed. "What about the future, then?"

"Patience. Firstly we shall see the obstacles that lie ahead of you. 'Asc'," she said, revealing to Millie a symbol shaped like an F, "the great ash-tree that links together the worlds."

"The ash-tree, why do I keep hearing about that?" Millie broke in, but the woman ignored her and carried on talking.

"In your quest you will have endurance and strength despite the fears and attacks that you may face."

"Fear and attacks": Millie wasn't sure she liked the sound of that.

"Next is the key rune, the best outcome that the future can bring. 'Eh', the horse rune. It represents carrying a task through to the end. But it is also associated strongly with travel and travel between the worlds. This final stone is your response, 'Daeg', the rune of day and midsummer. A positive change. Your heart is guided by the belief that light will prevail over darkness. The future looks promising, Millie, but remember, these are only possible futures, you must take into consideration the runes as a whole."

"How do you know my name?" Millie interrupted, but the woman put her hand up to request silence as she copied the symbols on to a piece of paper for Millie.

ᛁ ᚣ ᚼ

ᛉ ᛈ ᚱ

ᚠ ᛖ ᛞ

"Do you know how to use the runes to make spells?" Millie asked.

"Only tamper with the unknown if you are willing to accept the consequences," the woman from the bus suddenly spoke. Then the other silent sister rose up from her armchair to pull open the purple curtain for Millie.

Millie stood up and squinted at the bright sun. A dozen more questions were on the tip of her tongue but the next customer had already entered and was eagerly handing over his three pounds.

She hurried back to the tombola stall, knowing she had extended her break time.

"Guess what? I've just had my fortune told!"

"What did you find out?" Becky asked, wishing she had gone with her.

"It was amazing! It seemed like they knew my thoughts!"

"Like what?"

"Like how I'd lost something and had lots of things I was trying to find out at the moment that I had to act upon now, and about how in the past I accepted that I couldn't change things." Millie babbled away excitedly, trying to remember everything that she had been told, and showed them the rune paper.

"Really, they knew all that?"

"Yeah, and what's more I had a dream last week about runes and stones and I am sure one of them was in it. Maybe we should paint the runes on the stones I found because there's twenty-nine stones and twenty-nine runes."

"Maybe they've given you a magical rune spell!" said Sam, jokingly.

"We could do it on the eve of the solstice."

"That's tonight!"

"Are you all actually being serious?" Lee laughed scornfully. "What *exactly* do you think will happen? That we'll get sent back in time?"

"Maybe nothing will happen but this is the only chance I'll get to try. If the stones and the runes are anything to do with George and Bobby, then it has to be done on the solstice," Millie said.

"Well, we'll just try it out for a laugh and if nothing happens then nothing happens. Do you think it has to be done at midnight?"

"I think just as soon as the sun goes down, cos then it's the shortest night. What do you think, Lee, are you going to help?"

"Yeah, okay," Lee nodded. "Something to do, innit? Got to be more exciting trying to time travel in a graveyard than watching telly at home. We might get a bit of stick from the paranoid oldies for going out late on the solstice, though."

"Yeah, that's going to be difficult," Sam agreed. "Still, if they believe in all that folklore that's all the more reason to do it. I'll bring some chalk to write on the stones and Millie, you'll have to bring a list of the rune symbols for us all, so we can copy them onto the stones."

Chapter Twenty: The Eve of the Solstice

On the evening of the twentieth of June Millie stood waiting anxiously at the church gates. They should have met up thirty minutes ago. The sun was already low on the horizon and she was finding it hard to avoid the suspicious glances of evening dog-walkers as she stood lingering.

"Oy!"

Millie felt someone push her from behind and spun round.

"Sam! Don't do that. You're so annoying."

"Sorry, Mills."

"Where's Becky and Lee?"

"They're just walking up now, see," he said pointing. "It took a bit of time getting out. I had to pretend that I was in my room on my Play Station."

"My Grandad decided to have an early night, so there was no drama at all."

"That was easy," Millie said. "I managed to look up sunset times on the web and it said 9.20 p.m. for tonight."

"Okay, great, we've got about half an hour then."

"Hiya. Sorry I'm late." Becky joined them in a breathless pant. "Got a bit delayed. All right then, what's the plan?"

"Well, I've made you a copy of the symbols from a rune poem Mr Gordon had, I've written down each rune symbol and then its name next to it." Millie handed them all a sheet of paper. "The last nine are the rune symbols that were in my fortune, so I'll draw those onto the inner ring of stones and maybe you three could draw the others on the outer ring. Did you bring the chalk, Sam?" Sam nodded and gave them each a stick of chalk.

"Are we going to be able to find all the stones?" Becky asked.

"You should be able to, they're an equal distance from each other and they're quite distinctive, not smooth and flat like gravestones. This is one next to this gate," Millie said, crouching down and touching it. "So if you imagine it's part of a large circle and follow it round, then it ought to be pretty easy. I'm not sure where all mine are, though …"

Millie left the others discussing who was going to chalk the first rune and went over to the centre of the southern part of the graveyard. It took her a while, but she eventually found nine oddly-shaped stones which seemed to fit into points of a circle. Even though the stone circles were well camouflaged amongst the gravestones, Millie thought it was odd that the stones had remained in place and untouched for so many hundreds of years, especially if they were as old as Grandad had suggested. Did the Wirde sisters know about them? Millie studied the piece of paper they had given her showing her rune fortune and copied the letters ᛁ, ᚢ and ᚼ onto three of the stones with the chalk.

To the west of the church the sun was now a burning red and a mist of orange glowed above the line of fields. Two more stones made up the corners of a burial plot with railings and three others were covered in ivy. The last one was partly concealed under the low branches of a yew tree; she decided to mark this with the rune ᛈ.

Sam, Lee and Becky had finished the outer circle and came over to meet Millie.

“What shall we do now?” Becky asked.

“Wait until the sun goes completely down, I suppose.”

“Do you think that's when it happens?”

“It's the start of the shortest night, isn't it?”

“Maybe I need to stand somewhere, like, in the middle or something?”

“Okay, that old tree stump seems pretty central, sit on that. There's only a few minutes left now.”

Millie sat on the large stump in the centre of the circle.

“Why don't you three chant out the names of the runes or something?” she suggested light-heartedly.

The minutes passed by and the sun sank out of view until only pink and purple light remained. With her eyes closed Millie tried to relax and listen to the chanting but instead she found herself becoming more tense. What were they doing? What if it really did work? She would be completely alone, in the dark, somewhere she didn't know, without any food or place to sleep. She should've at least brought a packed lunch. And how was she ever going to get home? What was she thinking?

Feeling scared, Millie looked across at Becky and saw the corners of her mouth were twitching. As Millie caught her eye, the grin that Becky had been trying to contain exploded into a fit of contagious hysterics. The mood changed immediately and they were all giggling, even Millie. Lee and Sam pretended to be wizards and leapt around the girls, turning the chanting into a rap: "Is, Yr, Rad and rhymes. Millie back to da olden times ..."

"Well it obviously didn't work, did it?" Millie said, but despite her disappointment she was relieved to still be on familiar ground.

"No, you are definitely still here," Becky replied, offering Millie her hand and pulling her to her feet.

"Feoh, Feoh, Feoh and Ger,

The Anglo-Saxons don't want her,

My Mann, my Mann,

I said Yr Yr Yr..."

Lee carried on rapping with Sam accompanying with a beat-box.

"Can you two shut up now! It doesn't even sound good," Becky joked with them and then turned to Millie kindly and said, "We can carry on doing it for a bit longer if you want."

"No, let's go back. One of our parents is bound to notice we're not at home."

"What about the chalk on the stones?"

"We'll rub it off in the morning when it's lighter."

They walked back towards the entrance. As Millie turned to shut the gate a flicker of movement caught her eye. She looked up just in time to see a figure scuttle behind a yew tree and then out of view. Someone in a scarf and long coat like she'd seen the Wirde sisters wear. Had they been spied upon?

"Are you really upset, Mills?" Millie was distracted as Becky slipped an arm through hers.

"Not really. I suppose it was stupid anyway," she replied.

"No, it wasn't. Not with everything that's happened. You shouldn't feel negative about it."

"You know I'm kind of relieved because if I *had* gone back, then what? I would have been on my own in a dark forest with wolves and bears everywhere. I probably would have lasted five seconds. I just feel like I've wasted everyone's time and it has got me nowhere. I've found out so much and yet I'm still just as clueless as ever. All I've achieved is getting you all a bad reputation in the village with Mrs Gordon."

"That hardly matters. We know something really strange has been going on. We've just got to keep an open mind and keep on trying," Sam said encouragingly and in his best sci-fi accent added, "The truth is out there!"

"Yep, it's out there somewhere."

"Why don't we try putting the runes in a different order? Didn't someone say it was like a spell?"

"Yeah, the fortune teller said the runes could be used as spells when arranged in a certain way and it did seem like she was hinting she knew everything I've been up to. But I could have been imagining it, or maybe it's another coincidence. And I know loads of amazing coincidences have happened since the storm but that's probably all they are: coincidences that I've just read too much into."

"Coincidences! Millie, that pot was made in the seventh century. That's a fact proven by science and your name is on the pot. There was a mobile phone in it and it was wedged between the roots of a tree. That's not a coincidence. What if your Grandad was right about time travel?"

"Yeah Mills, there's loads of stuff that we don't understand yet. What if there is some gravitational force that the stones give off when you do something to them?" Lee suggested. "It could be some type of exotic matter that physicists haven't discovered yet!"

"Yeah, like magic exists and is part of science as well," Sam agreed.

"But I don't have the spell, so there's nothing I can …" she paused. "Wait a minute. Mr Gordon had a book on the shop counter that was something about spells from the Dark Ages."

"Well, let's go and get it."

"Are you serious? After last time?"

"We just won't get caught."

"Oh come on Lee, how's it going to work? She's going to be home, we can't just sneak in."

"Because, Becky," Sam said excitedly, "I've still got the boxes from the fête, with the tombola stuff and tablecloths in, at my house. If we take it back to Mrs Gordon's we'll be doing her a favour so she doesn't have to come to us. Then while we are helping her put it in the garage, Millie can grab the book."

"I don't know …"

"It's perfect! Nothing can go wrong. The garage is right at the end of the garden, you'll have ages. Look let's take the stuff round there. My mum's going to nag me about it anyway, and if you really don't want to go in, then don't. But it's the solstice tonight, so …"

Millie was reminded of the rune 'Is' that she had picked out in her fortune: things weren't always resolved by themselves.

"Yeah, okay let's do it then. What about you, Becks?"

"Okay, but it is a bit late. She might be going to bed soon."

"Let's hurry, then."

The four of them headed up the street towards the other end of the village. The boxes were in two enormous carrier bags in Sam's conservatory.

"Right, Mills, we'll take these and you follow behind. I'll try and put the door on the latch so you can get in."

With the bags heaved over their shoulders, Becky, Lee and Sam stood on Mrs Gordon's step and rang the bell. She opened the door wearing her dressing gown and slippers. She scowled at them.

"It's a bit late, isn't it? Do your parents know you're out? Oh, are those my tombola things?"

They nodded and she opened the door to let them in.

"I'll just get the garage key."

She disappeared into the dining room and Sam quickly slipped the lock onto its latch. Mrs Gordon returned wearing her shoes and holding a large bunch of keys.

"Come on! Make sure you close the door properly."

Millie heard footsteps heading down the garden path and poked her head around the corner. Quick as a flash she crept into the house and swiftly made her way to the dining room. She went over to the mantelpiece but the china pot was empty! Mrs Gordon must have moved the key. Where would it be? Millie checked all the shelves but couldn't find it. She was running out of time! In desperation she pulled a clip from her hair. It was far-fetched but maybe she could unfasten the lock herself. As Millie gripped the door handle it spun round. It was already open! Mrs Gordon must have forgotten to lock it, or else not bothered. Millie stepped into the dark room and, using the torch on her mobile, she shone the light down the piles of books on the shop counter. There it was! A large red book sitting right at the bottom of a pile - *Spells from the Dark Ages. A Complete Translation of Remedies and Spells taken from The Lacnunga and other Ancient Manuscripts.'* [3]

Millie pulled it out and flicked through its dusty pages. There were all kinds of spells: a potion to stop flying venom using oaken brand, a poem to shrink black ulcers, a magical drink of herbs boiled in butter to cure elf sickness, but what about time travel? There was no index at the back or contents page at the front. Then Millie saw there was a silk ribbon bookmark dangling from the bottom of the book. She turned the pages to where it lay. The left-hand page was entitled 'Travel in Time'. This must be it! Mr Gordon had thought it important enough to mark it. Could it be the rune spell?

The paragraph that followed was an early twentieth-century interpretation of the spell and described the effect on gravity and energy when stones of a certain composition were used with the following spell. Underneath the writing was a picture of a stone circle labelled 'A Hearg'. It was nearly identical to the diagram in the folder, but with arrows drawn joining the stones together like a dot-to-dot. Sketched next to it was a picture of the earth in relation to the sun throughout the year. Curved lines and dates showed the distance between the stars and planets during the different months. Millie looked over to the next page: it was a charm for dispersing a swarm of bees! Confused, she looked for the page numbers. A page was missing! She opened the book right up so the covers were touching and saw a jagged edge of paper along the spine where a page had been ripped out.

Millie frantically hunted through the piles of books and paper on the counter, but it wasn't there. Time was ticking by. She opened the drawers but there was so much clutter and junk, they were almost impossible to search. Keeping hold of the book Millie glanced around the shop, hoping that some other clue would jump out at her. But it didn't and now she really had to go. As she made her way to the front of the shop she passed the old costume that Becky had pulled out. If they did ever find a way back she wanted to be more prepared. Millie took it off the shelf and stuffed it inside her jumper with the book, just in case. Then she stealthily left, via the shop entrance.

Millie leant against the front wall of the house, guarding her treasure with one hand over her stomach. She heard Becky, Lee and Sam bidding goodnight to Mrs Gordon and waited for them to appear around the corner.

"Did you find anything?" Sam asked.

"Looks like you put on a bit of weight, Mills!"

"Shhh, keep your voices down."

Millie pulled the costume and the book out from under her jumper.

"You found it, then! What's that? Is it the peasant tunic I put on?"

"Yeah, I thought I might need it if I ever went back. It was pretty easy getting in there, the door wasn't even locked. I found a rune spell for time travel and using the stones, but some of the book has been torn out." She showed them the page where the book mark was. "There's just the beginning."

"That's annoying. At least the fact it's missing shows it obviously was important," Sam said.

"But the rest of the information is no good without the spell." Millie felt like giving up again.

"Maybe we could carry on looking for it and then try doing it at the winter solstice? There's bound to be another copy of the book somewhere," Becky suggested.

"No. I know you're only trying to make me feel better, but December's a really long time away. If it was going to happen, it would have been tonight."

"But you've tried so hard."

"Exactly, and I still haven't helped get George back."

"Mills, you've done everything you could have done. You even risked your life by going to Mrs Gordon's, twice! I'm sure George would be really grateful."

"Yeah, Sam's right, there's not much more you can do. We'll keep an ear out for you, when you go home to your Mum and Dad's place, and we'll let you know if anything strange happens."

The friends traipsed wearily along the main street, their footsteps echoing past the centuries-old cottages that stood silently. The full moon now shone and in the north-western sky the bright outline of the plough constellation twinkled its ancient light. They passed Sam's house, and Lee's and then the lane to Becky's; then Millie was walking alone.

She let herself in, fearful of being told off for staying out late, but her grandfather was asleep in his chair and snoring contently.

Chapter Twenty-one: When the Sun Stands Still

Millie was dreaming about the events of last night when a banging at her bedroom door woke her. She glanced at the alarm clock. It was already nine a.m.

"Millie! Millie! Are you awake? Can I come in?" Millie was surprised to hear Becky's voice.

"Yes, I am now," she replied.

Becky came into the room. "My mum's outside in the car. We're going into town to pick up some hair straighteners she won on eBay. I thought you might like to come, we're going to be driving past your parents' house."

"But I'm not dressed yet."

"I don't mind waiting. You said you had something you wanted to pick up from home."

Millie remembered the old phone charger. "Okay, give me a minute and I'll be down."

Mrs Hockley's car was as messy and chaotic as the Hockley house. Millie pushed aside some empty crisp packets and juice cartons and made a space to sit down. Mrs Hockley seemed pleased to see her and at once launched into a long account of all her many previous eBay purchases. She was still talking as she dropped Millie off outside the house.

It was strange being home without her parents there. With the familiar smell of home came a longing for the comfort of being near them. Millie wandered through the rooms, checking everything was as it should be, and then went up to her bedroom. She bent down under the bed and rummaged around for the large shoe box she kept old electrical stuff in. It was right towards the back of the wall. Millie had to squeeze herself under the bed to reach it. She opened it and found her old mobile. Exactly the same make and model as the one of George's they had found in the den (except with a pink stripy case) and there was the charger!

Millie put them in her bag and shoved the box back under the bed. As she was shutting her bedroom door she felt drawn to George's room. She hadn't been in there for a long time. She turned the handle and walked in. All of George's clothes and belongings had been boxed up and put in the loft. The same blue paint remained and the football pictures were still hanging on the walls, but it was now the spare guest room. Millie closed her eyes and tried to picture him here, looking up at her and telling her to "Get out!" She closed the door and went downstairs. While she was waiting for Becky and her mum to pick her up she decided to go online. She had really missed not having the internet at Grandad's. She typed "Solstice" into Google and read through the pages that came up. A horror film remade by Hollywood; Stonehenge; Wikipedia; and an essay entitled Understanding the Solstices. It was this last one that she clicked on:

Solstice comes from the Latin word sol (sun) and stitium, (stoppage), because twice a year at the winter and summer solstices, the sun stands still as the seasonal movement of the sun's path comes to a halt, before it then reverses direction.

In the summer the sun reaches its most northern point relative to the celestial equator on the celestial sphere, and in the winter the sun reaches its most southern point. This is due to the 23.5-degree tilt of the Earth's axis, which makes the sun shine above the horizon for different lengths of time during our different seasons. Of course it is not actually the sun that moves, it's the Earth.

During the day of the summer solstice the sun makes such a high arc across the sky that everyone in the northern hemisphere will experience the longest duration of daylight in the year. And in the winter the sun's arc is so low, we will experience the shortest amount of sunlight.

The summer solstice is often mistaken for being a full day, but it is in fact the moment that the sun is shining farthest to the north, before it begins its journey south again. This year on Sunday June 21 the Sun will be in its highest annual point in the sky, standing at 23 degrees above the Northern horizon. The actual event of the solstice in the UK will take place at precisely 17.38 (BST), the moment the sun changes direction and starts moving back towards the south.

On September 23 the sun will pass the equator at the autumn equinox, and move into the Southern Hemisphere at 09.20 (BST), and on December 22 the sun will head north again at 04.48 (GMT).

The solstices are largely connected with the seasons. In the past the year was divided into only winter and summer; therefore the solstices marked mid-summer and mid-winter. Although now we recognise autumn and spring, we mark the solstices as the start of summer and the start of winter. Many festivals have arisen around these events, for example festivals during the winter and southern solstice include Christmas, the Slavic pagan holiday Karachun, the Persian festival Yalda, the African-American Kwanzaa, the Roman festival Saturnalia and the Anglo-Saxon Yule festival.

Festivals during the summer and northern solstices include the Christian feast of St. John, the pagan festival of Litha, the Vestalia festival of the Ancient Romans, the South American We Tripantu festival and the ancient noise festival of the Atacama people.

Many temples and monuments have been built through time to mark the solstices. Two of the many examples of these are the Kukulcan temple built by the Mayan civilisation, where at the exact moment of the summer solstice the appearance of light and shadow on the surface of the temple seem to split it in half; and Stonehenge where when the sun rises on the day of the summer solstice, it lines up with the heel stone and shines its first rays through a stone archway in the centre circle.

So the summer solstice wasn't just a day in the year but an event. It was a single moment that occurs at a different time every year, and this year it would be specifically at 5.38 p.m., Millie concluded. There was a chart adjacent to the essay that listed the last twenty years and the corresponding times of the solstices and equinoxes for each year. Millie looked back three years before, when George had disappeared, and saw that the summer solstice had occurred at 00:09 on the 21st June. She had assumed that George had gone missing on the eve of the solstice, but no, he had gone missing on the actual day of the solstice.

"Beep beep!" Mrs Hockley had pulled up outside the house and was sounding the horn. Millie turned off the computer and, grabbing her bag and keys, went out to meet them.

"Did you get what you wanted?" Becky asked turning around in her seat as Millie got in.

"Yeah, it's in my bag. Did you pick up your new hair straighteners, Mrs Hockley?"

"Oh yes, dear. Becky and I will have a completely new look by tonight."

*

Millie's hand shook with excitement as she plugged the charger into her old phone and saw the screen flash up with the battery symbol. Now she just had to wait for it to fully charge as the countdown to 5.38 p.m. began.

Maybe, just maybe, she had another chance. She would go to the churchyard on her own this time - maybe it was only alone that Millie could discover the "hidden things that only she must unravel". But this time she must also have more faith, truly believe and be more prepared.

While she was waiting for the phone to charge Millie busied herself by packing the essentials. She dug out her grandfather's old leather satchel from under the stairs and went into the kitchen to raid the cupboards. Her grandad always went to the local pub on a Sunday afternoon and she was free to help herself without interrogation. She packed some oranges and apples, crisps, a pack of Penguin biscuits, a large chocolate bar and a bottle of juice and, as an afterthought, some Paracetamol as a first-aid kit.

The phone had been charging for an hour now. There should be enough battery in it to turn the phone on. She prised off the rubber camouflage case from George's phone. It had started to disintegrate with age and small flakes of it fell onto the bed. Opening the back cover Millie replaced the battery with her charged one. She said a quick prayer and pressed down the ON button at the top.

There was nothing. Not even a flicker of light on the screen. She held it down again, this time for longer, but still nothing. Maybe the battery wasn't in properly? Millie sat up and took the cover off again. No, there was nothing wrong with the battery. She wondered why she had ever expected it would work: it was over a thousand years old! Millie felt defeated once again. She lay on the bed in misery and stared up at the ceiling, hoping a solution would come to her. But it didn't. She took the battery out, ready to throw it away, when she noticed the SIM card. Of course! How could she have been so stupid! She could just put his SIM card in her old phone! Millie carefully took George's out and put it into her old phone with the battery. She pressed the ON button again and the screen lit up with George's welcome note.

Chapter Twenty-two: Dreaming of home

On the morning of the solstice George walked with the other villagers to the stones. He climbed the bough of a tree on the edge of the circle and sat watching as the villagers lay their offerings of withering herbs to the gods beside the world-tree, in assurance of a good harvest.

For three years George had speculated as to what force or power had brought him to this time; pondered the existence of magic and the facts of science. Intuition had told him that the stones marked the place in which he had left Wybrook and that they somehow held the key for returning to the twenty-first century. He was also convinced that his arrival on the solstice had to be of some special significance and not just coincidence.

So it was to the stones that George came on this long day, not to leave offerings for the gods but to wait and hope for something to happen or for someone to come - although he did so with an increasingly pessimistic heart.

This solstice was the end of his third year in East Seax. In the past years of the solstice he had sat high up in the same oak tree where he sat now. Two branches stemmed off from the same part in the trunk, making a comfortable dip for him to lie in. His spear lay balanced on the branch next to him to offer protection, should he need it.

The morning drew on. Two wise men had travelled here and drawn the runes onto the stones, in the same manner as they had been when George had first arrived, and now most of the villagers had left their offerings and gone back to work in the fields. George found himself hoping that the gods would be pleased and favour them all with a good harvest, so that they would have enough provisions for the winter. How much he had changed! The longer he was here in Widurok, the more superstitious and like-minded he found himself becoming. He had been here such a long time that his past life often felt far away and out of reach. It was almost as though it had never existed for him but had been part of somebody else's life.

George hoped nobody would notice he was missing back in the village; living in a tight-knit community, it was difficult to do anything without everybody else knowing about it. Still, he could always make his excuses when he returned. In previous years he had told them that his sister had promised to visit one year on the Litha and the Hearg was the best known landmark to Widurok. It was almost the truth. If only she would find his mobile. He thought of it lying buried just the other side of the trees and had to force himself to resist the temptation to jump down and check it was still there. It had been a stupid idea, of course. How would Millie ever find it? Even if she did, it probably wouldn't work by the twenty-first century and she wouldn't know what the runes were or what Saberht meant. Oh, *why* had he never kept his battery charged! He could have written a whole essay on his phone when he had first arrived.

George had only been a thirteen-year-old boy then. He was sixteen now - that was adulthood here. Would anybody in the twenty-first century even recognise him now? All the work in the fields had broadened his shoulders and beefed up his muscles. Although he relished the adventure and experience, it was hard work living in these times.

Every solstice the feelings that George usually kept locked inside him rushed to the forefront of his mind - mostly the longing to be home. Thoughts of his sister Millie, his parents and his close friends flooded his thoughts. He longed to tell them about the adventures he had, what it was like to go out hunting all day for wild bull, or the adrenaline rush of running from one when it attacked and the roles of hunted and hunter were reversed. But George was a world away from them all.

"This is the last year I come here," George promised to himself as a tear rolled freely down his cheek. It just made him sad and aware of how alone he was in this world. George got on well with the villagers and had found them very welcoming, but they could never relate to the life he had known or share his wavelength. The weight of keeping his past a secret burdened him and made him ill at ease. It was only Leof that he had ever been able to confide in; but Leof believed that the gods had brought George here and that this was the place where he belonged now.

George desperately wanted to chat about football teams and current music bands, or just lie on the sofa watching a film or playing computer games, or just taste smoky bacon crisps and chocolate once more! George even worried about all the schooling he was missing: he should be taking his GCSEs with the rest of his class. Now he would never catch up, although he was certain he could get an A in history and probably in crafts, woodwork and farming too!

"No magic is sending you home and no rescue party is coming for you. Stop putting yourself through this, George," he muttered to himself as he closed his eyes and, in the hook of the branch, drifted miserably off to sleep.

Chapter Twenty-three: A Journey through Time

Millie scrolled down the menu and into the Messages option. There were three texts in the Inbox waiting to be opened:

9.34 Hope you're looking after Grandad, don't forget to hand your trip money in today, miss you, mum xxxx

19.42 Hi George, when u back? football training has been changed to mon, Phil

11.34 Have u still got my ps game? Harry

Millie went back to Messages and into Drafts. There was a message waiting to be sent!

Millie/whoever, hope u get this. Am in Widurok 7 century. Ok but don't know how 2 get back. Maybe need stones/rune spell, check photos.

Millie could scarcely breathe. She had been right, George *had* gone back in time! She knew now for sure! She opened up Photos and there was a photo of some of the stones! They were looking rather less weathered and slightly taller than the ones she knew, but they *could* be the same. Next there was a photo of a parchment document with the rune spell she so badly needed! She counted the runes and wasn't at all surprised that there were twenty-nine.

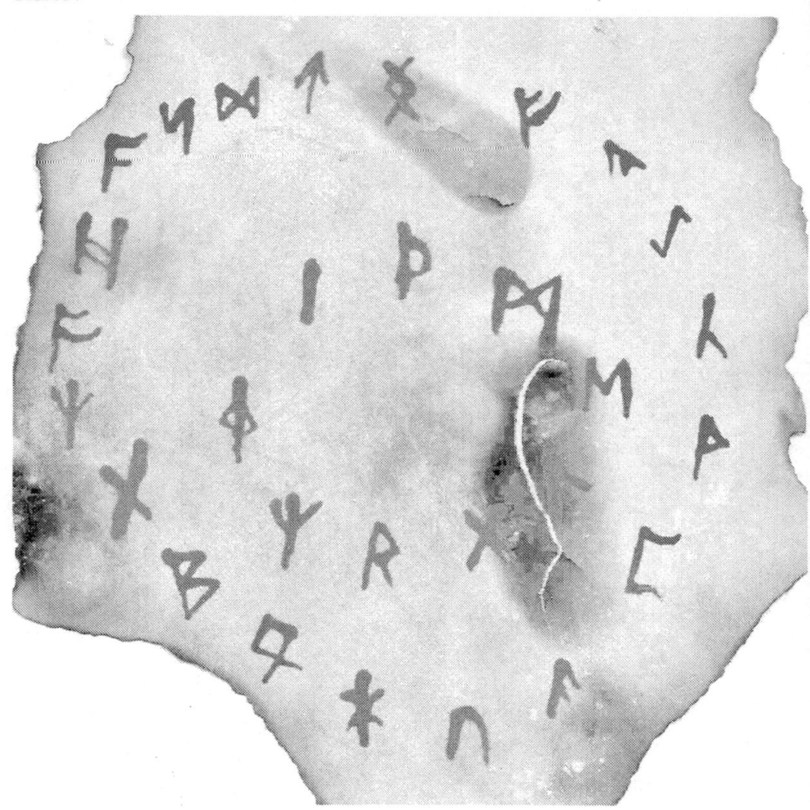

Millie got the diagram of the stones in the churchyard and compared it to George's photo of the stones. In his photo the nearest stone distinctly had a ᛠ marked on it, the rune Ear. Behind that stone she could see the other was ᛄ, Ger. It was clear in the photo that these were two stones from the inner circle. The stone with ᛠ marked on it was a triangular shape with a steep slant. Millie recognise which stone it was in Mr Gordon's diagram and remembered also seeing it yesterday, as it was quite unique. She wrote ᛠ and Ear on the corresponding stone on the diagram. Now she knew one stone she realised she could easily work out the others. She looked back at the diagram in the spell book. The arrow started from a stone at the top of the page and ran clockwise around the outer ring to the stone next to where it started. It then moved to a stone in the inner circle where it ran clockwise until the last stone and then pointed to the middle of the circle, having linked all the stones together.

Using the parchment photo alongside the rune poem which told her the names of the runes, Millie busily began filling in the symbols and their names onto the remaining stones in the diagram. Then she copied onto it the arrows from the spell.

Millie glanced at the clock: 4.47. She stuffed the tunic, maps, church diagrams, the page from the spell book and her old mobile into the bag and put a stick of the white chalk in her pocket. Now she was ready.

Millie felt a huge pang of guilt knowing the emotional trauma she would put Grandad through again if she succeeded. She could only hope that he would understand and left a simple note in the kitchen, "Gone to find George, xx".

Millie left the house and walked towards the church alone. As she pushed open the wooden gates she felt a change had come over her. She felt different inside. She wasn't just little schoolgirl Millie but Millie who was embarking on a great journey. The fear she had experienced earlier was gone.

"*Ing*" Millie said aloud as holding the diagram in one hand and the chalk in the other she drew the symbol ᛝ on the first stone. "*Feoh,*" she said moving on to the next. "*Yr Eoh Cen Wynn Peord Aesc Ur Ior Ethel Beorc Nyd Eolh Os*

Hagol Ac Sigel Daeg Tiw Thorn Mann Eh Lagu Gyfu Rad Ear Ger Is."

Millie put down the chalk and looked at the circles around her. Bearing their new marks, they seemed to hold some kind of mystical significance.

Her phone now said 5.30. There were only a few minutes left. Millie took her jacket off and carefully tucked it under a nearby tree with her phone inside it. She put the tunic on over her T-shirt and hoped that her canvas trousers wouldn't look too modern. Now appropriately dressed for the seventh century, she walked over to the tree stump and stood on it.

Millie stared out to the sun and waited. The seconds passed by like hours. Just as before nothing happened. She looked at the sun, standing still in the sky. Was it 5.38 p.m. yet? She couldn't help but doubt her newfound belief in magic and time travel.

"No," she said, strong-willed, "I *must* have faith."

As Millie spoke she began to feel a pressure building in the air surrounding her. She thought it must be her imagination and waited for it to pass, but instead it intensified. It was as if she was on the Hearts and Diamonds ride at the fair. The force seemed to be pulling her down onto the tree stump. Unable to move, she tried to scream, but her face was immobile under the intense pressure. Her mind filled with fear, her body felt as though it was going to explode! Desperate for help Millie saw three figures amongst the stones: the Wirde sisters were watching over her… as they had been from the start and all along. She closed her eyes. Then very suddenly the pressure stopped and Millie fell to the ground, panting for air. She looked up and saw that in the place of the tree stump was a great ash tree.

PART TWO

Chapter Twenty-four: Reunited

A small thud woke George on his branch. He instinctively grabbed his spear and dropped down from the tree. He was expecting to see someone from the village, or perhaps a wild animal, but instead he could only hear a wheezing noise like someone short of breath. It was coming from the other side of the ash tree. He walked cautiously towards it and saw a girl crouched on her knees trying to catch her breath. A girl with bobbed, high-lighted hair, very conditioned and shiny.

The girl lifted her head and George saw her face.

He reeled back in shock. Was it...? No, it couldn't be! He must still be dreaming. The spear dropped from George's grasp and he stood in amazement.

"Millie," his voice was barely audible, "is it really you?"

Millie turned at the sound of her name. In front of her was someone that she had once known as a shorter, slightly more fashionable-looking, pre-adolescent.

"*George?*" Millie felt confused. "You've come home!"

"No ... I don't think so. You've ... you've come to my time," George replied hesitantly.

"Oh," she uttered quietly in realisation. It had worked. The spell had *really* worked. And here she was. Here she was with George!

Millie stood up level with her brother so that they were face to face. For a moment there was a shyness between them. The years of childhood they had missed together meant that they were almost like strangers. But those missed years, years of wondering if they would ever see each other again, were at last over. That endless pain of worry and longing was finally gone and despite the strangeness between them, they both felt in their hearts more pleased to see each other than ever before.

"I can't believe I've finally found you! We haven't even known if you were alive or not!"

George shook his head slowly in disbelief. "I am *so* glad to see you."

He put his hands on Millie's shoulders and took a good look at the ten-year-old sister he had left behind who had now blossomed into a teenager. Despite the contrast in hair colours, different gender and George's dark tan from working in the fields, they were easily recognisable as brother and sister. They grinned at each other as the unfamiliarity between them began to melt.

"You've got no idea how many questions I've got to ask you."

"No, you've got no idea how many questions I've got to ask *you*!"

"But how did you get here? Did you ever find my mobile? I only buried it a few days ago," George said excitedly.

"Yes, just recently, but it wasn't working so I had to put your SIM in my old phone."

"You're a clever girl, Millie."

Millie smiled. He was still the same older brother she had always known.

"Here, I brought you some presents." She reached in her bag and handed him a packet of crisps.

George snatched them from her in excitement.

"Smoky bacon! I was just thinking what I would do for a packet of crisps."

He immediately tore open the bag and let the incomparable taste of deep fried potato and artificial flavourings excite his taste buds once again. But the aroma brought memories of home that had laid dormant in him.

"Wow, it's been so long. I mean ..." George's eyes welled up and he turned away to hide them from her. "I've been gone *so* long. Has it been three years for you, too?"

"Yes, three years today. The first year was the worst - Mum and Dad found it really tough. They tried so hard to find you. Everyone joined in the search but no one knew where to look. We all did everything we could to help find you. But there was nothing, no clues, no suspects. You just vanished into thin air. The police didn't have anything to investigate. I guess that was because you really *did* 'just disappear'."

George hung his head in shame. "Please don't tell me anymore. I feel so guilty about what I've put everybody through."

"Don't be stupid! It wasn't your fault. You didn't plan to come here, did you?"

"No! Of course not! All I know is that I went out really late that night and when I took a short cut through the churchyard I tripped over. I bumped my head pretty badly and then when I stood up everything seemed different. I was surrounded by trees and I couldn't work out where I was." He smiled. "Turns out I was here, in the Dark Ages, walking around these woods in circles."

"Well, you're not the only one here now."

"No, I'm not. How did you manage to time travel and break the basic laws of physics?"

"I don't understand the science of it, but I heard old rumours about other villagers going missing in the past. I started investigating and then a lot of research and guesswork got me here."

"What about Mum and Dad?"

"Well they kind of blamed themselves a bit - I guess parents do when bad stuff happens to their kids. They've just learnt to carry on as normal now, although they still seem a bit sad sometimes. They're in South Africa again at the moment."

"No, I mean, did they help you to get here? Why didn't they come too? You *have* told them, right?"

"Of course not! They would never have allowed me to come, or even believed me for that matter!"

"Hey, what's that noise?" George said, interrupting her.

In the silence they could hear a murmur of voices approaching them.

"Pilgrims," George explained. "Lots of pagans come ere on the Litha. They'll be lighting fires for the gods as art of their celebrations."

"Litha?"

"Yeah. It's a festival they have during the solstice. Come on, let's go somewhere else. I know a place that might make you feel like you're still in Wybrook. Follow me."

George led Millie along a muddy track, leaving the stone circle behind them. The path soon brought them out onto the mossy Roman road on which he had first travelled down with Leof.

"Recognise it?" George asked.

"Recognise what?" Millie asked, not sure what she was meant to be looking at.

"The stone marker you're standing next to!"

Millie crouched down to study it more closely.

"Wow, is this the stone next to our den? I guess that makes sense if we've just come from where the church is. And look - the footpath's a proper walkway!" The landscape was so different from her present day with its large open field and dried-out ditch. It felt like a completely different place altogether.

"This is where you buried the pot."

"Yes, it's under there now."

"It's only by chance that I found it. It was unearthed by a freak hurricane that uprooted the tree."

"It was a long shot. I thought if you ever found the phone you would recognise it and then wonder about the urn. The Saxon settlement is mostly in the same area of Wybrook that the old buildings are, back in our time, but this stone is the only solid landmark I had where I knew you would go. I once tried to work out where Grandad's garden is, but you know how he always lets it grow wild: it would never have been found." George sighed and shook his head in disbelief. "I slept out by the stones on all the solstices, but I never really believed that this day would come, or that anyone one would ever be able to get here."

Millie felt a tingling of fear and excitement. "Gosh, I really am back in the six hundreds!"

"Same *place* you were when you left, it's just that it's now 610AD."

"Really? Is that the year we're in?"

"According to a messenger from London. No one else seems to work by set dates. Most of the villagers don't even know how old they are, or care."

Millie looked around them. "There are so many trees here, it even smells different. Are there this many trees everywhere?"

"Yes, I think so, although I haven't gone much further out of Widurok. I think the climate is a bit hotter too; the people all manage to live through the winters in wooden huts. Wait till you see the village, then you'll *really* know you're in a different time!"

"I can't even imagine what it's like."

"If you want to find out, we can stay for a few days before we go back. I'm definitely going to miss a lot of people here."

"Er ..." For the first time Millie realised that she had never given proper consideration to the return journey.

"You *did* find out how to get back, didn't you?" George said slowly.

"I never really thought about that part. I guess I was too preoccupied with trying to get here. Sorry, I mean ... I didn't completely believe that this would actually happen."

George looked at Millie in horror: now they would both be trapped here! So much for going home.

"I brought a copy of the spell with me, it's in my bag." Millie said, patting her satchel.

"It's not enough. I've tried chalking the spell on before. Nothing happens."

"Maybe it depends on doing it at the right time. The solstice is a particular *time*, not the whole day."

"No Millie! It's not enough, I've tried all day on the solstice for the past three years. Being able to get back was more important than you finding me!" George sat down on the stone and put his hand to his forehead. "What about Mum and Dad? How do you think they'll feel losing both of us?"

"I'm sorry, George, I wasn't thinking. I just really wanted to see you and I was running out of time. Maybe we can just wait until the next solstice and try something then?"

"Like what? I've been trying every solstice since I got here."

They sat in silence for a while. George couldn't help feeling frustrated with his sister. He had foolishly assumed that she would have the solution for getting home. Now he would have someone else to worry about besides himself. Millie turned her back on him and walked towards the muddy track.

"Millie," he called after her. "I'm sorry. It's just that life is hard here, there are illnesses and famines and a *really* high mortality rate. Right now there are rumours of a disease spreading. It hasn't reached the north of the kingdom yet but it might. I don't want anything to happen to you."

"What kind of disease?"

"Some type of plague. Lots of people are convinced it's because our king, Saberht, has angered the gods by becoming Christian."

"Sounds like the Saxons are really superstitious."

"They are. Missionaries have been here talking about building a church by the stones and it's set the villagers panicking: they think the pagan gods are going to punish us all. Plagues are very real in this age, they can wipe out a whole settlement."

"Well, the stone circles are in the churchyard, so a church is bound to be built there sometime soon."

"Are all the stones still there in the future? I never really noticed them before and Grandad never mentioned them."

"Yes, they're all there. Some were buried in the church walls, or half underground."

"Tell me about the rumours you heard and how you got here, I want to know everything."

George perched on the stone again and Millie sat beside him and relayed the events of the past few weeks in as much detail as she could remember. Then, in between mouthfuls of chocolate, George told her of his experiences, how he had settled into the East Saxon culture and had learnt to live a whole new way of life. He told her about Leof, who had become his closest companion and the adventures they had had together, and of his horse, Elvina, who he had found as a wild young foal curled up against her lamed mother deep in the woods.

They talked and talked. There was so much to catch up on and so much to say. However, George was becoming increasingly aware of the time passing and that he would soon be missed from the village. He wanted to avoid any curiosity about where he'd been. It was time to introduce Millie to Widurok. Using their hands as shovels, they buried the crisp and chocolate wrappers in the earth so as not to leave any evidence of time-travelling. Then George briefed Millie on how to answer any difficult questions from inquisitive villagers and persuaded her to let him do most of the talking.

"I see you've dressed for the occasion already," he said, commenting on the clothes from the old shop.

"Do you think I look okay?"

"I guess you could just about pass as an East Saxon girl, although I'm sure we can find you something better tomorrow," George grinned.

He led the way along the Roman path to a crossroads. From here Widurok could be seen a few hundred metres to the west, a group of wooden huts in a clearing with a few swirling wisps of smoke rising here and there.

Millie felt a buzz of nervous excitement.

"Come on, then, we're almost there." George said giving her a nudge of assurance.

As they walked into the village George took his horn from his belt and blew on it, signifying the arrival of a friend and not a foe. A group of small children flocked to meet them.

"Who's that?" they asked, pointing at Millie.

"This is my sister, Millie, she's just arrived."

"Hello." Millie smiled at them and the youngest ones squealed and tried to hide behind each other. To Millie they appeared scruffy and thinner than the children she was used to seeing, but they seemed to have a healthy glow.

The children followed them as they made their way through the village.

"Did you travel here on your own?" one of them bravely asked.

"Her travelling companions have gone on to London, I mean Lundenburh," George answered, correcting himself.

"That's where the King's court is," an older child said with an air of authority to the younger ones. "It's in a Roman palace that was built by giants."

The children drew closer to Millie and one of them stroked her hair, amazed at its softness and shine.

"It feels like a new-born chick."

"How did you make it go like that?" another asked. More of them crowded around her, all now trying to touch her hair.

Millie tried to step away. "Erm ... we wash it in special herbs."

"What herbs?"

"Where have you come from?"

"Is it far?"

"A village very similar to this one," she replied honestly. She gave George a desperate look. She wasn't use to all this attention, or so many questions.

"Come on you lot, shoo. Leave her alone, there's work to be done." George waved them away with his hands.

"The Wolf Slayer said his sister would come one day," one of them called back to Millie as they ran off.

"The Wolf Slayer?" Millie laughed.

"Yep, that's what they call me." (George had yet to tell her *that* story.)

"Well the Wolf Slayer was right," she shouted back.

George felt relaxed knowing that Millie's sudden arrival was perfectly acceptable to the villagers. With no means of email, phones, or postal service, they had limited communication with the outside world. They were used to families and friends leaving on an indefinite journey, or to fight in battle, without knowing when - or if - they would return.

"Hey Millie, whenever someone new comes to the village everyone always wants to know any news," George warned her. "So you're going to get asked what's been going on, what's happening with the Christian missions and the West Saxons and the Britons and stuff."

"But I don't know anything."

"Just try to give as vague answers as you can or make something up. I'll butt in if I can."

They were walking in the direction of an open shelter where three boys were turning a pig roasting on a spit.

"Leof!" George called out to one of them. A skinny fair-haired boy a year or two older than Millie and with piercing blue eyes turned round. "I'd like you to meet my sister, Millie."

"Wes Hal, Millie!" Leof greeted her in surprise. "We were beginning to think George had made you up, he's been talking about you coming since he got here! How was your journey?"

"It was good, the time seemed to fly by."

"Are you joining us for the feast?"

"Yes, George has been telling me about it."

"Well, George is *meant* to be helping in the hall. You're going to get yourself into trouble with the headman if you're not careful," Leof mocked.

George grinned. "Yeah right. Come on, Mills, I'll take you over there."

Millie couldn't help looking around at everything in fascination. Not only was everything so different visually, the sound was also different. Instead of traffic, the background noise was of animals and children, and the smell in the air was of sweet smoke from cooking and of animals and straw thatch. This is what they mean when they say the past is a foreign country, Millie thought. Watching her, George was reminded of how he had felt when he had first arrived, and his child-like amazement back then.

As they approached the large building of the hall Millie almost stepped on a hen, which flew up at her, flapping in protest. Millie shrieked, jumped back to avoid it and nearly fell over two goats standing behind her.

"Watch out for the livestock, they're everywhere," George laughed. He had forgotten how accident-prone she was. "Wait till you wake up with a goat looking straight at you."

Millie flashed him a sarcastic smile. Their sibling bond was the same as ever.

Chapter Twenty-five: The Mead Hall

Over the grand doorway of the mead hall, lavish bunches of flowering yarrow had been placed in honour of the celebrations. Its white and yellow flowers hung low to avert disease and bad spells, causing both George and Millie to bow their heads as they entered. Once inside, Millie could immediately sense the importance of the hall by its size. Wooden beams stood thick and proud like great pillars reaching for the skies, and the walls were decorated with embroidered cloth depicting scenes of animals and gods.

Amongst these pillars villagers were busying themselves carrying food and utensils to the rows of tables. At the sight of the new arrival, a general hush swept the room as people turned to stare in curiosity. From the end of the hall the headman, Freodheric, came striding across to greet them and introduce himself.

"Ah, so the Wolf Slayer's sister has finally arrived. My youngest son told me it was so. Wes Hal, Millie, I hope your journey was a safe one. You are alone now, I hear. Your companions have travelled on?"

"Yes, that's right. The journey was uneventful, hopefully it will remain so for the others," Millie replied nervously.

"Well, what news do you bring? How's the kingdom north of here? Do the borders remain the same?"

"It's been peaceful," George answered, "and no plague to report, thank the gods."

"There must be *some* news," Freodheric asked again, redirecting his question back to Millie.

"There was a rumour of a Viking attack further up the coast. But actually our headman is hoping I *bring* news back with me. It has been quiet and so far the crops have been growing well. We are looking forward to a plentiful harvest." Millie hoped this was enough information to satisfy him.

"Humph, well that's good I suppose, although I was expecting more. We don't like to be kept in the dark about things - it's how villages end up being raided and burnt to the ground." He frowned. "I'm expecting one of the King's men to pass through this week; hopefully he'll bring tidings from the towns. But come! We shouldn't worry about such things now, we must prepare ourselves for merriment!"

Freodheric beckoned over to his daughter to bring them a large drinking horn. He raised it in the air towards the two of them.

"To the safe arrival of loved ones," he toasted and took a swig, before passing it onto Millie. "Welcome to Widurok!"

As Millie put the horn to her lips she could smell a strong aroma of alcohol and sweet honey. She coughed and spluttered, as the mead burnt her throat, causing both George and Freodheric to chuckle.

"The feasting will begin soon, but first we must finish the preparation. Wolf Slayer, you should you be helping Leof with the hog roast. Ladies," he called over to a group of girls who were bringing in bowls, "take Millie with you to help."

Freodheric left clutching his drinking horn and three teenage girls came over and ushered Millie away from George.

"I'm Sifelda, this is Alwun and this is Edyth," one of the girls said, introducing them. They seemed the same age as Millie, maybe a little older. They appeared friendly and were keen to ask Millie similar questions as the children had.

"Aren't you going to change out of your travelling clothes before the feast?" Alwun asked, looking at Millie's attire.

It was very different to what they were wearing, despite what George had said. The girls were dressed in long garments which were tied at the waist with a rope-like belt and from this hung various practical and ornamental accessories. Millie suddenly felt very self-conscious dressed in the old brown woollen tunic.

"I don't have anything else."

"Come on, let's get you an outfit." Millie felt she could be with a group of teenage girls from any era as they excitedly went off to find some clothes for her. Inside a nearby dwelling there was a pile of linen on a shelf.

Sifelda and Alwun held up different garments to Millie while Edyth determined the right length and which would suit her the best. Millie took off her clothes and was grateful that she had only worn a plain t-shirt that morning, as the sight of this alone evoked a careful study of the foreign cotton fabric and the perfect stitching along the seams.

After their amazement had subsided, the girls helped Millie into a full-length yellow underdress made of linen. It had long sleeves which fastened at the end with a braid and a drawstring neck, which they tightened around her to fit. Over this they put on her a red pinafore dress which they called a peplos. It too was long and was clasped onto the under-dress at the shoulders. Around her waist they tied a yellow belt in a special knot, like their own. Millie's canvas shoes were left, although they also drew much astonished discussion, being very different to the leather sandals the girls wore.

They were suddenly disturbed by the long note of a horn being blown: the feasting was starting! The girls stood in front of Millie, studying their subject's new look.

"She needs a brooch or a necklace," said Edyth.

"I've got a pendant she could wear," Sifelda replied and took a yellow stone from a pouch on her belt.

"That's perfect, it'll match the underdress," said Sifelda excitedly. "There's some leather cord here. Let's plait it and we can hang the pendant on it."

"Okay, but quickly!"

The girls hurriedly made Millie a necklace and then proudly put the finishing touch around her neck.

"Thank you," said Millie gratefully, not feeling like such a stranger anymore.

They ran over to the great mead hall. Large bowls and plates of food had been brought in and put on the tables. A whole cooked pig had been placed at the centre of the top table where Freodheric sat with his family and the more important men of the village. Millie noticed they all had beards, some very long and some quite short. Even George had a little stubble growing.

Already sitting at one of the tables, George scanned the room looking for Millie. In her new attire he had trouble spotting her. He finally recognised her by her hair and waved her over to the seat next to him and Leof.

Freodheric tore apart the first chunk of bread and the feasting began. Copying everybody else, Millie took a piece of bread and spread onto it a white paste. It looked like the fat left over from cooking a roast chicken and tasted salty, but at least it made the bread a little less dry.

George was helping himself to some purple and black vegetables in a bowl.

"What are those?" Millie asked.

"These? They're carrots. Orange carrots haven't come to Britain yet."

Millie took a bite of one. It certainly tasted like a carrot and was the same shape, only smaller.

"There's quite a lot of food we don't have, potatoes, oranges, tomatoes, even corn. I remember Dad saying that a lot of food came into our diet after the Americas were discovered. Here, have some pork, it's cooked with flower petals. It tastes really good, especially with the raspberry butter," George said, pushing a dish towards Millie.

Millie realised she had quite an appetite. George was right, the food did taste good. Vegetable and bean soups were served, smoked trout, roasted beetroots and squash, chicken and cherry sausages and a rubbery type of cheese. The dessert was even nicer, flat cake with fruit soaked in honey, custard pies with raspberries and strawberries and thick cream as a topping.

When no one could possibly eat any more, the food and empty dishes were cleared from the tables and jugs of ale and a communal goblet of mead replaced them.

Millie couldn't help feeling overwhelmed by her new scenery. It was only that afternoon that she had left Grandad's house in Wybrook, yet it seemed like days ago.

"Let's have a riddle!" a voice shouted out. A murmur of agreement echoed around the room and a young man was pushed to the centre of the hall.

"This is a favourite game of theirs," George whispered to Millie. "It's a bit like their version of a quiz show."

The man began,

Upon this earth there exists a wonderful warrior.
Made for the use of mankind by two dumb creatures
He is created, glowing brightly. Enemy bears him against enemy
To wreak harm. Although a woman can often tame him,
Despite his strength. He is an obedient
Servant to women and men
Who care for him and feed him well,
And brings comfort and joy to their lives.
But, this warrior will savage anyone who allows him to grow proud.
What am I? [4]

The great mead hall was silent for a moment as the villagers sat thoughtful, then a bubble of noise broke out as they cried out possible answers.

"Is it a god?"

"No," the riddler replied, "it is not a god."

"What about wood? Wood glows."

"It doesn't savage us, though."

"Is it the sun?"

"I know, fire!" shouted someone with the correct answer.

"Who were the two dumb creatures, then?" the man next to Leof called out.

"Steel and flint, of course!"

The man who had answered correctly stood up to take the young riddler's place.

The wind bears these little spirits
high over the hillsides. Bright creatures they are! Black, and
darkly clothed. They move in flocks,
loudly singing out their songs.
The cliffs they stop at, and sometimes
the houses of men. They name themselves. [5]

"That's easy, swallows!" a woman in a red dress shouted. Too easy: the man was heckled by his audience and made to sit down again.

"Let Millie tell us a riddle from her village!"

"Yes Millie, come on."

Millie's mind went blank as the focus of the room fell upon her. She tried rapidly to think of something whilst the villagers egged her on to take the floor.

"Don't worry," George muttered, "you'll be fine."

"But I don't know any riddles!" she protested.

Determined not to wither under the pressure Millie got up from her seat and stood before the audience. There was a silence of anticipation as Millie looked around desperately for inspiration. Her eyes rested on a fruit bowl.

"I am sometimes red and sometimes green,
Through the summer I hold on tight to my mother's fingers,
Until others pull me away.
Some bite me, some chop me,
And some will keep me through the winter months.
What am I?"

"A lamb or a calf."

"A leaf on a tree."

"You don't keep leaves for the winter."

"Pears."

The debating continued until finally Millie heard a voice shout, "An apple!"

"Yes!" she cried and a cheer went up.

"Well done," George whispered to Millie as she reclaimed her seat.

The riddles carried on until the villagers grew tired of them.

"Now it will be time for the poems, although they're more like stories," George told her. "What's amazing is that they learn them by heart just from listening to other people recite them. Most people can't write so they develop unbelievable memories instead and can remember lines and lines of verses. They also have a stringed instrument a bit like a guitar, that they call a harp. They play it while they're talking ..." he was interrupted by Freodheric, who stood up and clapped his hands together for attention.

"This evening we have with us a well-travelled harp player and poet who brings to our Kingdom a new Christian poem."

Freodheric didn't seem too enthused about the topic of poem but beckoned the entertainers forward with a zealous hand gesture. A musician emerged from one of the corners of the hall holding a strung instrument that looked like a wooden board. He began to pluck at the strings and the hall filled with a gentle melody of changing chords. The board on which he played was about two feet long and made from maple wood. The top half of the board was carved out in the middle and over it stretched six strings. The player stood in the centre of the room under the illumination of the candle light. When the melody ended he was joined by a large man wearing a hat with a fox's head on the brim. As soon as the hall was quiet the man addressed them. "Tonight we shall perform for you *The Dream of the Rood.*" The entertainer's voice was rich with emotion and drama, and his audience was held captivated.

Behold! The most virtue of dreams I shall tell,
Which came to me in the middle of the night,
While all of men lay asleep in their dwellings.
It seemed to me that I saw an incredible tree
Stretching up high and surrounded by light
Its trunk shone brightly - a beacon
Encased in gold; gems gleamed
With beauty at its earthen base
and five more decorated
The shoulder-span... [6]

The poem carried on through many verses. Millie struggled to keep her eyes open as the soft incessant melody of the harp and the strong mead lured her to sleep. George felt Millie's dead weight leaning against his arm and decided it was time to get some fresh air. He shook her awake and discreetly motioned her to the small door behind them. Hoping that their empty seats would go unnoticed and not be taken as rudeness, George led the way outside into the late summer's evening. One of the "unfree" families stood on the other side of the door, guarding it. The man nodded at George in recognition, who responded with a nod back.

"Sorry, George, I'm so tired," Millie stifled a yawn. "Where am I going to sleep tonight?"

"I sleep in a hut with some of Leof's family. I'm sure we can find space for you. Come on, I'll take you there."

Outside, the village was in near darkness. In the absence of street lighting there was no light pollution and the stars shone a thousand times brighter than Millie had ever remembered seeing them. She stared up in wonder.

"Do you think any of the villagers suspected we were lying?" Millie asked, as George took them through the village towards the hut he slept in.

"No. They may believe in the gods but they would never suspect that you had come through the stone circle. Anyway, why ..." The sound of a horse exhaling suddenly silenced him. Through the darkness the shadowy shape of a horse and rider emerged.

"Wes Hal, friends! Don't be alarmed, I am one of the King's messengers," the rider called out. "I sounded my horn but with all the celebration of the Litha, I don't think I was heard."

The rider dismounted. They could see he was a tall, wiry figure of a man but his face remained hidden from them by the shadow of his dark hood.

"You'll find our headman in the mead hall," said George.

"Thank you, I'll try there first. And what are your names?"

"They call me Wolf Slayer" George answered reluctantly.

"And the young lady?"

"My sister."

George cursed himself as the messenger walked away.

"He wouldn't have heard you - and if he did, he won't know what you meant by the stone circle," Millie said, trying to set both their minds at ease.

George nodded in agreement, not wanting to worry her. He remembered his first night in the village and understood how his younger sister must be feeling. He showed her the spare bed in their sleeping quarters and Millie gratefully crawled under the thin covers. As she closed her eyes she realised she had forgotten something.

"I left my satchel in the hall! It's under the table."

"Don't worry, I'll get it."

"Thanks," she muttered and a moment later was asleep.

George lay on his bed opposite and thought about what a long and strange day it had been. After spending half the day with Millie he almost felt as though he *were* back home. He had been isolated from his own culture for the last three years and had had to hide away much of himself in order to adapt to East Saxon life. He prayed to all the gods that he and Millie would find a way back home.

George dozed off for an hour and woke to the sound of singing outside somewhere. He stood up and checked that Millie was still sleeping soundly. Then, feeling wide awake, he headed out back to the hall. The sound of laughter rang out from across the meadow to his left, he turned to see the flickers of a large bonfire around which people were dancing and singing songs. He was tempted to join them but first he needed to get Millie's bag.

As George approached the hall he saw the messenger standing just inside the entrance with the headman. He didn't want to interrupt them and be questioned as to why he was there, so he decided to wait out of sight by the side of the building. There was general talk of trade that had been taking place and news of battles in neighbouring kingdoms. Then discussion turned to the King's concern that the new religion would anger the old gods and bring a bad harvest or plague. On and on they talked, as if they would never stop. George decided to go and see if the side entrance was open. But just as he was walking away he heard Millie's name being mentioned. They were talking about her arrival and the messenger was questioning Freodheric about where she had come from - a little too intensely for George's likening. He heard his own name too, then the conversation went back to trade. George felt uneasy. He didn't want news getting back to the capital that strange foreign people had been arriving on the solstice, especially if a bad harvest or plague *did* come. He and Millie needed to keep their heads down and be sure not to draw attention to themselves.

Luckily the side entrance was open and the satchel was sitting untouched under the table.

Chapter Twenty-six: The Cake

The next morning Millie awoke as George was leaving to do his duties. He told her to go back to sleep and that he'd return soon. Despite the racket the livestock were making at the excitement of dawn breaking, Millie managed to get back to sleep. When she woke again the village was quiet and she could only assume that many of the villagers were out in the fields or busy somewhere. She lay staring up at the rafters while she took the time to collect her thoughts and reflect on yesterday's events.

The silence grew eerily loud. Just like at home when Millie would come back from school to an empty house and lie relaxing on the sofa. At first it was silence but then the clock would start ticking louder and louder, then the buzzing of the fridge, the high-pitched whine of the TV on stand-by, the faint bass line of someone playing music next door and the sound of the occasional passing car. There was never really a silence at all.

There wasn't silence here in the hut, either, but the sounds were different. Millie could hear a goat rubbing against the other side of the wall to which it was tied, chickens pecking at the ground near the doorway, a cry of a baby from somewhere, a rhythmic thud of a woodsman chopping wood and birds whistling from the roofs.

Millie was too restless to wait around for her brother. She stood up and straightened her new dress, which she had slept in, and adjusted the belt. Next to her bed was a mug of milk and a chunk of bread, which she presumed George had left for her breakfast and she hungrily ate. As she was summoning up the courage to go off exploring by herself, there was the sound of giggling by the door. Two young girls peeped shyly into the hut.

"Hello," Millie said.

"We're going to wash the clothes, do you want to come?"

"Okay," she replied, pretty sure there weren't going to be any washing machines or dryers anywhere.

They each carried a bundle of garments wrapped in a linen cloth down to the village stream. Sifelda, Alwun and Edyth were already there and had in fact sent their younger siblings to fetch Millie. The girls were still very curious about her, as she was about them. Their lives and upbringing had been so very different and yet the more Millie got to know them, the more they found they had in common. Not only were they close in age to Millie and the same gender, but they had a similar sense of humour and seemed fun-loving and adventurous.

They soaked each garment in turn in the stream and scrubbed away at any dirt they saw. The work was hard, but they put an equal amount of effort into chatting and gossiping and splashing each other as they did in cleaning the clothes. Once the clothes were done, the younger children took them and hung them up to dry in the low branches of a nearby tree. It seemed to Millie that the older girls looked after the younger children for most of the day whilst they worked. Despite there being no school, the day still had order to it and the younger children were constantly being taught skills by their peers.

Washing the clothes in the morning was a daily activity during the summer and was part of Millie's new routine that took shape over the following days. After the washing, the girls would play games with the younger ones, then there was preparation of lunch and eating lunch, followed by washing the dishes down at the stream again. The afternoons were usually spent sitting outside the huts weaving baskets with the older women, or mending and making garments. Once the men came in from the fields it was time to cook again.

The girls were frequently shocked at Millie's lack of knowledge and practical skill in things that seemed to them second nature, like being able to light a fire, sew stitches or skin a rabbit. But they were equally amazed by the things she taught them. New games to play like noughts and crosses, skipping rope games and ball games; different ways of styling hair that they had never seen or thought of; and an endless repertoire of stories Millie told to the children - Peter Pan, Little Red Riding Hood, Hansel and Gretel.

Two months passed by in this manner and soon it was August. Millie was enjoying being in Widurok and felt so absorbed in her new life that she had almost forgotten her purpose in coming here. It was like being on an endless kids' adventure camp and it felt good escaping from normal reality and the pressure of school and exams.

George was not so happy and worried about their fate. He knew the dangers of living here: the threat of raids and attacks by neighbouring enemies; diseases that could spread like wild fire; that the average person was lucky to live to the same age as that of their mother and father; how tough it could be during the winter and at the end of the winter when food supplies where low; and that a poor harvest could be catastrophic. With this knowledge George felt burdened with the responsibility of protecting his sister and getting her back home. He had no idea how he would do this. He could see that for Millie this was a honeymoon period but there had been several occasions when she had woken in the night calling out for their mother in her sleep. Soon there would be a time when she would long for her old home comforts so much that her heart would ache as his did.

*

It was in late August that events took a turn. Millie was teaching some of the younger children to play hopscotch in the afternoon sun when she heard the horn of a messenger arriving. She looked over and saw Freodheric greeting him and taking him into the mead hall. Even from a distance Millie could see he was the same tall, wiry messenger as before. Several minutes later she saw them both reappear outside. The headman motioned to the slave to secure the messenger's horse and then they began to stroll together through the village. When they reached Millie they stopped for a while to watch their game. Millie strained her ears to catch what they were discussing over the shouts of the children.

"The King's daughters are sick ..." "... epidemic will spread throughout the Kingdom ..." "... appease the gods ..." "... not allow panic ..."

They must have seen she was listening for they looked at her and suddenly stopped talking.

"What is this game?" the messenger asked.

"We call it hopscotch," Millie answered. "You mustn't jump on the chalked squares the stone lands on."

"Strange, I've never come across it before." They left them and continued walking and discussing the troubled kingdom.

Millie felt she should speak to George and tell him what she had overheard. Where would he be? The children would know.

"Your brother?" one of the younger boys answered her. "I saw him go over to the lake to fish with Leof and a couple of others. They're trying out the old boat they fixed."

Millie headed off towards the lake - the same lake that was by Bernard's Woods in "her" Wybrook. As she drew closer she heard shouts of workers in the fields calling to one another in alarm. They were all looking towards something ahead of her and some had now dropped their field tools and were running. A commotion had broken out, something serious. Were they being attacked? No, they wouldn't have dropped their tools. What, then? Millie felt a wave of panic: something had happened at the water! She began to run too, past the sparse wood and root plants, down to the fishing lake.

Millie couldn't see the water at first for the line of villagers surrounding it. She pushed through them, worried that something had happened to George and alarmed at the barking of Leof's dog. A few metres out she saw George. He was diving into the water next to the boat that was floating upturned on the water. Suddenly George was visible again and holding onto an arm. Leof! He was motionless! Some of the villagers had their hands held up to their faces in horror. Leof must have fallen in. The East Saxons were a farming community - not many of them ever learnt to swim. George remembered his lifesaving lessons in the school swimming pool and swam on his side with Leof's bloated and lifeless body pulled up under his arm. He got to the edge of the water, close to where Millie stood, and a couple of the men in the village helped to heave Leof out. Some of the women started wailing and the men shook their heads with moist eyes. But Millie and George took no notice.

"Millie! Do you remember mouth-to-mouth?"

"I think so, we only did it a few weeks ago."

Millie tilted back Leof's head and checked his airway was clear. A little uncertainly she put her mouth to his and breathed into his lungs. Then she paused and put her ear to his mouth to listen for sounds of breathing. Three times she did this, but nothing.

"Here, let me try pressing on his chest."

"Okay, you're meant to do it thirty times, at the rate of a hundred a minute."

Millie waited as George repeatedly pressed down hard on the place he thought Leof's heart was, then Millie tried again to resuscitate him with her breath. This time Leof made a spluttering sound, his body shook and they rolled him over while he coughed up the lake water he had swallowed. The villagers who had been watching the pair stood back in disbelief and utter shock. Leof had died and now he was alive again! They had never seen anything like it. Murmurs of "sent by the gods", "Eostre herself, goddess of rebirth!" and "worker of miracles" turned into shouts. It was something people only talked about in myths and stories: a boy had died and had been brought back from the dead! Millie had breathed the gift of life back into Leof's body.

George watched the excitement of the villagers apprehensively, praying that Millie wouldn't be criticised.

Some of the villagers poked Leof to check that he was real, then one turned to face Millie and George and bowed down before them in awe.

"You are the son and daughter of the gods."

Millie gave a surprised laugh.

"No, we just resuscitated him. It's easy, anyone can do it," George said, trying to play down their role and avoid any deity status being put upon them. But the villagers weren't listening.

"We must take Millie to the headman immediately."

"Look, here he comes!" The headman was rushing towards them, along with the messenger.

"Are you from Asengeard, Millie? Is that where you came from too, Wolf Slayer?" asked one of the villagers.

"Of course we're not from the home of the gods. We're just normal people. You know that!" George was aware their actions could just as easily be interpreted as being sinister as divine. "It is normal practice in our village. Anyway, Leof wasn't dead, he just had too much lake water inside him."

"And where exactly is this village that you're from?" The crowd parted as the messenger approached, the headman following behind.

"It's ... a very small settlement, north of here," stammered George, taken by surprise.

The messenger frowned and gave him a long stare. George could sense there were other thoughts going through his mind.

"They are both Wiccan children."

"The gods have sent them."

"What other magic can they do?" the villagers continued to gossip.

"What exactly has happened here?" the messenger asked Millie.

"Nothing much. This boy was having trouble swimming, that's all ..." but Millie's modest words were again interrupted by the villagers.

"We have all just borne witness to this girl's magic. She breathed the soul back into Leof when he was drowned and dead. Now he walks! Look!" Leof, who was pale faced, had been lifted to his feet by two of the women and was being helped back to the village.

"Come on," called the headman, keen as always to keep the peace. "Let's get back to our work. I hope you managed to catch some fish as well as drowning each other."

Gradually the villagers reluctantly dispersed back to their fields and to Widurok. George stayed behind to drag the upturned boat from the water and up onto the bank. Millie waited for him and they walked back to the village together.

"So much for keeping our heads down," said George.

"What choice did we have? We could hardly leave Leof to ..." Millie stopped and looked suddenly bewildered.

"What?" George asked "What is it?"

"We saw all this in a picture."

"What picture? What are you on about?"

"Me and Becky saw this scene, with me resuscitating Leof! It's in a medieval painting on the church wall in Wybrook. How is that possible?" she paused. "And Mr Gordon had a copy of it. He must have known it was linked to Bobby disappearing."

"If it's painted in the church then the people of Widurok will still be telling this story in years to come. That means this won't be going away."

"I'm sure it'll be okay, George."

"No Millie, you've got no idea how powerful the spoken word is in these times."

Millie looked hurt.

"Sorry, but we could be in a lot of trouble."

"But we saved Leof's life!" Millie protested.

"Yes, I know. It was the right thing to do. I'm glad we did, only ... there are going to be consequences. I wonder what the messenger and Freodheric are saying about us?"

"I heard them talking before I got here. I think they might have some other issues on their minds." Millie briefly relayed to George what she had overheard.

George wondered if a plague were really spreading or if it was just paranoia. From what Millie had told him it sounded serious, but disease was fairly common and there hadn't been any news of an increase in fatalities. Also, it was generally thought that Saberht's conversion to Christianity was political and influenced by the King's powerful uncle, Athelberht I of Kent and not due to the faith of the East Saxons. So maybe the epidemic was just a rumour - fed on the fear that the pagan gods would respond angrily. If so it was a rumour that was getting out of control.

Once they reached the village Millie went to join Sifelda, Alwun and Edyth who were weaving baskets. George wanted to check Leof was okay and guessed that he had probably been taken to his bed. On the way he passed the great mead hall and noticed there was no sign of the messenger's horse. Had he left already? Maybe he should take this opportunity to speak to Freodheric.

George opened the door and went in. The hall was empty and lit solely by a dim lamp hanging from a rafter. He was about to leave when he heard a low voice from the far end of the hall and saw it was Freodheric sitting alone on his wooden throne. George was sure that the headman had noticed him but as he drew closer, George realised that he was in some kind of trance and muttering a chant. He was asking the gods for their guidance and divine inspiration. George felt uncomfortable, intruding on something so private. He quickly slipped back outside and hoped they would find another time to speak.

Chapter Twenty-seven: Slippy

The creature lay in the windowless stone stable. Edgar, his groom, perched beside him brushing his dark grey mane. Although it was summer, it remained cold and damp down here in the old Roman cellar under the baths.

It was three years ago that Edgar's master, Prince Saeward, and two huntsmen had dragged the horse down here, kicking and neighing, in the dead of night. "Slippy" Edgar had named him, as if he really were Woden's own horse Sleipnir. He understood why they had felt it necessary to hide Slippy down here and out of sight, but it had pained him to watch the horse slowly change from a fine gallant beast into a weak, thin and broken nag. The horse was near lame now - the dark confined space and the damp had ensured that. He probably didn't have the energy to escape even if he could. He seemed to be just waiting - waiting for a time when he could breathe his last on Middangeard and join his master at the gates of Waeheall. As though the horse could hear the stable boy's thoughts he closed his eyes and sighed loudly through his nostrils in agreement.

"There, boy." Edgar stroked his long nose affectionately.

Edgar knew Saeward felt guilty about Slippy's imprisonment and his worsening condition. The prince feared he had angered Woden and was ever remorseful that he had even thought to capture his horse.

"I was young and foolish, trying to impress my father," he had once said to Edgar during a visit. But those visits were scarce now, as they only caused Saeward's guilt to deepen. Still, as long as Edgar's food and lodgings were paid for, he would happily spend his days looking after this creature of the gods.

From the street above them, two tradesmen stopped to talk. The sound of their conversation flowed clearly through a high grate in the wall and Edgar couldn't help but overhear. It sounded like the tradesmen were discussing their travels.

"… anyway it don't sound right to me."

"It's as true as the sun is shining. She breathed the boy's soul back into him and he lived again."

"Where did you say this happened? Land of the gods, was it?"

"No, up in the north, the village by the stone hearg. One of our messengers was delivering news about the plague and he saw it with his own two eyes. The boy was dead and then he lived again."

Edgar pricked up his ears. God-like magic in the north of the Kingdom! Now this was interesting.

"Who is this girl, then?"

"Said she was a visitor. No one seemed to know where she was from," he replied mysteriously. "She arrived on the day of the solstice, same as did her brother several years before."

"Oh, don't be stupid, what's that got to do with it! Anyway, you'll believe anything."

The tradesmen carried on walking and their voices drained away. Edgar patted Sleipnir goodbye and hurried out of the stable, locking the door behind him. His master would want to know about this. It was too much of a coincidence. Walking quickly, he left the old Roman town and headed to the new Saxon trading port of Lundenwic.

Edgar soon spotted Saeward leading his own horse through the marketplace and overseeing the delivery of some new armoury.

"What is it?" the prince asked upon seeing him. "Is Slippy all right?"

"I just heard a messenger is back from the north of the Kingdom. There's been a girl arrive at the solstice in the village by the stones. She's been performing magic!"

Saeward frowned.

"You know the place, where the world-tree is, that you found Slippy."

"Yes, I know it. It's just strange because a while ago I heard there was a boy who showed up in that village on the same solstice as Slippy."

"I believe she's the boy's sister."

"Are you sure?"

"That's what they're saying."

"Do you think they both came through the world-tree looking for Slippy? Woden must want his horse back." The Prince's eyes flickered with fear. "I need to persuade my father to have them brought to us. Maybe I have a chance to right the wrong I have done and the gods will forgive me and spare my sisters."

Chapter Twenty-eight: The journey begins

Over the following week George and Millie found themselves being treated differently by the villagers. At first George thought he was just imagining it - a few suspicious glances, whispered conversations. But by the end of the week it became obvious that they were being talked about. No one knew what to make of the siblings. Even Leof found he was being given the cold-shoulder and treated with hostility.

"They think I am only half-living. It's like they are scared of me."

"It will pass," Millie said, reassuring as always. "People will see you are the same, it'll all be fine in a few days." In truth she too was finding things hard. Sifelda, Alwun and Edyth hadn't come to find her once that week. She had had to search them out and whenever she approached the group, the conversation became stilted and unnatural.

George was in one of the fields using his horse, Elvina, to help Leof and his brothers with the crop when the headman's servant came over, calling out to them.

"You are wanted in the mead hall, you and Leof," he puffed. "There is a messenger again from King Saberht."

"Both of us?" George asked.

"Yes."

"What can the King want with us? Are you sure?"

"Yes."

George handed the Elvina's reins to one of Leof's brothers and walked back towards the village. He felt worried. Had it been found out that they were not from where they'd said? Would they be interrogated or banished for using bad magic? He looked behind to see Millie following him. He cursed himself. Millie had only been here a couple of months and already their lives were in jeopardy.

Freodheric was sitting in his chair talking to a messenger they didn't recognise. He rose when he saw them enter.

"George and Millie" he greeted them, "news of the miracle you performed on Leofwine has reached far." George held his breath wondering what 'word of mouth' had added to the story.

The headman nodded at the messenger who spoke excitedly.

"The King is asking for you. He is holding court in Lundenburh at present. His daughters are deathly ill with plague and he wants you to cure them. He has asked that Millie and her brother travel there immediately."

"But we're not doctors!" Millie exclaimed. "I don't know anything about curing plagues!"

"Of course no one here would deny the wishes of the King," the messenger replied coldly.

"No, we all seek to assist the King!" the headman intervened. He could see this would be a simple solution to easing the tension that was building up in the village. "You will travel at once. Leof will go with you as proof of the work of the gods - I mean of the miracle of our Christian god," Freodheric hastily corrected himself.

"How will we know how to get there?" George protested.

"I will arrange an entourage with our finest warrior for your protection and a fierce dog and horses." He was just as keen for the three of them to leave Widurok as the messenger was for them to travel to Lundenburh.

"Good. It is settled then. The King will be expecting you."

*

Millie packed Grandad's leather satchel with the essentials, keeping in there everything she had brought with her from home. She was worried. She didn't want to go to London, let alone meet the King! The plan was to rescue George ... No, she thought, that wasn't strictly true. She had never really had a plan further than actually finding George. But instinct told her the stones were their passage home and she didn't want to travel too far from them, or be proclaimed a fraudster by the King.

"Yep, we've really kept a low profile." George came up to her with Leof.

"George! Well it was your fault for messing about on that stupid boat!"

"I could have coped with Leof on my own."

"You both should have left me for dead, then we'd all be better off," said Leof crossly.

"Don't be silly, Leof. We all just want everything to go back to normal."

"Yeah well, the villagers have got their own beliefs. No one can reason with them," Leof replied.

"Do we have to argue? Let's just see what happens when we meet the King," George said, but Leof was walking away.

"Maybe going to London will be a good thing," Millie offered. "It might be a chance to find out more about the stones and the world-tree. We could meet a Druid or someone there who knows about them. I mean, *someone* must know about their magic."

"Well that's what I've been hoping for the last three years. But you're right. I've never been very far outside Widurok and there's got to be an answer somewhere."

*

Wigheard, one of Leof's uncles was chosen to accompany them. Not only was he Widurok's finest warrior, having fought in battle against the Gewisse, but he had also travelled down to Lundenburh before. He was a large man, well-built, and always carried a finely crafted sword with him. Down one side of his face was a long scar that ran from his ear, under his chin, and ended somewhere hidden by his tunic.

The next morning as the sun was rising, the three of them went to meet Wigheard by the great hall. Elvina was tied up next to Wigheard's stallion, Tiw. Wigheard was busy loading the horses up with food and supplies, including a stock of arrows. He also had a large bundle of yarn and some pottery that the headman had asked them to take to trade for iron. The messenger had already left to tell the King they were coming and Wigheard began at once to take command.

"Leof and Wolf Slayer, make sure you both have your seax knives with you and that they are sharpened and ready for use. Millie, you will carry the bow and a couple of arrows."

George took the seax from his belt and ran his fingers over the curved blade with its distinct notch. Yes, it was sharp enough.

"We will be travelling through thick forest," Wigheard continued. "The bears and wolves should not bother us too much this time of year, but I'm not taking any chances. Millie, you will also carry the horn to sound when we approach any farmsteads or villages. We need to be on our guard for other travellers and thieves that live in the woods. The horses will carry our food but we will go on foot. Lundenburh is about four days from here. We will stay the second night with our good friend Bordley at Walla, but we will need to find a safe place to bed down for the other nights."

Millie thought about the train journey they normally embarked on to get to London, which took just over an hour.

Wigheard now turned their attention to the supplies. He wrapped up what looked like lard in a linen cloth, and some bread, cheese and dried meat. He threw over to George and Leof four water-tight pouches made from animal stomachs.

"Here, fill these up at the stream."

"What's the furthest you've ever been outside Widurok?" George asked as they went off to fill them.

"Probably Colneceastre. That's about two days' walk. I suppose I should be excited about getting out of here for a while. I've wanted to go travelling since I was little, but I've always been left behind. Too many bears and wolves. Still, you and Millie have much more experience of these woods than I do."

"I don't think so. You're actually the one with the wolf-slaying experience."

"Yeah, guess we're finally even, now that you've saved my life too. Thanks for that." Leof looked at George sincerely, but George sensed Leof still resented him for it. "Is Millie really from the gods?" Leof asked.

"Definitely not, she's just my sister!" George answered in surprise. "I don't know how we can help the King, we can't cure a plague. What do you think they'll do to us when they find out?"

"Kill you both probably" said Leof. It was a light-hearted remark but George knew there was truth behind it. "Don't worry, the headman knows it. He just wants someone to go to Lundenwic to trade the yarn and pottery, and to get rid of us for a bit. We're starting to cause a disturbance."

"Lundenwic? I thought we were going to Lundenburh?"

"We'll go to both. Lundenwic is the new Saxon trading town a mile west of Lundenburh. But Saberht likes to hold court in the old Roman buildings; guess it makes him feel more important."

They got back to the hall to find the horses were all packed up and ready to go. Leof's dog, Fen, was waiting there too. Some of the villagers had come to see them off, including Leof's close family and the headman.

Leof's mother hugged him as though she might not see him again and kissed him on the cheek. "Take care, Leof, and make sure you come back. At least it's the end of summer and the forest beasts will all have their bellies full. May the gods be with you!"

Leof reddened at the attention and tried to pull away from her motherly grasp. Wigheard gave both the boys a horse each to guide and led the way with Fen through the village to the western meadow. They walked up the path that went towards the stones, then veered off to follow a track that ran in a southerly direction through the forest.

Wigheard was a quiet and moody companion. Millie felt a little afraid of him knowing that he had fought in battles, although she was happy that he had been chosen as their protector. Fen dropped back to walk next to her and she took comfort in having him close by. Although a few times he turned and growled into the dark forest, which made her feel uneasy. Each time Fen growled, Wigheard turned his head too and stared warily into the trees. Millie wondered what he was expecting to see. She glanced back at George and Leof but they were busy debating the best way to catch fish from the lake.

Suddenly Millie saw a movement from her left. Fen growled again but Wigheard turned around and ordered him to be quiet.

Millie slackened her pace to join the boys.

"I really think someone's following us."

"Don't be silly, it's probably just your imagination. We've got Wigheard with us anyway: he's done this a thousand times."

"It might be kids from the village. I used to try and follow my brothers when I was little," Leof said.

Millie still felt uncomfortable. She had never walked through such thick forest and certainly not one that had bears and wolves roaming in it.

After an hour of walking they heard the noise of running water. The path ended and three long planks of wood were joined to form a bridge over the narrowest part of a river.

"Must be the Chelmer," Millie muttered to George as they crossed over.

"Maybe. It must pass this way."

The forest began to open into a clearing where they could see a few wooden buildings ahead of them together with some old Roman remains. Wigheard slowed down so they could walk together.

"We have reached the Dunmadu crossroads."

The crossroads was a meeting place of five Roman roads. The buildings seemed to be mainly used as stables - an Anglo-Saxon service station to refresh your horse and take a rest.

"Stay here and mind our horses," said Wigheard. I'm going to find out if there's any news on the roads."

He disappeared and left the three of them standing on the wayside. Next to them a weathered stone signpost left from the Roman era pointed down each of the five routes open to the traveller. Coamulodunum XXVI to the east, Caesaromagus XIIII to the south, Londonium XXXVI to the south-west. To the west and north-west the signs were broken, with just XI and XVIII remaining legible.

"Guess we're heading that way," George said, pointing south-west.

That sat down on the grass verge and waited for their leader. Leof wandered off for a moment into the open grassland and began to pick flowers from a small bush. He came back with a bunch of little flowers like daisies. He wafted them in Millie's direction and she could smell their citrus-scented leaves.

"Feverfew," he said matter-of-factly. "It's what the women use to treat headaches, fevers and stomach pains." Using one of the stems he tied them upside down onto Elvina's saddlebag.

"Let them dry for as long as possible then boil them to make an infusion. It might give the King some faith in your talents."

"Thank you," Millie said, grateful for his help and hopeful that Leof's mood had brightened. But she was wrong.

"You don't know much about our medicines, do you?" he said haughtily.

"No, nothing really."

"You don't know much about anything to do with us, do you?"

"What do you mean?" Millie asked feeling the tension rise.

"You and George always talk about how you go to school and learn loads of stuff, but it seems to me you don't know much at all. You don't even know how to get back to your home. Or are you going to stay in Widurok forever?"

"We *will* find a way," George retorted defiantly.

Leof looked annoyed and walked off to find Wigheard.

"What's his problem?" Millie muttered to George.

"The villagers are giving him a hard time about coming back to life. He thinks he won't be accepted back there when we return. He was trying to distance himself from me all week, to convince them he's nothing to do with us, but then this trip makes it worse again. He'll be all right by tomorrow. Where *is* Wigheard?"

Wigheard emerged from the dark doorway of a dwelling opposite and came over to them, followed by Leof. He said nothing about any news, which George decided to take as good news.

"We will travel through the valley of the Hrothingas people until the road ends," Wigheard said, marching towards the path signposted to Londinium.

"Come on, Fen," Leof called out. Fen appeared out of a bush and came running after them with his tail wagging. Leof trailed behind with Tiw, still angry at his predicament.

The Roman road was in good condition considering the Saxons had done little to maintain it since the Romans left two hundred years before. George recognised where they were and remembered the road as he had known it, with endless fields on either side as far as the eye could see and the smooth tarmacked surface that the cars raced over at seventy miles an hour. Here, in this time, there was nothing but forest on either side with some patches of open woodland where red deer were grazing. Millie was also paying attention to the landscape and had noticed that she hadn't spotted any rabbits or pheasants. She mentioned this to Leof, who shook his head, seemingly not to want to talk to her and muttered he didn't know of such creatures, although the rabbit sounded similar to a hare.

Millie reverted back to walking with George.

"How well do you trust Leof?"

"He's my best friend."

"He must know something more about the stones and the world-tree, some rumour or gossip he's heard."

"He knew about writing the runes on the stones, but not much else. He would tell me if he did."

"Maybe we can get him to find a Druid when we get to London?"

"Okay, I'll ask him when we get there; hopefully he'll have calmed down by then."

George handed Millie Elvina's reins while he stopped to relieve himself. He waited for the others to gain some distance and then walked into the woods. As he looked up he saw two men moving between the trees. They kept looking over to the road ahead and didn't seem aware of George. George was more taken aback by their appearance than their presence. They were both tall with long fair hair that flowed loosely over their shoulders and they moved almost as if they were dancing. On their backs they carried a very small bow and what looked like an arrow holdall - only it was minute. Were these the elves he had heard about in stories they told in Widurok? Surely they didn't really exist? They must just be Saxons who had a diet that made them taller and more agile; or perhaps they had a different ethnic background. Either way, George felt he should be very wary of them, especially as they kept darting behind foliage so as not to be seen. He hurried back onto the path and hastened to the others.

"What's wrong?" Millie asked seeing George looking anxious.

"I think you were right about someone following us!"

Chapter Twenty-nine: Elves, druids and a bear

The road had become quite dark now as the forest lowered over the road, cutting out the sunlight.

"What is it?" Wigheard asked, as he slackened his pace.

"George thinks he saw someone following us in the trees," Leof said.

"Two men, very tall with small bows."

"Elves, it sounds like. Hmm ... I wonder what they want. They don't normally steal from travellers. They probably don't mean any harm but be prepared if little arrows start firing at us."

George's hand instinctively curled around his seax.

"Have you ever met any elves?" Millie asked Wigheard.

"No, not in person. But most of us have felt the presence of elves, especially elf shot."

"What's elf shot?"

Wigheard looked at her as though she was from a different world - which in a way, she was. He lowered his voice. "When you feel a sudden twinge of pain in the arm or the head somewhere. That's where you've been shot by one of those tiny arrows that the elves carry, even if you can't see it. Elves aren't quite of this world. The dark elves usually stay in their own world but the light elves like to dwell in the forests. They have magic which even the wisest of us don't understand."

"Why are they following us?"

"I don't know, it's not often they follow men. Maybe they heard of your magic and are protecting you for the gods."

It was the most Wigheard had spoken to Millie since they left Widurok and she hoped he wouldn't revert back to his aloofness.

Up ahead in the distance, smoke rose above the trees. They were approaching the Hrodingas tribes. The forest landscape was soon replaced by wild grasslands, with a scattering of small dwellings. Wigheard nodded at Millie to sound the horn. She lifted it to her mouth and blew loudly three times. A woman appeared from one of the buildings and a man stopped his work in a field to watch them pass. They waved at the group and then carried on their farm work, paying them little attention.

"Keep themselves to themselves, this lot do," Wigheard commented. "But we've had some good soldiers from them."

"Did you fight in battle with any of them?" George asked as they plodded on.

"One or two, but a long time ago, probably when you lot were just babes."

"What happened?"

"Before King Athelberht was King of Kent he led the Kentings army against the Gewisse Saxons at the battle of Wibbandum. Of course back then his sister was married to our old King Sledd and was busy bearing our future kings. We were all in allegiance to Kent, whether our King wanted to acknowledge it or not. A great many of our warriors crossed the border to fight alongside our cousins but we were too few in number and were overcome by the manpower led by Ceawlin and Cuthwulf. It was not a victorious battle for us."

"Is that how you got your scar?"

"Cut nearly in two by a seax. I was lucky." Wigheard gave a wry smile. "Luckier than the man who cut me. You know what Wigheard means?"

"War brave," answered Leof.

"Yes, only I didn't feel so brave crawling across a field of my own slain men to follow our retreating warriors. I was waiting to hear the whiz of an arrow and to begin my journey to the afterlife in Neorxnawang. Yet none came and I was chosen to live and return to the village."

He sang out a little tune to them,

So spoke the wanderer,
Mindful of hardships,
Of brutal battles
And the fall of beloved kinsmen. [7]

George could not imagine having to crawl through a field of severed limbs and dead bodies, especially when they belonged to your friends. The stories he had heard of battles were all about glory and gallantry. Maybe the East Saxons only retold the tales of the victories they won.

They had been walking for nearly two hours since Dunmadu and had just passed another Hrodingas settlement when suddenly the road up ahead seemed to swerve sharply to the left into the trees. The Roman road had collapsed into the river and beyond it, weeds and other plants had grown up between the stones.

"Wait here," Wigheard commanded. "I'm going to look for another way to cross the river."

Whilst they waited, Leof untied the now empty water bottles from the horses and bent down in the river to fill them.

Wigheard returned some time later. "There's no way across near here and the road the other side is too overgrown. With the horses and all their load we will have to follow the track around and cross the river further up. Hopefully we can pick up this road again later."

"What about the track to the left?" asked Leof.

"No, that goes east to the settlements of the goddess Eostre. We need to travel south."

They followed Wigheard at a much slower pace than before as they fought their way through dense thicket and over uneven ground. They were grateful when the land finally opened up again and they were able to see the landscape around them. There was a flock of sheep in a large enclosure some way off and more deer grazing on the grassland.

Leof, who was walking alongside Millie, suddenly pointed excitedly to the trees on the other side of the enclosure crying, "Look! Look!"

"What is it?" asked Millie concerned.

"There's a bear in those woods! Can you see it walking between the trees there?"

Millie squinted her eyes: yes, she could see it! "Do you think it'll attack us?"

"No, it seems to be more interested in the sheep. It's pretty far away from us, anyway."

Millie gazed in wonder at the land that was so different from her time. Where had all this wild grassland and meadows vanished to, in just a millennium? Where were all the trees and open land that animals could graze freely in? In fact where was the wildlife in her time? It was like Grandad had said. Man had taken over everything, built houses and fenced off and named every section of land. Any spare inch was dug up and ploughed. The rest of nature were left with nothing, their numbers reduced to just a few, however plentiful they had once been. What she was seeing now was so rich in life. This was what her world had lost.

"You're so lucky to live in this time," she told Leof.

"What do you mean?"

"You have so much life in your world and harmony in how you live with it. It's not like that where I come from. Nearly all the forests have been cut down and the wildlife has shrunk to almost nothing. All you ever hear about is the damage we are doing to our planet and the animals that are endangered or becoming instinct. But here everything is just as it should be."

"It sounds very different to now. Don't the gods curse you for it?"

"No, they were forgotten long ago, too."

Leof looked at her in horror.

"But the balance of the world relies on us living together. We all need each other! The trees hold great power - you mustn't cut them all down! Without them, how would we live?"

Millie thought about global warming and the building up of carbon dioxide that was melting the ice.

"I think we all know that, but we've just lost contact with our roots. We don't see nature as our mother, or as being that important."

"What is important, then?"

"Technology and ourselves I suppose."

"Technology?"

"It's a way to make life easier by inventing and creating more and more things with science. I guess we've become a bit obsessed by it."

"Doesn't sound like a good idea to me, if you're destroying your own world."

"Well, there's more people in my time. We've got about seventy million people on this island alone; compared to that, you've got about one million. Besides we *have* got the technology to protect our environment."

"Why don't you use it, then?" Leof said confused.

Millie wanted to defend her time and way of life but she felt unable to. Leof was right and so was Grandad. How great it would be if the country was still like this.

They had seemed to be walking for ages when the road forked in front of them. They decided to turn right in the hope that it would meet up with the road again. But just up ahead the track forked once more.

"Well, which way now?"

"It can't be right again, we'll be going round in circles."

"But left is the wrong direction. We're meant to be going south, remember?"

"Maybe we should split up into twos and have a quick look down both routes."

"I don't want to split up. We could end up meeting that bear or worse!"

"I'm not sure where we are but from the position of the sun I say we should head right again."

"Okay, let's stop here and eat. We've been walking for hours," Wigheard decided, sensing they were getting tired. "I think we lost those elves anyway, as well as ourselves."

Wigheard took the saddle-bags from the horses and led them down to a nearby brook to quench their thirst. Millie and George flopped to the ground whilst Leof searched the bags for the food he had packed. As he was doing so, they heard the sound of voices and looked up to see two men approaching from the path on the right. Both men were dressed in grey robes and were carrying tall sticks.

"Druids!" George said. "They'll know where we are."

"Wes Hal," one of the Druids said in greeting.

To Millie they didn't look much like wizards from fiction books, more like elderly men in long dressing gowns.

"Quite a feast you've got there," the other said, noting the bread and cheese Leof was unwrapping. "Where are you travelling to?"

"We're on our way to Lundenburh, but we lost our bearings when we passed the Hrothingas Bridge. The road has collapsed and we couldn't find a way across."

"Yes, it's been that way since last autumn's rains," one of the druids said, shaking his head. "But who among us has the skill to mend it?"

"Do you know which track we should take?"

The Druid waved his stick to the way they had just come. "This track here goes west but it will lead you towards the Eppingas and onto Lundenburh. It's a clear path, you should have no trouble."

"What about you, where are you heading?" Leof asked.

"We are on the way to one of Hrothingas settlements. We have promised to try and cure an illness that is destroying the cattle there."

The Druids bade them farewell and went on their way. The group sat and ate their meal of rye bread and cheese and washed it down with the river water. Afterwards they packed up the remaining food and set off in a westerly direction.

Their pace was a lot slower after their late lunch and the afternoon soon passed. They needed to find somewhere to rest for the night. As they grew wearier they came upon a mound surrounded by a dried-up moat. The mound rose high enough to give them a good view of their surroundings. They scrambled to the top to find a flat area the size of an average garden, with what looked like a large stone picnic table in the centre - two dark pudding stones with a large flat stone lying across them.

"I know this place," Wigheard said. "This is the grazing land of the Lagefare. We will be safe here tonight."

They untied the saddle-bags again and let Elvina and Tiw loose to graze. Wigheard took the bow from Millie and went off with Fen to hunt for their dinner. While he was gone they set about collecting dry leaves and kindling wood to start a fire and a stock of sticks and small fallen branches to keep it fuelled. Leof rubbed together two flint stones until their spark lit the dry leaves. Then he carefully added the kindling, blowing through a gap to encourage the flames to take hold. Once the flames were strong enough they added the larger sticks and then slowly the small branches. Wigheard came back with two large birds and a handful of small eggs. The boys plucked the game and put the meat on sticks ready to roast while Millie wrapped the eggs in large leaves. They balanced the birds over the hot embers and placed the eggs around the edge of the fire. The feast was consumed hungrily with bread at the stone table, and washed down with a swig of sweet honey mead.

After the meal it started to get dark. The moon was full and a silvery glow began to take hold. They lay down on the mossy ground with woollen blankets to cover them. The sky was clear and bright with stars and the night was warm.

"Do you know the story of Day and Night?" Wigheard asked, and before they could reply he went on. "Long ago one of the first giants who live in the mountains bore a beautiful daughter called Niht. She had dark skin and black shimmering hair that flowed down her back. As soon as she was old enough she married the brightest god in Asengeard. They had a child they named Daeg. He was bright like his father and beautiful like his mother. Then Woden gave Niht and Daeg two horses for them to ride and put them high up in the sky to circle the world from the dawn of day until the end of night. Niht leads the way riding upon Frosty-Mane and Daeg leads in the dawn and illuminates the sky as he follows behind on his horse, Shining-Mane. Of course, they never see each other or meet, as they are to follow each other forever. Until Ragnerok comes." [8]

"What about the moon?"

"The moon? The moon stretches her light from Asengeard, over us in Middangeard and into the plains of Hel. She's the one that sprinkles magic over the Druids' plants and pulls up the oceans and moves the tides. Some say she even moves the liquid in our brains when we are born and it is from this that our destiny is created."

The moon looked down upon them where they lay. Its deep craters were the same as in modern times. Millie and George could almost imagine they were in the twenty-first century looking up, only here there was something mystical, something undetermined. A place where there were different and new possibilities, where boundaries were unknown and each man faced his fate anew with the dawning of each day.

Chapter Thirty: Thieves

"Looks like they're asleep."

George woke up suddenly to the sound of whispering. He kept still, pretending to be asleep, and squinted from the side of one eye. Dawn was just starting to break and the dew was fresh on the ground. George couldn't see the speaker and guessed he must be behind him. He could see Wigheard was still asleep next to him.

"Do you reckon they've got any gold on 'em?"

George felt a hand tug on his leather pocket. Instinctively he sprang to his feet, grabbed for his seax and whirled around to face the offender.

"What do you want?" he shouted fiercely, hoping to wake the others.

Three bearded men in their early twenties looked back at him defensively. "We ... we were just checking you're okay."

Wigheard, Leof and Millie were woken by the commotion and got up to stand beside George, suspicion on their faces.

"What's going on?" Wigheard demanded.

"These men were just checking we were okay," George replied sarcastically, but lowered his weapon. Then he noticed that Fen had been tied to a tree a few yards away with a rope wound around his mouth to stop him barking.

"Don't like dogs," one of them said, following George's gaze. Leof angrily went over to untie him.

"You local boys?" Wigheard asked.

"Yeah," replied one of the men pointing to the east. "We're just out doing some early hunting. You're on our land, as it happens, and we need to take some payment off you for that."

"It's no one's land."

"It is if we say it is."

"We are travelling to Lundenburh. We have a meeting with the King."

"Off you go then, but the horses stay here."

Wigheard's face darkened and he reached for his sword pulling it from the long sheaf.

"Get back to your woodland hovel," he said slowly in a low voice. "You'll take nothing from us without a cut to your throat."

The man grinned wickedly. "The horses are on *my* land, so they're *my* horses."

Millie suddenly screeched. Wigheard span around to see one of the men had grabbed Millie with a rough arm and put a knife to her throat.

"We'll have that nice shiny weapon as well." The man motioned to Wigheard's sword.

"Then we'll be having all that nice wool you got there to trade." A fourth man had crept up on them with his bow drawn and an arrow pointed directly at George and Leof. They were surrounded and unevenly matched.

Two of the men bent down to search through the saddle-bags but Wigheard swiftly took the opportunity to kick the man closest to him hard in the face. Before the man had recovered Wigheard dashed to claim back his sword, but was leapt upon and thrown to the ground by one of the accomplices.

"Tie them up," the oldest of the men commanded.

Seeing his master being man-handled, Fen jumped up and sank his teeth into one of the men's legs. He shouted in pain and tried to prise Fen off, but to no avail. The fourth man fired his arrow into the dog's soft belly. Fen yelped and immediately let go of the assailant and limped away into the bushes, blood gashing from his wound.

"Fen! Fen!" Leof cried, desperate to go after him. But he struggled in vain against the rope that was being tied tightly around him, Millie and George. Wigheard stood in front of the other two men, clenching his sword as they encircled him with their seax knives drawn.

"Your sword!" the older man demanded.

Wigheard surrendered his sword once again, throwing it bitterly to the ground. "Whoever carries my sword will be cursed," he spat.

The man looked suspiciously at the weapon. Then, deciding it wasn't cursed, he bent to pick it up. At that same moment a very strange thing happened. There was a slight whooshing sound followed by the man wincing in pain and clutching at his neck. He yanked out a tiny arrow no longer than a man's finger.

"Elves!" the man said in surprise, then looked up just in time to see Wigheard had recovered his sword.

Wigheard swung the weapon at the man who ducked and swiftly dug his seax knife deep into Wigheard's chest. Wigheard gasped in shock but lashed out again with his blade, ignoring his injury. This time the sword struck and the man fell back with blood oozing freely from his chest. Millie, George and Leof watched in horror as the villain's companions rushed to his aid. But as they approached him, they too began to grab various parts of their body as more tiny arrows whizzed out of the shrubbery with amazing accuracy. Millie, George and Leof craned their necks as they tried to see where the arrows were coming from. But they were unable to catch a glance of anyone.

With tiny arrows embedded in their skin, the four men ran and limped as fast as they could through the bushes and down the mound.

The seax was still in Wigheard's chest. He pulled it out and wiped the blood off on the grass. Then, clutching his side, he cut the rope that entwined the three teenagers. As soon as they were free they hovered by his side, concerned he might be mortally injured. But Wigheard pushed them away.

"I'm fine, it's just a flesh wound," he growled. "Go and find your dog, Leof."

Wigheard leant with an arm each on Millie and George and stumbled to the stone table to rest. He took off his tunic and washed the wound with water from his pouch. His scar was now visible right down to just below his chest. Millie ripped at one end of the blankets and it tore easily into a strip. It was a little coarse but all they had for a makeshift bandage. She tied it around Wigheard's chest. The wound was deep and she knew it was more serious than he was letting on.

Leof came back looking tearful. "I've called Fen's name and searched under every bush but I can't find him, he's gone!"

"Those imbeciles!" George said fiercely. "At least he got a good bite at one of them."

"He's probably crawled somewhere to die," Leof's voice quavered. "I've had him since he was a pup."

"I'm sorry, Leof." George patted his friend sympathetically on the shoulder. "Were they outlaws?" he asked Wigheard.

"Probably. There's plenty of folk living out in these woods. Sometimes people are cast out from their village and end up banding together."

"How do they survive?"

"They live off what the forest can provide or they take from strangers. Come, we'd best be getting on."

"But you need to rest," Leof protested.

"I've had worse scratches than this, little nephew."

Wigheard got up and tried to stagger towards his horse but he was clearly in no fit state to walk.

"We'll carry the bags and you ride on Tiw," Leof said.

The three of them packed up their belongings while Wigheard lay on the ground breathing heavily.

"If I don't ... make it ...," he said between breaths, "you must ... find Walla. Travel south ... and allow the sun ... to be your compass. If we pass over the ... Roman road again ... we've gone too far."

Elvina was loaded up with the heaviest of their belongings and the rest was shared out equally between them. They helped Wigheard onto Tiw and continued along the path they had been following the day before, through the open grassland and onwards to the dark forest, as Wigheard had instructed them.

Their stride was slower now that they each carried the extra weight. Leof's concern for his dog was replaced by concern for his uncle, who was quiet and at times seemed to drift in and out of consciousness. It wouldn't be far to Walla. At least there they could stop and rest in safety with Bordley. As they entered the woods, the sun was reduced to just an odd sliver of light along the path. A sense of an unease fell upon the group. And again there was a sense that they weren't alone - that something might be lurking in the undergrowth. Wigheard held his arm out and let his hand brush against the low tree branches as the horse stumbled along. Adding to the eerie atmosphere, Wigheard began to sing softly:

I sing a true song of myself,
Tell of my travels, the hardship endured
Days of toil and times of suffering
Bitter sorrows have gripped my heart
Known aboard my ship many worries
The terrifying waves rolling, as I kept night watch
Often in the narrow stern
When she tossed near the cliffs.
Frozen with cold were my feet
Bounded by the numbing of frost.
Then the cares burnt hot into my heart,
Hunger tore within my sea-weary soul …[9]

It was a song sung with sorrow and sadness. The emotion flowed from Wigheard as the colour drained from his face. Fortunately though, despite all the morning's drama, the journey to Walla was uneventful and Wigheard had guided them well. It was with sheer relief that they finally arrived, with Millie sounding out the horn. Walla was much smaller than Widurok, with just enough dwellings to house thirty or forty people. The children ran out to greet them, followed by a bearded man in his early forties.

"Travellers, how can we help you?"

"Is this place Walla?"

"Who is asking?"

"We have travelled from Widurok on the way to Lundenburh. We are looking for Bordley."

"Then look no further, fellow men ... though I don't think I know any of you."

"You might know my uncle, Wigheard. We were attacked this morning and he has been badly hurt."

Bordley went over to Tiw and looked at the ailing Wigheard.

"He's barely conscious!" he said, alarmed, and shouted to the two oldest girls urgently, "Quick! Fetch your mother and tell your older sisters to make up a bed for this man and heat some water!"

The girls rushed off into the one of the buildings. Bordley took Elvina and Tiw by the reins and walked them in the direction the girls had gone. A woman rushed out to meet him and together they lowered Wigheard from his horse and managed to carry him into the hut. A teenage girl with long fair hair came out of the building to tie the horses to a post. Once they were secure she came over to the three of them.

"Greetings. I'm Burhwynne, Bordley's eldest daughter. Do you want to come with me?" she said softly. She took them to another dwelling. "You can unpack your belongings in here and sleep on the hay over there."

They had unloaded the heavy packs they had been carrying and took the saddle-bag from Elvina. Then they went to see what had happened to Bordley and Wigheard. Bordley heard them approaching and came out of the hut. He looked grave.

"Curse those damned thieves."

"Is it bad?" Leof asked.

"Yes, it's a very deep wound. He will need lots of rest if he's even to have a chance. He certainly won't be fit to travel to Lundenburh."

"Can we see him?"

"He's in a deep sleep, he shouldn't be disturbed. But he's in good hands. Agilwith, my wife, is sitting with him." Bordley put his arm around Leof's shoulder in a gesture of kindness. "If you need to stay a few days, you are more than welcome here."

They saw no choice but to take up his offer and were grateful for the hospitality. After they had tended to the horses and washed in a nearby river, they joined Bordley and his family for an evening stew.

"Do you often get bandits attacking people around these parts?" George asked.

"Yes, it happens now and again. People get desperate when they don't have much, or are short of food."

"Yes, I guess if people get cast out from their village there's no one to help them."

"That's right. They can't just move house and go and live in another town." (Millie frowned: what did Bordley know about moving house?)

"But you moved from Widurok to here?"

"I married into my wife's family. Widurok is a fantastic village to be part of, though. I often miss it and its people. Were you all born there? I detect a bit of an accent."

George retold their fabricated story of hailing from a northern village.

"Oh yes, that's right, you are the brother and sister. I heard about you two from a messenger when he came past not long ago." Bordley gave George and Millie an odd look that made them both feel a little uncomfortable.

"Anyway, nice to meet you both, and you Leof. As it happens your arrival is quite well timed for us. We're building a new shelter to house the livestock this winter. If you are going to stay around for a few days I wouldn't mind a bit of extra man-power. What do you say?"

"Of course. We would love to help."

Chapter Thirty-one: The journey continues

The following days were spent assisting Bordley and his extended family to erect the frame for the new hut. It was a big heavy job and it was no wonder that Bordley was grateful for their presence. Unfortunately though, Wigheard was no better despite Agilwith's and Burhwynne's diligence and care, and Leof's many prayers to the gods. On the third night Wigheard's condition took a turn for the worse. His temperature had risen, he was barely conscious and sweating heavily with fever. Leof didn't want to leave his side and sat with him through the night, aware that it might bc Wigheard's last.

George rose at the first light of morning to see Leof's bed was empty. He guessed he was still with his uncle and thought he might need a friend. As George entered the hut, Leof stirred from his slumber and opened his eyes, yawning.

"Is it time to get up?" Leof asked loudly, forgetting where he was.

"Shh!" George said. "Wig is still sleeping." He nodded over to where the man lay.

Leof frowned and walked over to Wigheard. He knelt down and touched the man's shoulder. He paused for a moment then looked back at George.

"No, he's not sleeping," he said with a distant look in his eyes. "The Waelcyrge have taken him."[10]

George joined him at Wigheard's side but found he was unable to look at Wigheard's empty body and turned his head away. He had never been so close to a dead person before and it unnerved him.

"We should cremate him as soon as possible," Leof said, immediately taking control. "It rained in the night so we will need to search for dry wood."

George wasn't sure if Leof was suffering from the shock of losing a family member or if he was just more used to death than he was. After all it was extremely rare for a family's siblings all to survive to adulthood.

Leof covered Wigheard's face with the blanket and muttered a prayer to one of the gods. Then he went outside into the fresh air to find an appropriate spot for a funeral pyre.

"He died saving us," George said. "I can never repay him for that, but I will *never* forget him."

"He died fighting a group of outlaws," Leof said with resignation. "This is how our world is. It's a fight for survival."

They walked towards the surrounding woodland in silence as they both reflected upon what had happened.

"I guess death is not such a terrible thing. It's just the start of life in the other world," Leof said thoughtfully. "I'm going to miss him, though."

"He was still young."

"He had almost reached his thirtieth year!" Leof contended. "It's a good age to live to, older than most."

"Do you really believe in the other world?" George asked.

Leof shrugged. "I suppose. It's a way of explaining things, a way that it can all make sense. We have a story about life and death, we say that life is like a bird that flies in from the dark cold of the outside and into a warm food hall, full of people and festivities. He flies around the room a few times and then like death he flies back out into the night."

It was a beautiful image and it was comforting to think of Wigheard flying free somewhere in the realms of the cosmos.

Millie came to join them having heard the news. Leof smiled sadly at her and she returned the same grimace.

"I'm going to help Leof collect some wood for a funeral pyre," George said, taking Millie's hand. "Why don't you start to pack our stuff up and prepare some food for the journey? Looks like we're going to have to find our own way to Saberht."

Helped by the village's inhabitants, the funeral pyre was quickly put together and the Wigheard's body was prepared and laid upon it. Leof lit the small tinder sticks underneath and in the strong heat of the day, the flames soon rose and engulfed the pyre. The three teenagers stood watching as the flames consumed their protector and their uncle. They uttered a few words in praise of his bravery, and in farewell. Then solemnly left the burning pyre to the elements.

Bordley was waiting for them outside their hut, next to their heap of belongings.

"I am going to help you get to Lundenburh. We will load up Tiw and walk south down to Teidana which sits on the river Hrothingas. I have friends there who will trade you a boat and a guide for Wigheard's horse. The river empties into the Thames, I mean the Temesa, and from there the guide will take you upstream to dock at Lundenwic. They will get you to the capital fast and safely. Elvina can stay with us until you return. But we need to get going straightaway; you don't want to arrive in the night."

Tiw was loaded up with the saddle-bags again and they were ready to leave. Bordley's family crowded round to see them off.

"You will return, won't you?" Burhwynne said to Leof, gazing deeply at him.

"Of course." Leof reddened, sensing George and Millie were giggling at him, although he couldn't help enjoying the girl's attention.

Walla was very close to the Roman road they had walked along from Dunmadu. The road here was in good condition and they were able to arrive at Teidana just a few hours later. Bordley seemed to know everyone in the small farmstead and quickly struck a deal as he had promised. A young man named Oswin was chosen to be their guide and took them down to a rowing-boat docked alongside a small pier. There was just enough room for the four of them to sit, with their belongings and the goods they had to trade heaped between them. Oswin was eager to leave immediately so they expressed their gratitude and thanks to Bordley, who then helped pushed the boat off and set them on a course downstream.

They were leaving a lot later in the day than was ideal, but luckily the current flowed with them. They each had an oar and pulled rhythmically under Oswin's instruction.

"The harder you row, the faster we'll get there," he kept saying, whistling cheerfully as though he felt at home on the water.

They passed several more farmsteads along the banks where women had come down to the river to wash their clothes, or children to collect water for cooking. In the shallow parts of the river, boys stood deathly still, staring into the water with a spear held in one hand. Millie blew the horn as they approached and the locals waved, although the fishermen weren't too happy to have the fish disturbed.

"I wonder what the King's daughters are like. Do you think they'll be any different from Sifelda, Alwun and Edyth?"

"How do you mean?" asked Leof.

"Well-mannered and educated ... posh."

"I've no idea. They probably keep themselves a lot better than we do. I imagine the King's three sons will be draped in finery. But otherwise they'll be just like us."

Up ahead the river began to widen.

"London must be just round the corner," George whispered to Millie.

"Bit further than that! We're going upstream now. I'd saying we've got a good many hours ahead of us. Be lucky to get there before dark."

They turned into the wide river of the Temesa. The current was against them and they had to row harder to make any progress at all. The light was also starting to fade. Millie had been expecting to see buildings as soon as they reached the main river. Now it dawned on her just how small London was.

"Why is it called London *burh*?" she asked George.

"Wigheard told me that *burh* means fort. I guess there's not much that can get through Roman walls. And *wic* means trading place - it's where the main port is. London's a big trading centre for Essex."

"So does the King have a palace in London, then?"

"Not exactly. He travels around the kingdom with his court. But London is a pretty important place. They've just built the first church where the old Roman temple was, which I think might be where St Paul's Cathedral is in our time. Anyway, it shows the city's importance and makes a statement to foreign traders coming here."

The land that banked the river was marshy and open, the trees sparser than they had been the whole journey. The Temesa was also much wider than the Hrothingas and riddled with small islands of sand and gravel, which constantly threatened to beach their little boat.

They were close to exhaustion when the Roman city walls finally became visible on the northern banks: a high barricade of brick and stone protruding from the landscape, in some places over six metres high. Spurred on by the sight of their destination, they rowed with greater speed and vigour. A grand bridge supported on stone pillars led out of the city and crossed over into the kingdom of Kent in the south. It looked as if it had been well maintained by its Saxon inheritors, although the buildings it led to were long since ruined. Beacons had been lit as the daylight dimmed and they illuminated the main dock close to the bridge. They rowed towards it and moored alongside the many others. Very happy to be able to stretch their legs, they clambered out of the boat onto an overgrown cobbled pavement. Next to them, a few metres away, three fishermen were unloading a cargo of fish and talking in loud voices.

"What kind of law is that, anyway?" "I'm not going to give any of my fish away cos of a vision!" "What vision? I ain't heard nothing" "Saba' thinks an angel took him across the river" "Don't talk stupid ..." The voices diminished as they walked away, heaving the day's catch up a flight of steps that ran alongside the bridge.

"We should follow them. That's probably the way up into the city," said George.

"Well, I'm going to go on to Lundenwic with Orswin," said Leof, jumping back into the boat. "We need to find somewhere to stay and unload these goods. If I don't see you again tonight, I'll come and find you both in the morning."

"Sounds like a good plan," George said, reaching into the boat for Millie's satchel and his leather pouch.

"Here, keep those bundles of yarn and pottery covered up. We might be able to get into the town without having to pay trading taxes! said Leof. "I'm hoping to get a good price for them."

"And I'm hoping we find the King in good spirits! See you in the morning! Thanks for bringing us here, Orswin," George said, shaking his hand. Millie and George waved goodbye and pushed the boat back on its way up river.

It was dark now and the three travellers were all in unfamiliar territory.

Chapter Thirty-two: Lundenburh

Millie and George climbed the stairs and found the entrance to the city was gated. Two armoured guards stepped out of the shadows to accost them.

"State your business!"

"We have been sent for by King Saberht," George answered.

One of the men raised a lit torch towards their faces. "Two young un's, boy and girl. What are your names?"

"Millie."

"George."

"Right you are. We've been expecting you." He nodded to his colleague. "Cyneward here will escort you."

Cyneward opened the gate and in the twilight they followed him along a paved street into the city, which by George and Millie's standards wasn't much larger than a small town. Some of the buildings seemed derelict and in ruins. Others seemed to have been patched up with crude attempts at the unknown art of masonry. Some were repaired in Anglo-Saxon style, with straw roofs and woodwork. Their footsteps echoed along the quiet, half-abandoned streets and through this sinister patchwork of buildings. Holding his burning torch, Cyneward led them down a street to the left of an inlet. At the end a stone building stood out from the rest, looking newly built and very imposing.

"Our first church, thanks to the kind endowment of King Athelbert," Cyneard said, catching Millie staring. She realised that this must be the site of St Paul's cathedral.

"It's papal policy that our churches have to be built in former Roman cities" he added.

They turned right and passed a once-grand Roman square that was now being used more practically as a market garden. The King's palace and court were situated in the northern corner of the city, surrounded by Roman walls. Towers - or what remained of them - protruded from each corner, as though it had once been the town's main fort. The entrance was through a large wooden door in one of these walls. Cyneward banged on it and a hatch opened. The face of a guard appeared, to scrutinize them.

"Who calls, this late in the evening?"

"It is I, Cyneward, with the magic-folk from Widurok."

"The King is at his meadhall in Lundenwic tonight, but the sons are here," the guard said and unlocked the door to let them in. "You must leave your weapons with me."

George untied his seax and Millie took off the bow. Before them stood another patched-up Roman building, but it was by far the largest building either of them had seen in East Seax. They crossed a courtyard to the palace entrance where a servant greeted them and invited them both inside, before scurrying off to inform the royal family. The building had been constructed from bricks and patterned tiles and had a cool, airy feel to it. A Roman mosaic, chipped in parts, decorated the floor of the entrance hall and on the wall facing them was a large modern tapestry displaying the three curved seaxes of the Essex coat of arms, each sword elaborately decorated. It was a strange combination of two very different eras.

In the background they could hear the chattering of people talking and laughing. This stopped for a moment as news of their arrival was received and a moment later a woman entered the room through an archway, holding a lit candle. She was dressed similarly to Millie but the cloth had been more skilfully woven and dyed a bright blue. The sleeves and shoulders were fastened with beautiful jewelled clasps and her braided hair with elaborately decorated clips. Her features were soft and gentle but she walked with an air of confidence and authority.

"Wes Hal, I am Queen Ethelgoda, King Saberht's wife. Please come into the dining room. I will get you something to eat. You must be very tired after your travels." She shouted out into the darkness and a servant appeared. She gave him a command and he hurried off to obey it.

George and Millie followed Ethelgoda through to a dining hall furnished with a large oak table and wooden benches cushioned with straw. Sitting at the table were two teenage boys, who stood up and motioned for George and Millie to join them. The older one was tall with brown hair to his shoulders and a serious expression; the younger was fair-haired and about the same height and age as George, although with a shyer manner.

"Wes Hal," the older boy said. "I am Prince Saeward, son of Saba, that is, King Saberht. And this is my younger brother, Prince Seaxred." He gave them both a long stare as he tried to judge their characters and then continued. "I apologise for my father's absence, he is at his mead hall and our younger brother, Seaxbald, is out learning the skills of a huntsman, but I hope we can make you feel welcome here."

Three servants entered, bowing, and carrying bread and bowls of stew. They laid the food along the table.

"Please eat and drink," Ethelgoda said, filling their cups from a jug of milk. They drank thirstily and broke the bread into their bowls.

"Did you travel alone, without a guide?" Seaxred asked.

"Our guide was fatally wounded in a fight with outlaws who tried to take our horses and belongings. But thanks to his bravery, we escaped unharmed." Millie relayed the incident in detail while George ate silently, lost in thought as he tried to recollect when he had last heard the name "Prince Saeward".

"Outlaws! Will this Kingdom never be rid of them?" Saeward exclaimed, reacting to Millie's story.

"That's why Saba, your father, has embraced Christianity," his mother said. "So we can be cleansed of such sinful ways."

"Don't you mean because father's uncle told him to, and because we have Mellitus on his mission from Rome telling us what to do?" Saeward replied resentfully.

("Mellitus"? Millie thought, remembering the book of Anglo-Saxon chronicles she had found in Mr Gordon's old shop. Wasn't he the preacher who brought Christianity to Essex and held the bishopric?)

"Shhh, keep your voice down," Ethelgoda said angered at her son's unpleasant tone. "Even kings must answer to somebody!" She turned and smiled at Millie, quick to change the subject. "We are very grateful you are here. Both my two daughters are deathly sick with plague and we are frantic with worry that they won't recover and that it will spread. We hope you are capable of saving them. We were told you have the magic of Frige in your blood."

"They fell sick the day father decided to build another new church at his hunting ground on Thorny Island," Saeward added curtly.

"Enough! Please!" Ethelgoda looked at George and Millie with shame. "It is true, the gods are punishing our family for bringing this foreign religion to the Kingdom."

"There seems to be a lot of conflict between the old gods and the new one. But I don't think that any god would mean you harm," George said to her. But if the plague was just exaggerated hearsay and fear of the wrath of gods, then what, he wondered, was the point of them coming here?

"Yes, I hope you are right. Yet we have become fearful of both now. As long as we owe allegiance to the King of Kent we must do as he says. He is my husband's uncle and a very powerful and ambitious man," Ethelgoda replied.

After they had finished eating Seaxred showed them to their quarters. Their room was as sparsely furnished as a prison cell, with two wooden cot beds and straw on the floor as a carpet. They thanked him graciously, nonetheless. For George it was a novelty not to sleep surrounded by wood. They slept almost immediately, worn out from the long day.

*

Leof and Oswin arrived at the port of Lundenwic and moored the rowing-boat. Leof could dimly make out the town in the background, a larger-sized Widurok as he had expected it to be. A merchant unloading his wares pointed them in the direction of a grand, impressive dwelling on the edge of the town, promising it would provide a warm bed and supper for them both. The door to the dwelling was wide open when they arrived, and they were warmly received by a plump woman who offered them hospitality in exchange for one of Leof's clay pots. The main building consisted of two large rooms: one was the dining room and the other a dorm-room for sleeping. The dining hall was full of rowdy men, many of whom talked in foreign tongues as they sat drinking ale and filling their bellies. Leof and Oswin found a space at a table between them and helped themselves to the stew that simmered in a large cauldron hanging over a fire pit. Leof felt a little uncomfortable and out of place but Oswin, who had made this trip many times before, seemed quite at home.

Their beds weren't as comfortable as Millie and George's, just straw laid upon the dirt floor and a rough blanket as cover, but they were tired enough not to care. Even the loud snoring of drunken men and the scuttling of rats that shared the room didn't wake them from their slumber.

In the morning Leof decided to find Millie and George before he went to the markets to trade. He still had the feverfew he had picked for Millie and tied to Elvina; she might be needing it today. Leof set off on the road to Lundenburh that cut between the sheep pens and the fields of crops which separated the new town from the old. The road neared the city and crossed over the Fleta River, which flowed just outside the walls. The entrance to the city was open and Leof strolled through it, awestruck. He had seen Roman ruins when he was younger, but never a city like this! Tall buildings made from bricks and stone, roofs still clinging to their tiles - it was like being in another of the seven realms! He passed down a street that led to a statue of a man carved in stone, more real-looking than any carving

Leof had ever seen. He climbed up to touch the man's face and to check for certain that he wasn't real. Leof wondered if the person represented by the statue had ever stood in this spot, all those hundreds of years ago. What would the city have been like then, buzzing with Roman citizens going about their daily lives? Leof was suddenly reminded of a song he knew and realised that now he understood the author's meaning. He began to it sing to himself;

Wondrous is this walled stone; broken by fate;
The work of giants wastes away.
The roofs have fallen, the towers ruined,
the gate posts are bare, frost covers the cement,
disused roofs are torn down, collapsed with
Age. The Earth has gripped
the great builders, dead and decayed,
in the hard grasp of earth, until a hundred generations
of people have passed by. Long this wall,
masked grey and tarnished red, lived through king after king,
standing sturdily under storms; though the highest walls have
tumbled. [11]

Leof continued his sight-seeing, happy to get lost in this strange world. At another entrance he met a guard who informed him that a boy and a girl had been taken to the King's court and palace last night and pointed Leof in the right direction.

Leof knocked at the palace door and was taken by a slave girl to Millie's quarters. Millie was very happy to see him.

"Where's George, is he not here?" Leof asked.

"No, he went hunting with Saberht's son, Saeward" Millie told him. "Did you find Lundenwic all right, and somewhere to sleep?"

"Yes. Everything was fine. But I must get back soon as Oswin will be leaving and he has our goods. I just came to give you these," Leof took the herbs from his belt. "I don't know if they can be of much help to you but perhaps they will give you confidence. They will ease any pain or a headache the daughters might have."

"What should I do with them?" Millie asked, taking them.

"Let the flower-heads steep in hot water for five minutes. When it is cool enough to drink, give it to the girls and utter this spell. It's something my mother use to say - part of 'The nine herb charm'."

Leof leant forward and whispered in her ear as though he were disclosing clandestine information. Millie was surprised; she hadn't been aware that Leof knew any witchcraft. He made her repeat it back to him a few times, until he was sure she had memorised it properly.

"I don't think it'll be enough. If they have a serious illness, I won't be able to cure them," Millie said nervously.

Leof frowned and thought hard. "Okay, what about this then. I know George can read and write, so I'm guessing you can too. Show them that and it will be enough to persuade them that you have a magic gift."

Leof seemed to be suggesting that a placebo effect might work: if the daughters *believed* they were being cured, they would *actually* be cured.

"But what do I write? I don't know runes that well and I don't have anything to write on."

"Ask one of the servants to bring you a tablet and write down the spell I just told you, then leave it with the daughters. Trust me, they'll be impressed. To write and read is magic to many of us. You *have* to make them believe you can help or else we are all going to be in serious trouble."

"I will. thank you Leof," Millie said, keeping hold of the flowers.

"Good luck. I will return after midday."

Chapter Thirty-three: The Prince's secret

Lundenwic's bustling market place was the largest trading area Leof had ever seen. There were people here from all the kingdoms of the island, Gewisse Saxons from the West, East Angles, Mercians, Kentings. There were even merchants who had sailed from the continent in their long boats with tall sails. They traded all manner of things: bottles and barrels of wine, spices from exotic lands, sea salt and cured meats, woven and silk fabrics, animal furs, precious stones and metals for making jewellery.

Leof sat watching and listening to the banter and the bartering. A few potential customers had shown some interest in his goods but his sales experience was very limited and he failed to make a profitable exchange.

"What wares have you there?" a man wearing a black cap asked.

"Fine wool from the north of East Seax and beautifully crafted pottery. Would you like to take a closer look?"

The man turned the spun wool over in his hands. "Is this all you have? It is a long way to travel for a couple of sacks of wool and some pottery."

"I was accompanying my friends on their visit to see the King's daughters."

"The King, you say? Who are these friends?"

The man seemed unusually interested in this and Leof reluctantly retold the story, keeping it as brief as possible. When he had finished the man angrily put down the wool and left in the direction of the old town. Leof wished he had said nothing.

"Why have you really come?" Leof looked down and saw a young boy of seven.

"Sorry, do you know me?"

"I'm Seaxbald. Your friends met with my older brothers last night. I saw you visiting the palace earlier."

"Should such a young prince be wandering about the marketplace alone?" Leof asked.

"I do it all the time," the boy replied in a blasé fashion. He was a bright child, outspoken like his oldest brother Saeward but with the same fair complexion as Seaxred. "I want to know why you have come, cos my brothers won't tell me."

"We came to save your sisters from the wrath of the gods. You must know that."

"No, I mean the *real* reason. Is it for the horse?"

"What? I don't know anything about a horse."

The boy looked at him suspiciously, as if trying to decide whether Leof was telling the truth. "What is it you want to exchange your goods for?" he asked changing the subject.

"I am trying to get our headman some iron cooking pots."

"I know an iron merchant who will be interested in the pottery. I'll take you to him if you like. Come on!"

The young boy took Leof back down to the port where a clean-shaven man with short dark hair sat in his long boat amidst an array of cooking pots.

The boy introduced them, conversing with the man in a foreign language. Leof showed him the items he had and the man turned them over in his hands, carefully studying the workmanship. He was interested and offered Leof two small metal pots for the lot. Seaxbald bargained on Leof's behalf and managed to secure Leof a large pot and two small ones. Leof felt Freodheric would be proud of him, and he went back to the market now confident he could sell the wool.

*

Early that same morning Saeward joined George for breakfast and the conversation quickly turned to hunting and the skills of archery. This led to Saeward insisting that George spend the day with him at Saberht's hunting lodge, an offer that George was happy to take up. Once they had finished eating they went outside to prepare the horses. The city looked very different now that it was light. George could see that the palace had been mainly constructed from reused bricks taken from ruined Roman buildings. They were in a square enclosure which was well protected from any invaders by the high Roman walls which loomed over the city.

Saeward's chestnut horse was the largest George had ever seen and had clearly been chosen for a member of the royal family. George's horse was large also and as black as a moonless night. The gateway was opened for them and they rode through the town together. They headed past the church Mellitus had ordered to be built and through to a gate on the west side just behind it. Livestock roamed the street just as in Widurok and they had to keep shooing them away. There hadn't been much opportunity to ride in Widurok as most of the hunting was done on foot and the horses the village had were strictly used to plough the land or by the older men of the village.

They passed through the grey walls and onto a road that continued west. George could see Lundenwic before them, wisps of smoke rising up from the many buildings.

The horses broke into a gallop. George held on tight and dug his feet in. He sensed that Saeward was challenging him to a race and he did not want to be outdone.

Saeward slowed his horse as they reached the new town.

"This is the port of Lundenwic," he shouted to George proudly. "It's the largest trading centre in the Kingdom."

"It's a good spot for a port town," said George without enthusiasm, feeling annoyed that he had only lagged behind because his horse was smaller.

"Yes, it is. Lundenburh is a crumbling ruin. It was wise of Saba - and you are aware there are not many of his plans that he and I agree on!"

"Your father probably does what he thinks is best for the East Saxons. I'm sure he has his reasons."

Saeward frowned. "Come on" he said and kicked his horse forwards. They took a longer route around the town's outskirts and then onwards beside small fields of barley and rye and the fenced enclosures of sheep and cattle.

After a mile or so they came to an island surrounded by the Temesa.

"Welcome to Thorny Island!" Saeward dismounted to stretch his legs.

The land was overrun with thorny bushes and George could see how it got its name. Next to the road up ahead was an open patch of land where some men were building foundations and cutting great trunks of wood. Upon seeing the prince, their chatter stopped as they suddenly became focused on the job in hand.

"Is this where they are building the church you talked about?" George asked.

"Yes, the result of a stupid vision one of the fishermen had," Saeward replied in disdain. "Apparently Saint Peter appeared to him and told him a church must be built here and now my father has agreed because he is worried about bad omens. He is a great man, my father, but he is too easily influenced by others, and too superstitious."

Suddenly there was a movement in the bushes. Saeward saw it too.

"A deer, quick!" They jumped back on the horses and urged them on to chase it, but the deer had darted out of sight.

"Let's get to the hunting lodge and get better equipped," Saeward suggested.

The hunting lodge was just like any other Saxon dwelling although it housed a large store of hunting weapons, food and beverages. They each picked out a handful of arrows with heads sharpened in various shapes, and a bow that was sized to their suiting. They also took a long spear each and quenched their thirst from a barrel of weak ale.

George and Saeward climbed back onto their horses, armed and ready for action. George didn't really expect to catch anything - nor did he really want to. The exhilaration of spending the whole morning galloping through woodland and meadows and chasing any movement they saw was enough excitement for him. Saeward too seemed to enjoy himself and his teenage sullenness melted away. Just as the horses began to tire, Saeward successfully managed to maim a wild boar with an arrow. The creature lay writhing and squeaking in pain, half-dead. Saeward gave it two quick jabs from his spear and the pig gave a final high-pitched screech before being still forever. George flinched. He had never quite learnt to take such a practical approach to the killing of animals, despite the many times he had had to lend a hand. They heaved the beast up onto Saeward' horse to bring back to Lundenburh for dinner that night. They rode back slowly side by side.

"What is your village like in the north?" Saeward asked.

"Widurok? Similar to most East Saxon villages, I presume. There are over a hundred of us, mostly freemen, but even those who are not are treated well. You may have heard of the strange stone hearg nearby."

"What stones are they?" Saeward asked, sounding slightly uneasy.

"It's a group of two stone circles with a large tree in the middle. Have you been there?" George clearly remembered the night he had arrived: was this the same Prince Saeward? It had to be.

Saeward looked away before he answered. "Yes, once when I was younger, a few years back." He paused for a moment in thought. "You know, George, there is another reason you came here, other than to help my sisters." He hesitated again, as though unsure whether to continue. "You must promise never to tell anyone what I am about to reveal, only speak about it to your companions that travelled here with you. Do I have your word?"

"Of course."

"You see, when I had just reached manhood I believed in my father's new religion and I wanted to prove to him what a great king I would make. It was stupid really. I was only fourteen at the time and it seemed important." He lowered his voice until it was barely audible. "I did something terrible which has angered Saxonet and Woden. I ... I fear that I have brought a curse upon this land."

"What do you mean? A fourteen-year-old can't cause a curse!"

"It was just before mid-summer. I had been allowed to accompany my father and his council as they travelled through the north of the kingdom. One evening I decided to go out on a hunting trip with some of the men. I wanted to explore a different woodland from what I was used to. I had heard so many stories of the creatures of Asengeard and elves and dwarfs living in those parts. I wanted to hunt one down and bring it to Saba as a sign of my commitment to his new religion. We hadn't been out long when I saw what would be the greatest of all gifts. I could barely believe my eyes! I followed it through the night, I was so determined to catch it."

"Did you catch it?" George asked eagerly.

"Yes, when the creature stopped at the stones," Saeward answered soberly.

George remembered the moment well; how could he ever forget the night his life had changed so dramatically?

"I shot an arrow at the creature and it fell instantly. The strange thing was that as I went over to finish him off, he lifted his head and looked me directly in the eyes. It was as though he could see into my soul! And I had a sudden revelation that we were all creatures of Saxonet and this was my own flesh and blood I was about to slay."

"Wasn't the animal just a wild horse, though?" George asked.

"It was Sleipnir, Woden's horse," Saeward whispered, as though scared the air would carry his voice.

"What? Sleipnir?" George was taken aback. He didn't know what to think. Sleipnir was the horse of the god Woden, a mythical creature with eight legs. Was Saeward being serious or was this some strange trick to test his pagan loyalty? But there again, the creature that George saw that night did seem to have many legs. He had thought at the time they were shadows cast by the moon - but what if they weren't?

"Shhh, don't speak so loud! When I realised what a sacred place we were in I felt terrified that the gods would *know* that I had done this and that the elves might be watching me from the woods. Instead of wanting to present Sleipnir to my father I knew I must save him and not let him die. I knelt beside him, unsure what to do. The arrow had gone deep but it was not fatal."

"Well, what happened to him?"

"I couldn't leave him there. He would have been easy prey for the wolves. So I swore my men to secrecy and we managed somehow to carry him back to Lundenburh by stretcher and boat. My brother and I hid him in the lower chambers of a ruin."

"Is he still alive?"

"Yes, although I am often too ashamed to visit him. For the past three years a stable boy named Edgar has been looking after him. But despite his care Sleipnir's health is very poor. In truth we don't think he will live much longer, certainly not though this coming winter. We dread to think how the gods will react when he is taken into the wind."

"So why are you telling me this?"

The prince drew in his breath and then let it out again slowly. "You were there that night. I know Sleipnir was waiting for you."

"*What?*" George was dumbfounded by the prince's assertion.

"You came to Widurok village on the solstice, the same as your sister! Sleipnir was standing by the world-tree that *same* night, waiting," Saeward argued, listing the facts that he knew to be true.

"If he was waiting, it wasn't for me!"

"We have messengers that bring news all around the kingdom to us. I have lain awake many nights thinking about why Sleipnir was at such a place. When I heard news that a foreign boy had arrived at the village by the stones on the very same night I was there, I grew suspicious. But then I heard about your sister's arrival too - also on the solstice - and that she breathed life back into the dead! You can't deny that you came through the world-tree. All the gods travel between the realms that way."

"But ... but ... you don't think that I'm a god?" George stammered. He was trying hard to keep his wits about him whilst struggling to think of the best way to deal with this sudden turn in conversation.

"I wasn't sure before I met you. Now I believe you were sent by one of the gods to carry out a task, maybe by Woden himself."

Saeward shot a sideways look at George to see if his reaction would reveal the truth, but George said nothing. He felt deceived and tricked. He had believed that Saeward had invited him hunting out of kindness and hospitality and to strike up a new friendship, not to corner him into revealing his most closely kept secret.

"I'm sorry, please don't be alarmed" Saeward begged, sensing George's sudden coldness. "We are so desperate for your help. That's why we devised a plan to persuade Saba that he must send for you both to cure our sisters.

George was even more dumbfounded. So it wasn't saving the sisters that had been their true agenda, but a horse! Could there *really* be an eight- legged horse somewhere in the ruins of Roman London? Surely it was impossible. He had become accustomed to stories of mythical creatures, but George had never believed in them as the villagers did. He may have grown a little superstitious but nothing he had witnessed was ever magical. George even viewed his time travel as having a scientific explanation, and saw the so-called "elves" in the woods as humans of different ethnicity. Surely they couldn't be magical or mythical beings? That was ridiculous.

Chapter Thirty-four: Millie and the Princesses

After Leof had left her, Millie asked one of the palace slaves for some writing materials. Instead of paper he brought her a wax tablet and a bone marker as a pen, sharp at one end and rounded at the other.

There was a commotion at the palace gate as someone important arrived on horseback.

"The King has returned!" said the slave and hurried out.

Millie knew she would be called for soon. She emptied her satchel bag and repacked it with the herbal medicine Leof had given her and the tablet and bone. Millie was reminded of the paracetamol she had packed when she was at Grandad's. It was still here, in the little side pocket and untouched.

There was a knock at the door and Seaxred entered. "Millie, my father is ready to see you. Come."

The King was in the hall untying his boots. He was a lot younger than Millie had expected, perhaps in his late thirties, although it was hard to tell with half his face hidden by beard. Around his shoulders was wound a long and elaborately woven cloak. On his head he wore a gold-threaded band to keep his hair in place.

"Millie?" he asked, rising to his feet. He looked her up and down, no doubt registering her youth, too! "I'm sorry I wasn't here to meet you yesterday. I hope you were well looked after?"

"Yes, very well, thank you."

"Well then, let me take you to my daughters, Sunngifu and Swanhild. They have been ill for nearly a month now. Anything you can do for them will be a blessing to us. Come, we must hurry before that meddling Mellitus finds you here."

Millie followed Saberht and Seaxred to a dark room at the end of the building.

The daughters were asleep but they woke when their father entered and sat up.

"This is my dear Sunngifu." Saberht took the hand of the youngest daughter who looked about six or seven years old. "And this is Swanhild," he said and gently patted the head of the other girl who was slightly older.

They looked very similar. Both were pale and thin and their long hair hung limply about their face. They gave Millie a weak smile and looked hopefully at her.

The daughter's nursemaid sat in the corner of the room sewing whilst she watched over the girls. Trying to appear confident and knowledgeable, Millie asked her what the exact nature of the girls' illness was. The nurse replied that they complained of stomach pains and headaches. Millie thought for a moment, very conscious of being observed, and asked the fire in the room to be lit and a pan of water to be boiled. As that was being seen to by Seaxred she asked the nurse to bring her a bowl and pestle so she could grind the herbs, a pot of honey and a horn for the girls to drink from.

"I see they are in capable hands, I will leave you to your work," the King said, knowing it was bad luck to watch for too long and having other business to attend to.

He left with Seaxred and Millie was alone with the daughters waiting for the flames to get going and the water to boil. She sat beside the girls to talk to them.

"How long have you been in bed?" she asked.

"A few weeks now," Swanhild replied.

"You would get better if you got up and walked around more. Lying in bed will only make you feel worse." It was something Millie's mother always said to her when she was recovering from an illness.

"But people are worried we will spread disease."

"Well I think that's silly. You need fresh air and exercise. Maybe a place can be found for you to recover away from others."

The nursemaid returned with the items Millie had requested just as the water started to boil. Millie took the pot from the fire and dropped the yellow and white flowers of the feverfew plant into the hot water. Next she ground the paracetamol and added it along with some of the honey to sweeten the bitter taste. She stirred the mixture as it cooled and repeated the rhyme that Leof had taught her, as best she could remember,

To poison that comes flying from the east,
or any from the north and south,
or any from the west among the realm of man.
Freo stands over sickness of every kind.

I alone know the running rivers,
and there nine adders beware.
May all the weeds spring up as herbs,
the seas slip apart all salt water,
while I blow this poison from you. [12]

With the bone marker, Millie etched the poem into the wax and placed it between the girls' two beds as a lucky charm. She then poured some of the liquid into a horn and instructed both girls to have half each now and then the same again before evening and in the morning. Millie felt a little uncomfortable being so bossy, but she knew she had a role to play. She instructed the nurse that the girls were to have a walk outside in the courtyard and to eat a warm simple meal at midday and in the evening, such as porridge, and the fire was to be keep lit and the room aired.

Having felt she had done everything she could, Millie bade goodbye to Swanhild and Sunngifu and promised to come and visit them the next morning. She went down the dark corridor to find the king. Would she and George be free now to go back to Widurok, or would they have to stay until the girls were fully recovered? Millie had done the best she could.

As Millie neared the hall she saw a man in a black cap being greeted by King Saberht. She stayed in the shadows, not wanting to interrupt them.

"Bishop Mellitus. How are you today?"

"I have come to question your faith," the man in the black cap said unpleasantly. "I hear you have brought a pagan leechcraft woman into your home to cure your daughters. Did you not think to ask God for His help?"

Was the bishop talking about her? What was leechcraft? Another word for medicine, perhaps?

"Yes, I have asked your god for help and this is the price I pay! Our gods are angry and will punish us all with disease and famine!"

"You should better understand the love of the one true God. Must I go to your uncle, who is, need I remind you, the King of Kent, and tell him how you revoke our religion?" Mellitus asked with obvious malice.

"I do not revoke it! In fact on account of a vision from your God, I have made plans to build a church on Thorny Island, where I will ask my sons to bury me when I die. Is *that* not piety enough for you?"

"Hmm. Right, well I shall see you in church later for mass." Bishop Mellitus turned his back and left the way he had entered, leaving a chilly atmosphere.

Suddenly Seaxred ran in from the other side of the hall very upset; it seemed that Millie hadn't been the only one listening in.

"Saba! You are not to be buried there! We shan't allow it. You belong with our ancestors, at the family burial ground where the river meets the sea."

Saberht sat down on a wooden bench and rubbed a hand across his forehead. Seaxred gave a snort and left the same way as Mellitus.

Millie couldn't hide in the shadows anymore and went over to the King. He looked up when he saw her.

"See how difficult it is to be king," he sighed. "I have wars to fight, borders to defend, famines to ward off, yet all the time I am being pulled in two by the gods. My sons keep imploring me to stop the new religion; my uncle insists on it. My sons are ambitious for East Seax to be a great kingdom and trade centre. But they don't understand that for trade to flourish we need to convert to the new religion, to allow greater ties with the Christian world and to honour our allegiance to Athelberht of Kent. Yet how can I banish the beliefs that I have taught my own children? It is that which Mellitus is most scared of." He looked searching at Millie as though hoping for an answer. "I'm sorry, what can a young girl know of such matters?"

"Very little, I'm afraid, but I hope I have helped with your daughters. I have done everything I can and I pray it may just be a fever. Either way, I don't think you should worry too much. Even kings can't control destiny." Millie was surprised by her own assurance and realised just how much she had matured since she had left home.

"Yes, you are right, kings can't control destiny or change, and there will *always* be change. We must find a balance between accepting the new and retaining the best of our ancestors' way of life." He rose to his feet again and stood up tall. "Thank you for your help with Sunngifu and Swanhild. We would like you to stay here until they are fit and well, through to the winter at least."

Until the *winter*! Millie was mortified. That would be three months! Surely Saberht could not be serious? She and George needed to work on getting back to the twenty-first century. Millie left the palace and went into the courtyard, wanting to go and find George or Leof.

Seaxred was talking to one of the guards at the gate but broke off when he saw her.

"Millie," he said coming over. "I hope you don't think I was rude shouting at my father. I saw you standing there in the shadows."

"Oh, I ... I was just waiting to speak to the King," she said, trying to explain herself.

But Seaxred didn't seem interested in her explanation. "My brother and I … we were ... we were ..." he broke off.

"Were what?" Millie pressed, surprised by his fumbling manner.

"Well, it's just ... there's something that you should know about."

"What? Has something happened to George?"

"No, it's nothing like that. It's probably best if I show you. It's a very ... delicate matter."

"Okay." Millie was even more curious now.

"Millie!" interrupted a voice. Millie looked to see Leof walking towards them and seemingly very pleased with himself.

"I've managed to trade the wool and pottery in exchange for all this iron!" Leof proudly dropped the hessian sack that was weighing down his shoulder and showed Millie the three iron pots and some rough lumps of iron he had acquired.

"That's excellent!" said Millie. "What are you doing now?"

"I thought it would be best to leave it with you. It'll be safest here until we head back to Widurok in a few days."

"Of course. Good idea," Millie said, failing to mention that a few days might actually be a few months. "I'm going with Seaxred now but stay here and we can catch up when I get back."

Leof went into the palace and Millie followed the prince through the gates into the city. She wondered what it was that he was going to show her.

"Is it something secret?" she asked.

"Yes. We must be very careful. I wouldn't normally visit him in daylight."

"Who are we going to see?"

"Shhh, keep your voice down. It is a creature from Asengeard."

"Asengeard! Do you mean the land of the gods?"

"Of course the land of the gods." Seaxred then looked directly at Millie and spoke very slowly as he emphasised the importance of his words. "It's a lost creature. We *know* you have travelled through the worlds to find him."

"*What?*" Millie said in alarm.

"Don't worry, your secret is safe. Woden sent you through the world-tree to bring back his horse."

"Horse! What horse are you talking about? Is that what we are going to see now?" Millie felt very confused. Where did Seaxred think she was from? Did he know about time travel too?

Seaxred frowned. "Please don't lie to me, Millie. We know what your true intention in our kingdom is."

Millie had no idea what this could mean. She had stood upon the tree stump in order to travel to this time, but there was never any horse involved, and as far as Millie was concerned the only other intention she had here was to find a way home. Still, maybe she could use this as an opportunity to gain some knowledge.

"I think you must be referring to the stone circles near Widurok. What do you know about travelling through the world-tree?"

"It is a door to our fate and to the other realms. I often sit high up in the trees thinking over difficult matters, but it is the world-tree that bestows the greatest inspiration."

They had been walking through the old streets but now Seaxred stopped outside a disused bath house.

"He's in here," Seaxred whispered. "Hidden in the old heating chambers underground."

Before he went to knock upon the door he turned his head to quickly check the coast was clear. It wasn't. He screwed up his face irritably and swore under his breath. Millie glanced back to see what bothered him and saw they had been followed - by Mellitus.

Chapter Thirty-five: A horse and a game of Tafl

"Damn," Seaxred muttered, "he must have overheard me in the hall and followed us here. Let's see what he wants."

"Seaxred! I see you are showing the young leechcraft woman around the old city. How nice," Mellitus greeted them with sarcasm.

"Hello, bishop. How are you?"

Mellitus ignored the question and continued, spitting out his words in disgust. "Do you think there is any part of me that actually wants to live here amongst you barbarians? Of course not. I have been sent to you by Rome and invited here by the King of Kent, your father's uncle. I do it for God and so that *you* might all be saved. Yet what gratitude do I get for my efforts and teaching?"

"We receive your new religion, don't we?"

"Six long years I have been here and still your father and family make no effort to persuade your own people to embrace Christianity. Instead - this!" He looked Millie up and down with an expression of contempt. "Now tell me where you were going. I demand an answer. I have the power to cut off the trade this kingdom relies on, you know."

"I was just showing Millie the city, as you said yourself," Seaxred replied angrily.

"Liar! Too often I have seen you sneak down here under cover of darkness. I've heard you whispering in corners with your brother and that boy Edgar. You will tell me!"

"I am free to walk where I wish. You don't have the power over us that you may think. There will come a time when my brothers and I are kings of this land and when Athelbert's son, Eadbald, is the King of Kent. You can be assured that when that time comes you will be expelled from East Seax and Kent forever!"

The bishop was taken aback by this defiant response but was not to be beaten. "Foolish boy. *You* give *me* threats of expulsion!" He turned and haughtily walked off.

Seaxred looked troubled.

"Don't worry," Millie said, "he won't find what you're hiding. What was it you wanted to show me? Was it a horse?"

"I can't show you now. We will have to come back later. I can't risk it with Mellitus hanging around."

"Okay. Maybe at dusk then, and I'll bring George and Leof."

"Yes, okay. Let's meet at the corner of the street there, rather than coming together. We mustn't draw too much attention to ourselves."

They walked back to the palace, passing by a marketplace where the Roman forum had been. Millie felt as if she were on the set of a period drama film, waiting for one of the great Roman generals to arrive on a grand chariot amongst buildings that were fully functional once again.

But now there were Saxon people here, and again - in her time - there would be another culture and way of living. Layers of different aeons, piled and buried one on top of the other ...

In the centre of the square a row of men were lined up and tied together by rope. Millie thought that they might be criminals but then noticed how they had a darker complexion and different clothes to the fair-headed Saxons.

"What are those people doing over there?"

"Oh, they're Britons. There is a slave market here today."

"They're being sold? As slaves?" Millie was shocked.

"Yes. We do a roaring trade, selling slaves to lands overseas."

"But that's really unfair!" she said, thinking about the families of Britons who lived in Widurok. They had fewer rights than the Saxons but they still remained part of the community.

Seaxred shrugged. "They get treated all right. They have food and a place to sleep. Most invaders kill the natives when they land, so at least they have their lives. These are the lucky ones." It seemed to be perfectly normal to him, as it was to the slaves and their owners.

Millie felt her stomach rumble. Seaxred must been feeling hungry too, for he ushered her away from the market and back towards the old fort where now the palace was and where food would be being served.

Saeward, George and Leof were already eating with some of the palace soldiers in the hall. George and Saeward were bent over a board game in which they were totally engrossed. Millie and Seaxred sat down and joined them.

The table was laid with pork, rye bread and a bowl of lettuce; over the fire was a cauldron of soup.

"How's the meat?" Millie asked Leof.

"Excellent, I was starving."

"Did you catch this when you were hunting today, George?"

George looked up and noticed her for the first time. "Yes, we had a good time hunting. How was your day?"

"Good," Millie nodded as she tucked into her food.

George went back to concentrating on his game of Tafl.[13] It was being played on a wooden board of nine by nine squares, decorated with carved snakes in the four corners. Saeward was representing the East Saxons and had eight dark glass pieces and a special blue piece which was the King. George was representing the West Saxons and had sixteen light glass pieces. The game started with the King in the centre surrounded by his pieces and the light pieces around the outside. Saeward had to move his King first. He could win the game only if he managed to get his King out into one of the corner squares. George could win only by trapping the King.

George had played it many times before in Widurok and participated with a competitive spirit. But once he saw Millie had finished eating he was keener to lose rather than let the game drag on, as it often did. He conceded to Saeward's King and motioned for Seaxred to take his place at the board.

The three travellers were reunited for the first time that day and sat together to swap stories of their time apart. Millie was relieved to hear that one of the daughters had been up and the other was a little better. The herbs and advice Leof had given Millie seemed to be having a positive effect. George and Leof were less pleased to hear that the King wanted them all to stay until the winter. Although they agreed that more time away would probably help the villagers in Widurok to forget the drowning incident.

There was the sound of the King's arrival and the guards and the King's sons left the hall to meet him. Now alone, George saw this was his opportunity to tell Millie and Leof what he had learnt that morning.

"Saeward told me the strangest thing whilst we were hunting. I'm not quite sure what to make of it."

"What was it?" Millie asked as she and Leof both leaned in towards him.

"Well ... he said that he and Seaxred persuaded the King to send for us to help their sisters. But that actually Saeward and Seaxred really wanted us here for their own reason. They want us to do something with a supposedly *mythical* creature that they have been looking after."

"Oh!" exclaimed Millie thinking of what had happened to her today.

"What creature?" Leof asked.

"Not a horse?" Millie suggested.

"Well, I don't know what to believe but ... Saeward says they have Sleipnir here, here in Lundenburh."

"You mean Woden's Sleipnir?" Leof was astonished. "But no man has ever seen him! He rides for the gods."

"Who is Sleipnir?" Millie asked.

"He is Woden's horse. A dark grey stallion with eight legs," Leof explained "But it can't be true. Why would Sleipnir be in our earthly realm. And how could he possibly have been captured?"

"Well, I would normally be more sceptical, but I think I was there the night that Saeward caught him." George briefly told them both what he had witnessed immediately after he had time-travelled and reminded Leof of the blood-stained grass at the stone circle on the morning that they had met. "Through their messengers, Saeward and Seaxred have worked out I was there and have somehow concluded that I must therefore have some link to Sleipnir."

"We shall all be cursed!" Leof went pale and fear darkened his eyes.

"There's no such thing as a horse with eight legs. It just doesn't exist," said Millie bluntly.

"Well *something* was shot down and injured."

"Seaxred tried to take me to see something very secret today. I think it was a horse."

"You saw it?"

"No, we didn't go there in the end. We were followed by Mellitus and so Seaxred thought it best to come back. But he said that he knew Woden had sent me through the worlds to find his horse."

Leof became even more ashen and sat shaking his head.

"Leof, it'll be okay. If the creature is real there's probably a logical explanation it's got an abnormal number of legs," George said reassuringly. "All mammals can be born with extra limbs. It could have occurred through a genetic defect or as part of a conjoined twin. It doesn't mean it's from the gods."

Leof looked at him in confusion, not really understanding what these concepts of biology meant.

"I agree. Leof, there's probably an explanation," Millie said taking his hand.

"I hope you're right, but if it is Sleipnir then there will be a famine across the land."

"Is there an old folk story about Sleipnir?" she asked, hoping to lighten Leof's mood.

"Yes, my mother used to tell it to me when I was very young," Leof replied.

"Do you still remember it? I would love to hear it."

"I think so." Leof altered his tone to that of a narrator and began his tale: "The story of Sleipnir begins long ago when the gods had only just arrived at Asengeard and our realm of Middangeard was very young. To protect their land from the giants the gods decided to build a high wall around Asengeard. However, the human stonemason who offered to build it for them was actually a giant in disguise. He promised to finish the wall within six months and in return he demanded from the gods the goddess Freo's hand in marriage, the moon and the sun.

"The gods were so sure that a human would never be able to build the wall in such a short time that they agreed and gave the giant use of a magic grey stallion to help him. It soon became evident that the wall *would* be finished in time and that the gods would have to repay their debt. The gods were so outraged that one of them devised a plan.

"A few days before the six-month period of work was nearing completion, one of the gods transformed himself into the most beautiful white mare and lured the giant's horse away into the forest. The stallion and the mare ran together all night and all day. The giant gave chase but could not catch his horse. Unable to finish the work on time, he returned to Asengeard in a terrible rage and began to tear down the wall. As he did so Thunor recognised that he was not a man but a giant and smashed him into pieces with his hammer.

"The horses continued to gallop together for many days and nights. Thereafter an eight-legged stallion was born. The foal grew to be the fastest and greatest horse there ever was, able to carry the rider over all the seven realms. Woden took the horse for his own and named it Sleipnir."[14]

"So Sleipnir was born from a god and the magic horse of a giant?"

"Yes, and he is the most admired of all horses."

Enlightened by this legend, Millie and George understood the importance of the horse to the King's sons. They must have been almost star-struck when they had first seen him.

That evening, as night began to fall, the three of them left to meet the two princes at the street Seaxred had arranged with Millie. This time she took extra care to ensure that they weren't being followed. Seaxred and Saeward were already both there when they arrived, waiting outside the entrance to the abandoned Roman baths.

"Hi, I'm glad you've come," Saeward said. He escorted them with a lit torch down some steps into the underground heating room where slaves would have burnt coal and wood to heat the water for wealthy Romans. To the side of the room was a wooden door.

"Before we go in, you must promise to Seaxnot that you will never tell a living soul of what you are about to see."

Millie, George and Leof each nodded solemnly and Saeward raised his hand to knock upon the door.

Chapter Thirty-six: Woden's horse

Saeward knocked three times, paused, and then knocked again four times.

"Who is it?" came a voice.

"It's us, Edgar - Saeward and Seaxred."

They heard the sound of a wooden bolt on the other side being slid back. The door opened just wide enough for them to squeeze through, one at a time.

Inside, the room was cold and damp. The only natural light was a dim ray that shone down from a gap close to the ceiling, which made a halo of light round the young boy who had let them in.

"This is Edgar, he has been looking after Sleipnir since the day we brought him here. Edgar, this is Millie, George and Leof from the standing stones," Saeward said, introducing them and shining his torch around.

Edgar nodded and stepped aside. Behind him a dark grey horse lay on a pile of hay, its body covered by a large blanket. He lifted his head and breathed loudly through his nostrils as Edgar knelt down and affectionately stroked his nose.

"You've got some visitors, Slippy. They've come to get you well again." Edgar looked up at them and then, on Saeward's nod, he pulled back the blanket and revealed the horse's true form.

Millie, George and Leof gasped! Not only was the stallion larger than any horse they had ever seen but protruding from its body were eight legs. As real as their own.

Leof at once fell to his knees and started uttering prayers to the gods. Millie felt like she was a little girl again, day-dreaming of mythical horses, and George frantically tried to rationalise what he was seeing. Could it be a long-forgotten breed that had almost died out or been hunted to near extinction? Or, as he had previous speculated, a horse born with a genetic defect?

Sleipnir moved his head slightly and studied them with tired eyes and then he closed them as if to sleep and a shiver ran through his body. Edgar quickly covered him with the blanket again, not wanting Sleipnir to suffer any distress.

"He is ill," Edgar said.

"Will he live?" George asked.

"He needs to be back in Asengeard where he belongs," Seaxred said.

"You will take Slippy back to Woden, won't you?" Edgar asked George.

"We don't really know how to do that," George replied.

"But you came through the world-tree to get him! You must take what it is you have travelled so far for. Then our people and kingdom will be safe."

"But we … we just came here to help your sisters," Millie protested. "We can't take a sick horse back with us to Widurok."

"He'll never make the journey," George agreed. "Is he not lame from where you shot him with the arrow?"

The horse raised its head again as though attempting to join in with the discussion of his fate.

"No, the wound is healed. It is three years being imprisoned down here that has made Slippy sick - but there is nowhere else we can take him, without being seen. I can't imagine how Saba, or Mellitus would react if they saw him, or anyone for that matter."

"That's why we were so excited to hear of you both, and George arriving on the solstice like that, the very same night Slippy was there!" Seaxred said. "We know you have come to this realm looking for the horse. You must be honest with us! I don't understand why you are making excuses. I see you are not gods, but you *must* save him and take him back where he belongs."

"We can try and help him to grow stronger and then take him to Widurok, but we're just not sure *how* to take him back through the world-tree," Millie said.

"Slippy will go with you this winter solstice. Woden uses the world-tree at Yule time when he visits us as Father Winter."

"So we have three months to get him well again." Millie was thinking of the time-frame Saberht had given her to stay with his daughters. No doubt the seed of this idea had been sown by Saeward and Seaxred.

"You know about medicine, you can help."

"What if we can't?"

"You will do it. And you will be well rewarded."

George didn't like the threatening tone in Saeward's voice. He, Millie and Leof would have to escape from Lundenburh very quickly if anything did go wrong.

"Okay. To be clear, what you're asking is that we return Slippy to good health and then take him to the tree in the stone hearg at the winter solstice."

"Yes."

George nodded thoughtfully. "We'll do our best. But in return we need to speak to the palace Druid, or whoever has the most knowledge about the stones. We will not leave with Slippy until we have spoken with him."

"I will find the most knowledgeable Druid in the kingdom and arrange a meeting. Hopefully they haven't all been banished by Mellitus."

Millie knelt next to Leof who was still sitting on his knees, dumbfounded by what he was seeing.

"Come and stroke his mane, Leof," Millie said as she ran her hand over the horse's soft coat. Leof shakily put his hand next to hers.

"He is beautiful. He shouldn't be down here."

"No, you're right. He needs fresh air and to get out of this damp," said George.

"We can't risk taking him outside."

"Can't we take him over to Thorny Island where we went hunting? He could get there by boat."

"No, Saba is there too often."

"Let's start by making him more comfortable down here. He needs to be cleaned out every day and given fresh hay." Millie had been riding many times and knew the basics about caring for horses. "Have you tried feeding him warm porridge?" she asked Edgar, who shook his head. "Then we will start with that in the morning. Seaxred, you must ask the servants to prepare it. We can't risk anyone seeing smoke coming from here. Tell them it is for your horse."

"Good idea! Have it left outside your stables and Leof or I can collect it and bring it down here."

"I suggest as soon as he can stand we must think of a way to move him out of this dark and cold, somewhere he won't been seen."

"Yes, anything you need we will arrange. Thank you, thank you both," Saeward said gratefully. "It was unwise of me to have brought him here and pointless to have shot him. I did it to please Saba ... and yet I never even showed Slippy to him! Instead I have carried three years of shame inside me. There's no excuse for what I did, only that we are all scared our way of life is coming to an end. Our world of the old gods is dying and a new Christian one is beginning. We are the rulers of this kingdom; we have to make the choices that decide all our fates."

They left Edgar as he got ready to bed down next to Sleipnir. Millie, George and Leof walked back to the palace separately from the princes so as not to cause any suspicion. It had been arranged that Leof would sleep in George's room. All three were exhausted from the day's events and were very happy to finally see their beds.

"Sleipnir *must* have been waiting for you to come through the stones when he was shot," Leof whispered to George as he lay down on his straw mattress.

The idea kept going round George's head as he tried to sleep. Despite his rationality he couldn't help wondering if this really was his purpose in being here, in this time. Had he been sent here by some ancient gods to help a horse get home? Images of Woden, giant ash trees and galloping through Asengeard dominated his dreams as he tossed and turned through the night.

Leof, too, lay awake thinking. For all the stories his parents and the elders in the village had told him about the gods and Asengeard, none of them had ever seen any of the gods themselves. They had only had heard Thunor through the roar of thunder or felt Frige's kindness in the good harvest. Yet he, young Leof, had seen Sleipnir with his own eyes. He had touched the very horse that bore Woden across the worlds. Oh, how he longed to tell the villagers! But he had made his promise to Saeward and was always true to his word. To Leof there was no doubt what he had seen, and he understood the princes' concern about the repercussions.

Chapter Thirty-seven: Challenges and responsibilities

George, Leof and Millie felt they had no choice but to stay in Lundenburh until mid-winter in December. Saeward's promise of finding them a Druid was the only hope they had of gaining knowledge about the way home; and anyway, they hadn't been given the choice of leaving without first fulfilling Saeward's wishes, or the King's.

They had no plan as to what would happen to Sleipnir if they took him to Widurok, but they decided between them that the best thing to do was to comply with the wishes of the princes and the King and cross that bridge when the time came. Maybe they could release Sleipnir into the wild woodland near Widurok? Millie and George strongly doubted that one of the gods would be coming to collect him!

George took on the responsibility of looking after Sleipnir and returning him back to health. Every morning for the first few weeks he went to Seaxred's stable to collect the pan of warm oats to take down to the disused baths. While Edgar made sure Sleipnir ate, George mucked out the old hay and replaced it with fresh stuff. Once the stable was clean, Sleipnir was groomed with a brush and George and Edgar tried to encourage him to his feet. George persevered with their strict regime and by the end of the second week the horse was walking around the stable in circles and out into the main chamber of the heating room. It was a wonder to George that any animal would be able to co-ordinate that many legs, but Sleipnir managed pretty well, considering.

Although George was happy at the progress Sleipnir was making, he felt frustrated that the space in the stable was so confined. What George really needed was to be able to take him outside and try and get him trotting and eventually galloping; but how to move him without drawing attention to his legs?

An idea came to George one day when he saw the slaves dressing Saberht's horse in a winter rug. George asked Saeward to instruct one of the weavers to make a dark grey rug that would fully cover a horse and drop to the ground, like a blanket. George gave Saeward the exact measurements to pass on and a week later the coat had been made and delivered. When the rug was draped over Sleipnir and tied under the tail at the back and around the front, the multiple legs were almost completely hidden. It also kept him warm as the weather grew colder and colder, for Sleipnir was very underweight and his ribs showed painfully through his skin.

With Sleipnir now in disguise the princes gave their blessings for George to venture with him out into the open. North of the town was an area of woodland and meadows that was reserved just for the King's family to hunt in. Away from too many prying eyes, this was an ideal space for Sleipnir. It was still too risky to go out in daylight so Edgar and George woke an hour before sunrise and left Lundenburh under cover of dark. The first time they ventured out, Sleipnir was so tired from the walk that all he wanted to do was lie on the grass and rest. But each day and each week he grew stronger and stronger, thanks to the fresh air and big open grassy spaces. Seaxred and Saeward frequently joined George and Edgar with their own horses. On occasion Seaxbald begged to come and Saeward would lift him up to sit in front of him. Being a herd animal, Sleipnir enjoyed the company of other horses and George could see that it lifted his spirits.

At first George didn't ride Sleipnir. He felt the horse needed more time to gain strength and felt uneasy that he might be seen as encroaching on Woden's property. But after a while it was necessary as Sleipnir became ready to trot, and then to canter and finally fit enough to gallop.

George felt a great sense of accomplishment as he witnessed Sleipnir's transformation back to a gallant stallion. He had been at death's door when George first met him and could barely raise his head. Now he was galloping and frolicking as though he had never been ill. Three months of patience and hard work had paid off.

*

Millie spent most of the autumn with Sunngifu and Swanhild. The medicine she had made for them only lasted a few days, after which Millie had no more paracetamol to grind up. Instead she gave them a weak tea from more of the feverfew which she and Leof picked from the nearby countryside. She was doubtful of its medical qualities but hoped it would make the daughters feel looked after.

It was arranged that the girls were to be moved to a warmer part of the palace, closer to where Millie slept. Their bedding was made fresh twice a week on Millie's request. In the morning she would wake them at sunrise and have breakfast with the girls to make sure they ate well and regained their strength. Like George, Millie too found it easier to work to a school-like regime with a daily plan. Every day after breakfast the girls dressed properly and walked with Millie to Lundenwic and back. In the first weeks this seemed too far and they would often turn around after they had got half-way, but as the girls grew fitter it stopped being such an effort. They spent longer exploring the new town and often brought spices and herbs to take back to the palace kitchen.

The girls took well to Millie. She was very different to the other women who had raised and cared for them. They looked forward to spending time with her and seemed to trust her judgement in what was best for them, which made Millie's task a lot easier. Sunngifu and Swanhild were both very thin when Millie first met them but over the autumn months they put on weight as they regained their appetites and grew more active.

As Millie had done with Sifelda, Alwun and Edyth, she introduced lots of new games to Sunngifu and Swanhild that they had never heard of, such as hopscotch, skipping rope rhymes, sticky toffee, tennis and rounders. Now it was colder outside she also played indoor games with them like snakes and ladders, which she drew out on the floor in chalk and made dice from wood. In the late afternoons she taught them how to do different hairstyles - French plaits, bunches and fishtails - letting them experiment and practise on her own hair. Millie also sang them chart songs she knew and dance routines she had made up with her friends back home.

In the late afternoon and evening the girls spent time with their mother, Ethelgoda, and if he was home, Saberht. By December they were very different girls. With their bedridden days long forgotten, they had regained their zest for life and were as happy and energetic as any other children. Millie felt her job was done; now they needed to be with their own people who would teach them the skills they really needed to be the daughters of the King - how to sew and make clothes, play the harp and keep the household. Millie noted how Saberht observed the girls' changing health and hoped that he would be happy enough to let her leave with George and Leof before the winter solstice, but not so happy that he wanted her to stay permanently as the girls' nanny. She could only trust that the princes had enough influence over their father to be able to persuade him otherwise, should this happen. For Millie's greatest fear, and the nightmare that sometimes haunted her dreams, was that she would somehow be left behind in Saxon Essex without George.

The late afternoon and evenings were the time Millie was free to seek out George and Leof and spend time with them. The daylight was getting shorter and shorter and most of the evening was passed in dim light. Only the King's family had the luxury of candles to light the hall and carry with them. The majority of Saxons used rush lights made from rushes that had been dipped in animal fat. They produced a good light and burnt slowly, but the smell of the burning fat made Millie retch. It seemed to her that most of the people had entered into a sort of hibernation, eating less and sleeping more to conserve energy.

*

As for Leof, he was very glad that their stay in Lundenburh was extended. Now he had experienced the excitement of being in a large town and meeting completely new people, he didn't think he would ever be quite so content living in Widurok.

For most of the autumn Leof spent his time down at Lundenwic's docks and in the marketplace. He was fascinated by the foreign crafts and goods that he saw and was keen to learn new skills and techniques from the many traders. Some of them would leave and return regularly each week, others had taken weeks or even months just to arrive here, having passed through many other ports on their way. As well as bringing foreign goods they also brought to the capital new ideas and ways of doing things that Leof had never seen practised before: pottery that was finished using a different glaze, that when put over hot embers didn't crack like the glaze they used; unfamiliar herbs they used to put in milk to kept it fresher for longer; how to cook with the spices that they carried and which ones complemented which meats.

The traders also had different ways of writing and talking, and Leof learnt how to greet them in their own tongues and could recognise which boats arrived from where and what goods they would be carrying. Some of the traders wore strange clothes and had skin and eyes darker than Leof had ever seen. They spoke of hot lands, dry deserts and warm seas. The gods they worshipped were very different and the stories and myths they told Leof could barely relate to, as he tried hard to picture what a camel or elephant might look like. Others told of the grand buildings of Rome and Greece - ancient monuments left over from a time hundreds of years ago, or the great pyramids that sat beside the river Nile. A long way from East Seax!

Leof's mind was filled with wonder and of the many tales he would have to tell everyone back in Widurok. He only hoped that when he returned there would not still be whisperings of his drowning. Maybe by sharing all the new stories he had heard, and the skills he had learnt, he would become a valued member of their community once again.

George and Millie also relied on Leof for his help in fulfilling their tasks. Leof had heard some very unpleasant rumours about the fate of those who had failed their rulers and he feared for the lives of his friends (and his own), should Sleipnir's and the daughters' condition deteriorate.

It had taken George and Millie quite some time to persuade Leof that they had not been sent from the gods to find Sleipnir. And even when Leof nodded in agreement he still couldn't help retaining some doubt. For there was no creature alive like Sleipnir on this realm.

Once Sleipnir was moved to a warmer stable it was arranged that Leof would sleep with Edgar in the stable and to be on guard for anyone that might come by. He also helped each day to prepare Sleipnir before sunrise for his trip to the northern woodland. He too witnessed Sleipnir grow stronger and his protruding ribs disappear into a healthy layer of fat and muscle.

*

As the weeks passed on, George and Millie waited patiently to be visited by a wise Druid, as the two older princes had promised. They were both beginning to wonder if this meeting would ever happen. Then one afternoon, just when George felt he couldn't possibly remind Saeward about it again, they were called to the great hall to meet a Druid of high repute.

The wise man was tall and dressed in a long grey cloak, similar to a monk's habit, but it was tied at the waist with an ornate gold-threaded belt. The man was very old, perhaps the oldest person Millie and George had seen in their time here. He had a long white beard that looked as if it had never been trimmed and his face was very wrinkled, like old leather. He was sitting at the table writing on parchment. To both George and Millie's relief they were alone and away from prying ears; they could ask the man's advice privately.

"I have been asked to meet with you," he said slowly rising to his feet. "What is it you want to know?"

"We have come from Widurok, near to the stone hearg and the world-tree; you may have heard of it," George said.

"Yes, I have been there on several occasions. It is a very sacred place. The tree holds great magic."

"We ... we believe ..." - George struggled to search for the best words to use - "We travelled back through time in the world-tree, but we're a little uncertain, well *very* uncertain, how to get back."

"Stanweard."

"Stanweard? What does that mean?" George asked.

"The elves that guard the stones. Not many folk have seen them but they are there, between the trees."

"Do they know how we can get home?"

"Yes. You will need to find them. But they will be watching out for you, no doubt."

George frowned; this was hardly much help to them. He had hoped the Druid would have the answers, not that they would be told to ask someone else. The Druid saw his frown and smiled.

"Don't worry, you are on the right track. The world-tree works different magic on the Modraniht than it does on the Litha. If one solstice carried you here, the other will carry you home."

"But we're not gods!" Millie proclaimed. "How can we be sure it'll work for us?"

"You got *here* somehow. You must have faith that it can happen."

Millie remembered the letters she had found, addressed to Mr Gordon. There was the postlady mentioned in them who had come back to Wybrook in the winter. Maybe the *winter* solstice was the key! They just needed to find the elves, and Millie was pretty sure they had already encountered them on the journey down here.

Chapter Thirty-eight: Back to Walla

Having gained all the knowledge Millie and George could from the Druid, and with the daughters and horse in good health, they felt the time had come to leave Lundenburh.

It was decided by Saeward and Seaxred that Millie and Leof would travel early the following morning by rowing boat for Teidana, taking with them two of the palace guardsmen as protectors. From there they would continue the journey by foot, on to Walla and Bordley.

As Sleipnir could hardly travel in the boat, George would leave separately under cover of darkness. He would ride Sleipnir, alongside Saeward and Seaxred and their horses. They planned to take the old Roman road that led north-east directly out of Lundenburh, which then meets up with the road they had travelled down on. It would be dangerous and cold travelling at night, but at least they would benefit from a full moon. And at Walla they would be reunited with Millie and Leof.

*

Millie, Leof and George rose before dawn the next day. Millie had her belongings packed and ready and Leof had his hessian sack of iron and some spices he wanted to bring as gifts for his family.

They went into the great hall and found the princes waiting for them with Queen Ethelgoda. On the table a bag of food had been packed for them by the servants, and a bladder filled with weak ale.

"You must be on your way as soon as possible, the winter daylight does not last long," Ethelgoda said. "There is enough food here to last you two days, in case you have to stop."

"Our father wishes to speak with you before you leave - George, you too," said Saeward and nodded over to the King's chair. They hadn't noticed him sitting there and bowed their heads in respect. Either side of him were sitting Swanheld and Sunngifu. They smiled at Millie then ran over to hug her farewell.

"Millie, George and Leofwine! Sadly my sons tell me that you must leave today while the weather is fine. Tomorrow is Thunorsday and no doubt the skies will open and let loose the rains."

On the table next to Saberht's chair lay a shining sword and its scabbard case, a small wooden box and a leather pouch. The King stood up and took the sword in his hands.

"These are gifts from the spoils of battle. My sons have asked me to reward you for your deeds to my daughters and country."

He beckoned to George to come closer and placed the sword in his arms.

"This is to protect you and your sister as you travel back to your homestead."

George turned over the sword in awe. Few men owned such a weapon - a valuable possession only ever handed down as heirlooms or received as gifts from kings. It was a lot heavier than it looked, being made of twisted iron on the inside and coated with steel to give it strength and sharpness. The pommel was animal horn and embellished with layers of silver and gold, with a garnet on the centre of each side. Down the side of the blade faint markings of runes were inscribed into the metal. George ran his hand carefully over one side of the long blade. Both edges had been sharpened and they tapered down to a razor-sharp point.

"It was won in battle by my cousin many years ago. I hope it will serve you as well as it served him," King Saberht said. He passed George the scabbard which was made from two pieces of wood glued together with thin leather covering them to make it watertight. On the outside a blue ribbon was wound around it, and on the inside it was lined with fleece to protect the sword.

To Leof, the King gave the small leather pouch. Leof emptied the contents out onto his palm. There were thirty silver coins and three gold thrymsas coins.

"Is that real gold?" Millie whispered to George.

"Yes. Twenty of those silver sceattas make up a gold piece."

Leof bowed down low to the King. He had never had such personal wealth and hardly felt worthy of it.

There was just the box left on the table which the King presented to Millie.

"Millie, your magic has woven its way into the bodies and souls of my dear daughters. They show no sign of fragility, look how well and full of life they are! I give you a gift of the Goddess Freo."

She opened it and inside was a necklace. It was set with amethysts alternating with gold beads to form a choker. In the centre hung a carved pendant depicting a Waelcyrge woman riding a wolf with a raven on her shoulder. It was beautiful.[15]

"Thank you," Millie said graciously, "but these gifts are too much. We can't possible accept them."

"All kings must reward their people. It is the duty of a king if he is to expect a long reign and loyalty in the battlefields," Saberht explained and looked over to his sons to direct this comment towards them.

As they left to board the boat Leof and George collected their two seaxes swords they had left with the guard. George could no longer carry his now he had the sword, so he gave it to Millie, showing her how to tie it horizontally at her waist.

They walked through the ruins and the Saxon buildings, silently lost in their own thoughts and worries.

"The next time you see this place it will be crammed with tall modern buildings and the streets will be full of cars and buses," George said to Millie as she clambered into the boat next to Leof and the guardsmen.

"Let's hope so."

It was early still and they had a good amount of daylight with which to make the journey. George watched from dry land as the boat was set adrift down the Temesa. He was uneasy and worried about the dangers they might face without him, but he knew he had to be strong. He had his own journey to prepare for: one that involved all the perils of the dark winter forest.

"Good luck!" Millie called out to George and stood up to wave as they floated away. She felt panicky to be leaving without him, although she knew that it was the best solution. She tried instead to think of all the positive outcomes there had been. The plague wasn't coming; the sons believed the gods would forgive them; Leof had traded all the yarn and pottery; the daughters were well; and Sleipnir was galloping around like a young foal.

*

The little boat followed the current of the river downstream and with two strong guardsmen in charge of the oars, it was only a few hours before they reached the entrance to the river Hrothingas. This time the flow of the water was against them and their progress was slowed by half.

They passed the same villages and homesteads that they had when it had still been summer, but now it was winter and the landscape looked very different. Not only had the leaves gone from the trees but the villages seemed almost abandoned. The sole indication of habitation was from the small spirals of smoke that rose from fires round which the villagers huddled as they hibernated inside their dwellings.

The guardsmen moored the boat for a late lunch and to rest their arms. The journey seemed endless and slow. The light was beginning to fade and large rain clouds had begun to settle over them. The pressure to reach Teidana was growing. They got back into the boat and took an oar each, to try and speed up the journey. The first drops of rain started to fall and before long it was pouring down upon them, drenching their clothes and filling the boat. They desperately needed shelter. Determined they rowed on, wet, tired, cold and hungry.

Millie and Leof recognised Teidana when they spotted the boat they had travelled in with Oswin, pulled up on the river bank. Almost crying with relief they moored their own rowing-boat next to it and dragged out their belongings.

Millie sounded the horn Wigheard had given her but the noise was lost to the beating of the rain. Regardless, they made their way up the path to the main dwellings. One of the guardsmen banged loudly on the door of the main hall. It was opened by a man who looked at them with suspicion. Beyond him they could see and feel the heat of the fire.

"Wes Hal! We are friends of Oswin," Leof said, shivering. "We come looking for shelter and warmth. We bring news from Lundenburh and the plague."

"Travellers seeking shelter," the man called back to someone inside. He waited for a response and then opened the door wide and hustled them in from the cold. "Come in and get yourselves warmed by the fire."

The room was filled with families drinking and eating their evening meal. When they saw how drenched their guests were, a few of the women rushed up to fetch dry clothes and blankets. Once the four of them had changed their garments, Oswin found them a place close to the roaring fire where they could warm up. He was very happy to make their acquaintance again and sat down between Millie and Leof. Their wet clothes were hung up to dry and their belongings placed next to them, near the edge of the fire. One of the women ladled out hot cups of broth from a large pot and brought them over for each of them. The four travellers were an object of curiosity and everyone crowded around them, keen for some fresh conversation and news to brighten the long cold night ahead.

"Tell us of Lundenwic," a man asked. "Are there many boats that sail there?"

"Does the King keep his court in the palace still, or is he elsewhere in the kingdom?"

"What news of plague?"

"How has the harvest been throughout the land?"

"The threat of plague has gone. The King and his family are well in Lundenburh and the gods have promised a mild winter," Leof said.

"Well, I'll drink to that!" One of the men lifted up his cup of honey mead and the hall cheered and drank with him.

It turned into a lively night as the weary travellers were persuaded to stay up late telling stories of the city many times over to the people of Teidana.

They slept in the hall, staying close to the fire as it burnt down to embers. Despite the throbbing of their arms from the hours of rowing, they all slept soundly and deeply, late into the morning.

The next day the weather was dry. They left the boat securely tied to the bank for the guardsmen to return in and set off on foot for Walla with their damp belongings. They took the same route they had come with Bordley, only this time they were warier of hungry wolves. The journey took most of the hours of daylight. As they approached Walla, Millie sounded her horn again, although she felt so familiar here that it didn't seem necessary. They were greeted with open arms by Bordley's family and were made to feel very welcome.

The family all wondered where George was and questioned the long period of time they had been in Lundenburh. Leof assured them that George would be here by the morning and that he was perfectly safe and well. They ate supper together, with Burhwynne making sure she sat close to Leof and that his every need was attended to. Before they turned in to rest, Millie knew she had to confide in Bordley about Sleipnir before George arrived with him. It was going to be too hard to keep the horse a secret and she felt she could trust Bordley. Maybe it was because there was something niggling at her about him. The colour of his eyes, the shape of his hairline and his accent, which wasn't the same as the others ... It sounded, well, more like hers and George's.

Millie didn't know how else to broach the subject except by being direct with Bordley. She followed him as he went to check on the livestock.

"Have you ever heard the name Bobby Gordon?" she asked.

Bordley stopped still in his tracks as though he had been frozen. It took him a moment to recover before he replied. "Yes. I do believe I have." He turned to face her and they looked at each other anew.

"I ... I haven't ever talked about this to anyone. In a way I've managed to cut that bit of my past from my memory." He paused and Millie could see the pain it caused him to reminisce. "When you first came here it brought it all back. I had my suspicions about you and George from the moment I saw you. Something about you reminded me of my true childhood and of course your names are so, well ... modern."

"Do you know how you got here?"

"No. But I've thought about it so much, it's almost driven me crazy. In the end I've accepted the 'not knowing' instead. I still think of my family, though: How are they? Are they even alive?"

"Your mother's well. She has always missed you."

"And my father?"

"I'm afraid he died a while ago. He never gave up looking for you. It was all the research he had done that helped me to work out what had happened to George and come here myself."

"Poor old Dad. My disappearing like that must have really destroyed him. Did he ever work out a way for us to get home?"

"No, I don't think so. But the King's Druid has given us some advice. It's possible that it is the winter solstice which enables us to go forward in time and the summer which has brought us back."

"You haven't got long then. I wish I could come with you, I want for nothing more than to see my mother, but I have a family to look after - seven children to feed. Or one less soon, if my eldest daughter manages to run off with Leof." A small smile flickered across his sad face. "Honestly, she's talked about nothing else!"

Millie laughed.

"There's also a small matter of a horse." Millie took her time to explain what had really happened in Lundenburh.

"Well, I'll believe it when I see it. Goodness knows what creatures live in these woods. You can put him in the stable with Elvina. He will be safe from any prying eyes, don't you worry. We'll talk again in the morning, about everything." Bordley (or Bobby) finished seeing to the livestock and they walked back to their huts to turn in for the night.

It was still dark outside when Millie and Leof were awoken in the early hours by the arrival of George and the princes. They were both relieved that they had all made it in one piece.

Milllie and Leof gave up their beds to the new arrivals and took the horses to the stables to feed them.

George and the princes slept on while Millie and Leof had breakfast and talked to Bordley. Millie and Bordley discussed everything that had happened to her since the day George had left three-and-a-half years earlier. For Bordley, talking to someone of a similar background was like turning on the tap of his memories. He eagerly quizzed Millie for every bit of news. Were his favourite bands still making music? Did his mother continue to run their shop? Who was prime minister now? Did Millie know any of his friends he had grown up with? Millie told him what she knew and described how the world had changed since he left. Leof listened intently and with amazement, unable to imagine how a mobile phone or the internet could work without magic.

The princes didn't stay for long. As soon as they had eaten they bade George, Leof and Millie a final farewell and galloped off with the two guardsmen in tow. Pious, gallant and noble, they already seemed like Kings of East Seax.

"We need to think about our own journey from here," George said to Millie. "It might be better to risk travelling during the day than in the night."

"I thought you were worried about being seen?"

"Being seen? I could hardly see myself in the dark, and it was so cold. Besides, we all rode horseback. Elvina will be carrying the food and belongings and there will only be Slippy to ride."

"You're right, daylight is the best option. The roads seem deserted anyway; we didn't pass anyone when we walked up here. Everyone is too busy trying to keep warm."

"I'd quite like to get warm myself," George said, and cupped his freezing hands to his face. They walked back to the main hall and huddled with Bordley's family close to the fire.

The next day they were all refreshed and ready to leave. George was delighted to be reunited with Elvina. He stroked her long neck and she nuzzled at his back, just as happy to see George.

"I have something for your family, Leof," Bordley said solemnly as he carefully put an urn filled with ashes from Wigheard's funeral pyre into Elvina's saddle bag. He also held something else in his hands, a child's T-shirt, very un-Saxon. "It's what I was wearing when I went missing."

"You kept it all this time!"

"Yes, it was the one thing I had to remind me of where I had come from. If you do make it back, could you give it to my mother for me? So she knows I really am safe. I've a letter for her too." He put a folded up piece of parchment and the T-shirt in the bag next to the urn. Millie and George promised that they would do everything they could to deliver the keepsakes.

Leof said an emotional goodbye to Burhwynne and the three teenagers set off once again, Elvina and Sleipnir between them.

Chapter Thirty-nine: The elves

They walked back to the Roman road that would lead them to the Dunmadu crossroads. For many hours they plodded through marshy land, open meadows and forests of bare trees. The road was wetter and muddier now it was winter and there was no warm sun to dry the ground. Their leather boots had thin soles and didn't offer the comfort that Millie was used to.

They took it in turns to sit on Sleipnir while the other two walked alongside leading Elvina. Bordley had given them directions that would take them around the fallen bridge in the Hrothingas valley without having to walk too far out of their way. They stopped briefly at the river for lunch and to refill their water carriers. They barely felt rested when they set off again, but it was on their minds that the days were short and that they had to find shelter before dark. They also needed to somehow make contact with the elves - that is, if they truly existed. As chance would have it, it was on the same stretch of road where George had previously thought he had seen the two elves, that he saw one again.

George was riding Sleipnir and was being extra vigilant for any sign of movement in the woods, making the most of his higher vantage point. Suddenly a figure darted across the path in front of him and straight over into the trees opposite, quick and yet with a certain elegance, almost as though its feet were barely touching the ground. An elf! It was almost like in invitation to follow. The others were walking in front and hadn't seen him. George shouted to them and tugged hard at Sleipnir's reins, pulling the horse into the forest to chase after the elf. He was no longer in sight but George carried on riding in the same direction, keeping his eyes peeled, until he was stopped by a small river. George turned Sleipnir around and found his way blocked by a tall, thin man standing right before him.

The man's face was young but his hair was so fair it was almost white, making him look older than his years. The long smock he wore was also white and added to his ghostly appearance. The man beckoned George to follow him as he turned without speaking a word and began to walk on. George jumped down from the horse and did as he was bade. He hoped Millie and Leof had come after him; he didn't want to risk going too deep into the woods and getting separated from them.

"My friends are waiting for me," George said, unsure of the intentions of this strange man.

"They will join you soon."

Millie and Leof hadn't seen the elf and were taken by surprise at George's sudden dash into the trees. They shouted after him but there was no reply and so they waited impatiently for his return and then decided to go after him. Sleipnir's hoof prints were clearly marked into the mud and were easy to follow. The tracks stopped at a river and then continued on almost at a right angle. The hoof prints were much shallower now and were joined by George's footprints and someone else's, whose footprints were very faint and much larger.

"Elves," whispered Leof pointing to them. "See how their print barely makes a mark, so nimble and light."

They followed the tracks through the woods until they discovered Sleipnir, alone and tied to a tree at the base of a long mossy mound.

"Slippy!" Millie cried running to him. "What are you doing here? Where's George?"

Sleipnir nuzzled at her ear, as though trying to whisper an answer.

"He can't be far from here. George! George!" Leof shouted.

Millie studied the earth for prints. The ground in front of them was banked up like old ramparts and it was at the base of this that the footprints ended. Millie frowned and knelt down on the mound. It felt hard underneath, harder than mossy ground should be, and it looked as if it had been disturbed. She knelt down and pulled at a clump of moss. There was a wooden panel underneath.

"Leof, give me hand! I've found something," Millie called.

Together they pushed hard at the wood and it flipped up to reveal some narrow steps descending down towards a dim light. Leof tied Elvina up next to Sleipnir and they cautiously climbed down into a large burrow. The space was clearly occupied and had seating and bedding as well as a kitchen area. It was a long narrow room. The floor was carpeted with moss and the walls and arched ceiling were decorated with plant and tree roots that wove their way in and out. The light was coming from a door which was ajar on the other side of the steps and opened at ground level onto a garden.

A man appeared at the doorway, merging into the sunlight in his white attire. He didn't speak but beckoned for them to come with him. They walked out into a garden that was beautifully organised into rows of winter vegetables. Somewhere a pipe was being played and a cheerful melody filled the air. It felt surreal, like they had happened upon a secret world. Millie assumed that this was where the people they called elves must live. Were they really magical creatures or just a different race, living parallel to the Saxons in their own separate society? Millie would have liked to have believed they were magical, as Leof believed, but her education made her doubt it.

The man led Millie and Leof through a row of holly trees weighed down with red berries to a circular hedged garden in which another elf sat at a round table. He too was dressed in white but his tunic was held together by a large gold brooch pinned to his shoulder. George was sitting opposite him, stroking a very happy dog with a wagging tail.

"Fen!" Leof cried in surprise and delight.

The dog leapt from George's side straight up into Leof's arms.

"You're alive! I can't believe it! I never thought I'd see you again."

Fen licked his master's face in excitement and Leof laughed with happiness, both overjoyed to see one another.

"The elves were there when we were attacked. They found Fen half-dead and brought him back here with them," George explained.

The elf from the barrow spoke in low tones to the elf at the table, then bowed his head to them and left.

"Please," the elf said, motioning them to sit.

The table was a large tree stump that had been carved out underneath to make a toadstool shape. The stools on which they sat were large logs which had been sculpted to match the table.

"Now you are all here, you may tell me what you want from us."

"We just want to get home," George said solemnly.

"To get to your home is not an easy task."

"So you know where we're from, then?" Millie asked.

"I know as many things as my place in this realm allows," he replied. "There is a way through the worlds that has been retold by our ancestors for many hundreds of years. The same way that Woden uses to travel."

"Do we have to wait until the solstice?"

"Yes, there are ten more days left until the winter sun is still. But first you must train your mind to endure suffering and patience if you are to be strong enough to face the journey." He looked at George and Millie and sadly shook his head. "I fear you will not be able to stand the hardship."

"We would stand *any* hardship! Please tell us what we must do." George insisted.

"Very well. To be able to travel through the branches of the world-tree it is necessary to first fast for nine nights and nine days to enable your mind to reach a state of purity. It is only then that you are able to travel forward through the worlds."

"What? You mean if we starve ourselves we'll be able to time-travel?" Millie felt disappointed. It seemed like nonsense again.

"You have little faith in the power of your mind. I think we cannot help you."

"We would be happy to try anything," George said quickly. "Fasting can't be much different from what the animals do when they hibernate."

"Are we to eat nothing?"

"You may drink."

"Is there anything else we need to do?"

"Whilst you lie in the trees' branches, you will wear cloaks woven with the magic of the Ése and the Wena."

"Who are they?" Millie asked.

"The Ese are the gods that decide our destinies like Thunor and Tiw, whilst the Wena are the gods of new life, like Freo and Eostre," Leof explained.

"Onto your two horses have been loaded the flax of the elves. You must take it to three sisters east of here and there you shall ask them to weave the yarn into cloaks. In return for the yarn, all we ask is for a cutting of your hair."

"Our hair?"

The elf ignored Millie's protest and carried on. "This flax was grown on our sacred mound. After it was harvested it was soaked in springs from the four edges of the kingdom: at the sacred water of Waecc's well in the west, Chich well in the east,[16] Rune well in the north, and Ceald well in the south. When the fibres were separated it was spun with threads of gold on a full moon at the eve of Yule. The sisters will weave into the cloth the pattern of your chosen destinies."

The elf man produced a sharp blade and a leather bag and put them on the table.

George hacked at a chunk of his hair and put it in the bag. He passed the blade to Millie.

"Come on, it will grow back."

"In three years, maybe! It's all right for you, you're a boy."

"It's the same! I don't want to have an odd bit of hair missing. Look, I'll do it for you."

Millie begrudgingly let George cut her hair from underneath. The elf thanked them and left with the bag.

"Now what?" Leof asked.

"I suppose we need to find the three sisters."

They left the hedged garden and walked back to the barrow. They wanted to thank the elves for their help but there was no sign of anyone. Instead they climbed back up the steps to the concealed entrance they had come through. Elvina and Sleipnir were where they had tied them and, as promised, attached to each of them was a bundle of flax yarn in red and yellows.

They followed a path running east through the trees, then came to the Roman road again. On the opposite side of the road the path continued in the same direction. It forked several times but they chose the path that kept the low sun behind them, and this acted as their guide.

Chapter Forty: The three sisters

In the final hour of daylight Millie, George and Leof reached a small dwelling. A woman was sitting outside the building in front of a large weaving loom which stood against the wall. The loom was made from a wooden frame of about four foot by six foot and from it hung woollen thread of many colours. The yarn was kept down at the bottom of the frame by clay weights which kept the vertical yarn straight. The woman didn't look up but carried on with her work. Her fingers flew nimbly over the loom, weaving the wool in front and then behind the vertical threads to create colourful cloth. The woman stopped suddenly and began to push the threads together with a small thread-picker to ensure the thread was woven tightly.

Millie wondered if she should sound out her horn, but decided instead on a polite greeting: "Wes Hal."

"What do you want?" the woman replied rudely and pulled her thick shawl closer around her body. Her voice and manner reminded Millie of the fortune-teller at the Wybrook fête.

"We are looking for someone to weave the flax of elves into two cloaks."

The woman turned to them and they realised she was blind.

"Let me feel it," she said and held out her hands expectantly.

George passed her a bundle of the yarn.

"Hmm ... spun on a full moon ... soaked in ... sacred waters. Do you wish me to weave into it the pattern of your destinies?"

"Yes, if it will help us."

"Then you must stay here with us while they are made. But it will be for a price."

"Of course, what is it you want?"

"Three gold coins and your white horse."

"I'm sorry but the horse is not for exchange," George protectively reached for Elvina's reins.

"Then we can't help you," said the woman and carried on with her weaving.

"Wait," said Millie and turned to George. "You'll have to leave her anyway, why not leave her here?"

"No. What if it doesn't work? I don't want to stay in Widurok and not have my horse."

"George, please. I'm sure they'll look after her."

"Can I not offer you my sword instead?" George asked the woman.

"Three gold coins and your horse there," she repeated.

"I don't mind giving up my gold coins," Leof said opening his leather pouch to count out his money.

"Oh Leof, you don't have to."

"They are only mine because I travelled with you."

Seeing Leof sacrifice the most wealth he would ever have prompted George to do the right thing and promise Elvina to the sisters.

"Okay, for the horse and three gold coins," he reluctantly agreed.

"The elves tell me you are fasting for nine days and nine nights," said a voice from the entrance to the dwelling.

They turned around to see a slightly younger woman of similar appearance, with long silver hair tied into two plaits, and seemingly with better sight.

"There are beds in here where you may sleep. Every morning you must tell us what you have dreamt so that we may learn of your destiny in order to weave it. When your minds have become focused for your journey, the cloaks will be ready."

"But we can't go without eating for nine days. We shall be so weak, we will barely be able to stand," Millie said, still protesting the idea.

"We shall make you a special drink each morning and night from milk and vegetables. It will give you the energy you need. There are many hours of the day when it is dark and you can sleep, for we have no candle-light to keep you awake here. When the sun has risen you may take time to meditate and clear your thoughts."

"We have got ten days until the solstice and we can't go back to Widurok with Sleipnir, so we might as well stay here and do this," George reasoned with Millie. "It'll make Christmas dinner seem even more special!"

"Yes, okay."

"Very well, you have chosen wisely." The woman smiled and called back into the hut, speaking in a tongue neither George, Millie nor Leof could understand.

"Come in and prepare yourself for the night. I will find somewhere for your horses." Neither of the sisters made any comment about Sleipnir and appeared to regard him no differently than Elvina.

The third sister came shuffling across to greet them. She was hunched over almost double and leant heavily on a stick. They followed her inside to where there was bedding laid out. Although the hour was early it was easy to sleep after such a long walk.

In the morning the women set to work as soon as it was light. Next to the weighted loom two other frames were pulled out from the hut. The sisters took the bag of yarn and began fastening the thread around the frame and weighting it down with the clay weights. On one loom the thread hung longer for George's cloak.

Only Leof had been given breakfast and Millie was already beginning to feel hungry. The younger sister brought her the milky drink she had spoken of and asked Millie about her dreams. Millie recollected she had dreamt of a hare, burrowing under a tree. She drank the milk and feeling a little more energised went to look for George. He was sitting at a nearby pond trying to catch some fish, which Millie thought a little pointless when they weren't going to be eating them. Millie sat and watched him, hugging herself as she tried to keep warm.

"Don't you have any hunger pains?" she asked George.

"I'm used to it. There was a bad harvest last year when mostly we only had a little bread soaked in sheep's milk. Not much difference from fasting, really."

"The whole winter?"

"For almost a month. Don't forget, we've been eating with the King's family all autumn. Most ordinary people don't have the luxuries that they do."

"Bread and milk doesn't seem like much to get you through the day."

"You'd be surprised how little a person can survive on. You must get liquid into you, though, can't live without that."

Back at the hut the sisters had many household tasks that they needed help with - logs that were waiting to be chopped for the fire, a loose wooden panel in need of fixing on the outside wall, water to be fetched from the nearby stream, sheep to be milked. The sisters were keen to make the most of having young manpower and Millie, George and Leof felt obliged to help as much as they could, especially in view of the frailty and age of the women. Although on the second day Leof announced to them, rather mysteriously, that he was going on a mission by himself. He left with Fen that morning and didn't return until the following afternoon, not saying a word about where he had been.

Millic found that the hunger pains were less severe if she kept busy and as the days went on she became more used to them, as did George. Every morning they told the sisters their dreams, which they both found they remembered more clearly than they usually did. One night Millie dreamt that she was sitting in the world-tree and a huge eagle was perched on the branch above her and then the next night she dreamt that there was a hawk hovering above her. George too dreamt about the world-tree, that its deep roots were being gnawed at by a dragon and another night that a squirrel was chattering and scurrying up and down the tree trunk. On the ninth and final night George and Millie both dreamt the same dream, that there were four stags eating the few remaining ash leaves on the world-tree. When they told the sisters this, they nodded at them wisely.

"Congratulations, you are now ready in mind and body for the journey ahead. Your time here is now over."

The sisters took the finished cloaks off the looms and held them up to the light. Flickers of gold shone through the red yarn and columns of rune letters woven in yellow ran down each edge of the fabric. The back of the cloaks were decorated with five symbols of the gods.

"Seaxneat's seax to ensure his blessing, Freo's boar to protect you from harm, Woden's raven for success in your quest, Frige's stork to help you home and the blessings of the Eostre hare which brings life with the new dawn."

Millie and George put the cloaks around themselves and felt instantly warmer and protected from the elements.

"Wow, they look amazing!" Leof said as he stopped chopping wood and came to admire the women's handiwork. Their years of experience as weavers was clearly noticeable in the intricate design.

"You must go now, children. The winter solstice will fall in the night."

They thanked the women for all their hard work and set about loading Sleipnir with the saddle-bags. George went to say goodbye to Elvina.

"We will take good care of her and her foal when it is born," the blind woman whispered in his ear.

George looked at Elvina in surprise.

"Did you hear that, old girl, you're going to be a mum soon!" George stroked her long nose and kissed her goodbye. Elvina nuzzled back at him but she made no attempt to follow him as he ran to catch up with Sleipnir and the others.

They walked along a path the sisters had directed them towards, leading to the crossroads at Dunmadu. The path was narrow and strewn with forest debris. Sharp brambles cut into their exposed skin and they took off the cloaks so as not to tear them. The weight of George's sword pulled him down and he longed to rest. But the thought of finally getting home spurred him on.

"I think we should go straight to the circle," George said to Leof.

"Don't you want to return to Widurok before you go?"

"I don't want to say goodbye in case it doesn't work. Besides if it does, it will be easier for you to explain our disappearance."

George desperately wanted to see everyone for one last time and was also disappointed to be missing out on the Yule celebrations, but he knew this was the best way. Leof could tell the villagers that they had been attacked by wolves in the night and that they had fled in different directions. If they were "feared dead", at least if they didn't get back to Wybrook they could then return to Widurok with a plausible explanation.

It was dusk by the time they got near Widurok. Instead of walking through the village they took the path that passed alongside the den and then cut across to the circle.

The runes were already marked on the stones; they could only assume that a Druid or elf had been here earlier and written them out ready for the Modraniht and start of

Yule. The great ash tree stood in the centre, looking very bare now all its leaves had fallen. Sleipnir went straight to the tree and stood by its side looking up at it as he had done before. Leof unstrapped Sleipnir's saddle-bags from him, and took the ironware and seax swords.

"Good luck. I'll be back in the morning to check you're not here," Leof said to them sadly. "I wish I could come with you. Who am I going to go hunting with now?" He hugged both of them tightly in turn.

"I hope you have a good life, Leof" Millie said.

"And both of you too. I've got something for you, Wolf Slayer." Leof reached into his pouch and pulled out a miniature glass jar tied onto a length of leather, like a necklace. He gave it to George.

"What's inside?" he asked.

"Seeds I took from this ash tree and some of its bark. You'll know what to do with it when you are home. From everything you've told me it seems to me that your land is missing the bond of man to nature. That all these forests and animals are gone."

"I don't think I'm going to be able to change that."

"Maybe not, but I hope you have learnt something from us, even if we do seem backward compared to your world," Leof said.

"Of course! I've learnt loads about history ..."

"No, not history, I mean about living in harmony with nature. Your time seems to have forgotten their own home - the earth - and what it provides for them. It *must* be respected and cared for! Failing to value your own home and to treat it with love, failing to plant trees when you cut one down; and failing to reuse things instead of throwing them away, will end in a fate too horrible to think about. Woden would surely weep to see what will come of Middangeard."

George put the ash seeds around his neck. "Yes, I understand what you're saying. Living in this time, I have really become aware of our place on this planet and how much we take our natural world for granted. Thank you, Leof. You have been a good friend to me."

"And you to me, George."

George and Millie took the cloaks and draped them over their shoulders. It was time to climb the tree. Leof gave Millie a leg up to the first branch and then George. Sleipnir seemed contented and laid down as if to rest for the night.

"Say hello to Woden for me, Slippy," Leof said patting his neck. "Wes Hal and happy Yule," he called in final farewell up to the tree, then he walked away with Fen, back to Widurok.

Millie and George found a place to half-sit, half-lie between the branches, although they could barely see each other for the large trunk that divided them.

"I feel like Bessie from *The Faraway Tree*. Do you think each branch takes you to a different land? Don't the Saxons believe there are seven different worlds? How do we know the tree's going to take us to *our* home?"

"I don't think we're meant to talk. The elf said it was important to reach a state of purity in our minds."

They sat silently as darkness surrounded them and they drifted in and out of sleep. After a while Millie awoke so anxious that she didn't feel she could tolerate staying in the tree any longer.

"This is stupid. I think I'm going to get down."

"Give it a chance. It's only been a few hours."

"But I'm so uncomfortable and it's freezing. How can this possibly work?"

"Concentrate your mind."

"How can draping a special cloak over ourselves, or not eating much for over a week, change time?"

"Maybe it doesn't, but maybe it'll work anyway."

Millie knew she had to stay where she was. She couldn't risk being left alone here.

A few hours later it was George that awoke Millie.

"Millie? Are you awake?"

"Hmm. No."

"Do you have any water left?"

"A little."

"Throw it over."

"No, it'll hit the trunk."

"Just swing it then."

Millie swung the water bladder by its strap and George managed to catch it.

"Do you think we'll be home tomorrow?"

"I thought you were asleep."

"You woke me, remember? Won't you miss it here?"

"Yes, I'll always miss it. But I'll still be *here,* in the same place."

The cold of the glass pendant tingled against George's chest. He slowly nodded off again, dreaming that the seeds were alive and trying to burst out and sprout up like Jack's beanstalk.

Chapter Forty-one: The Twenty-first century

They were both woken from their sleep by a hard bump on the side of their bodies. They groaned in pain and realised they were lying on the ground. They must have fallen out of the tree.

"Millie, are you okay?" George called out to the darkness.

"I think so." She said, picking herself up and rubbing the thigh on which she had landed. "Did you fall off the branch, too?"

"I suppose I must have done." George looked around him. Although it was still night it didn't seem quite so dark. There was a faint orangey haze and ... where was the tree they had just fallen out of? All he could make out was the outline of a tall building some metres away. He could hardly dare to believe it!

"Millie ... I think we're home! *I'M HOME! I'M HOME!*" he shouted, as the notion took hold of him. He started laughing and danced around her in circles. "Millie, we're home!" He grabbed her hands, pulling her up and spinning her around with him.

"I can't believe it!" she said, grinning. "I'm so happy! Mum and Dad are going to be ecstatic."

Millie had been missing for over six months now. Their parents would have spent that time completely distraught, having lost both their children.

"Maybe we need to think of a story first."

"No, let's tell them the truth, we owe them that. We can make up a story for everyone else, but they need to know the truth, and Grandad too."

In the cover of the night they made their way to the churchyard gates. To their surprise an untidy-looking white horse was tied to the gate, the same animal Millie had seen outside the Wirde sisters' tepee. Millie smiled to herself, knowing the women were somewhere in the shadows watching them.

"I guess this is our lift home!" she said.

They mounted the horse with George at the front and rode through Wybrook's tarmac streets, lit by electric light and lined with modern brick buildings. At the old shop George pulled on the reins and Millie jumped down. She took the letter and the old T-shirt Bobby had given her and pushed them through Mrs Gordon's letter-box.

Then into the night they went, towards their home town, their minds filled with thoughts and reflections. Some of the journey they took on road and some along the bridleways.

As they entered their town George dismounted and, holding the reins, led them towards their house. He remembered the way as though he had walked it just yesterday. He took them down the side path into the back garden, where Millie dismounted and tied the horse to the clothes line pole. George retrieved the key that was hidden in the shed, where it was always kept, and unlocked the back door for them. The kitchen clock told them it had just gone six; their parents would still be sleeping. George looked around the room. The same crockery set sitting on the shelves and the blue saucepans provoked flashbacks to his childhood. He felt a sudden panic of being displaced and of being a stranger in his own home. Almost as though he, the person he had become, didn't belong here. What if he didn't recognise his parents, or if they didn't care about him anymore?

"Shall we wake Mum and Dad?"

"It's a bit early. I don't want to freak them out. Let's just crash on the sofa." George needed some time to get used to this place again and recover from the shock.

George took the sword off his belt and tried to lean it carefully against the table, but it fell, knocking over a glass which fell to the floor with a clatter. They froze but no one came. In the lounge, Christmas tree lights dimly lit up the room, ready for the celebrations in a few days. Millie noticed how few presents there were around the tree and wondered if any were for her, but she didn't have the heart to look. They flopped onto the sofa with the intention of staying awake until light, but sleep soon took over.

"Ahhhh!" A scream woke them. Their mother was standing at the bottom of the stairs. She was staring at the sofa and at George's sword, which he had left on the carpet.

They both sat up.

"Millie! Oh my goodness! You're okay! I've been so worried. I didn't recognise you with that hair and in that cloak! Thank goodness, oh my goodness, thank you, thank you, you're okay!" she cried emotionally. She threw her arms around Millie and hugged her tightly. There was a loud thumping on the stairs as their father ran down to see what the commotion was about.

"Millie's back!" their mother wept.

George watched them shyly. Their mother hadn't recognised him and had long since given up hope of seeing him again. But their father stopped still and looked straight at his son. He knew that face, those blue eyes and that shade of blonde-brown hair.

"George?"

"Hi Dad," he replied softly.

Ann let go of Millie and stared at George in shock. The emotion was too much for her and she broke down in tears again.

"It's okay Mum, I'm back home now," George said and put his arms around her.

*

The next few weeks passed in a whirl. Journalists and locals alike were caught up in their story. Millie, the missing girl, whose clothes were found in the churchyard last summer had returned home with her brother George - who had himself been missing for over three years! It was a sensational story. Of course no one could be told the truth so instead the family told the police and media that George had run away and had contacted Millie in June, when she had set out on a mission to persuade him to return. The story was believed by most.

George enrolled in college, having missed his GCSE's. He decided to study farming techniques. He had worked for so long on the land that he felt drawn to continuing with this, though his mind was very unsettled. All these years he had lived so differently from his friends and family and had seen things that they would never experience. It was just as hard from him to relate now to the modern world as it had been for him to adjust to the old world. Sometimes George even wondered if he should have stayed in Widurok. Although of course his family were so happy to have him back.

One year in spring Mrs Gordon put her house on the market and started to sell off her belongings. The last anyone in Wybrook ever saw of her was on the day before the summer solstice, when she bade a fond farewell to all of her friends, announcing that the house had been sold and that she would be leaving the next day. Only Grandad knew that she was really going to live out her remaining days with her long-lost son and the seven grandchildren she had yet to meet ...

Once life for Millie and George had settled back into a routine, Grandad thought it was high time he told them all that he knew. Starting with the letter he kept locked away. The opportunity came during lunch one day when George and Millie were staying with him in the holidays.

"In Mr Gordon's search to find out what happened to Bobby, he stumbled across something that related directly to the two of you, something I kept from you."

"What is it?" Millie and George both asked, Grandad's words immediately seizing their attention.

"It seemed like a coincidence at first, I mean Millie was only a toddler at the time, but the two names together? Millie and George? Who else could it be for?"

"What are you talking about?"

"A letter. It was found when the baptismal stone font was replaced at the beginning of the last century. It was placed in a jar to protect it and pushed into a hollow part of the stone. After that it remained amongst some papers in the vestry until Mr Gordon found it. He left it to me after he passed away. I imagine he thought it very peculiar that I'd had two grandchildren named Millie and George, and was trying to warn me."

"Is that the letter I found that day?"

"Yes. I tried very hard to stop George disappearing but I couldn't. So when it came to you, Millie, I thought the best thing to do was to let fate guide you along and just gently push you in the right direction." He passed the jar over to George. "I think you're both ready to read it now."

George carefully pulled out the ancient scroll and read aloud.

Wes Hal Millie and George,

I am writing this letter with the vague hope that it may one day reach you.

Many, many seasons have passed since I last saw you and yet in these final moons of my time on this earth I am still wondering how you both are and if you did arrive home. The morning after I had left you I returned to see if you were still in the tree but you had gone, as had Woden's horse.

I remained in Widurok throughout the winter but the people still regarded me with suspicion and I felt unhappy and restless. When Bordley arrived one summer to meet his mother I was quick to take up his offer of work at Walla and soon after was wed to Burhwynne. They were happy times and I will remain forever indebted to Bordley and his mother for their patient tutoring which enabled my writing studies to develop.

The kingdom changed back and forth between Christianity and the old gods. We ordinary folk never paid this too much attention, but when the first monastery was built I decided to become a monk. My wife had passed on and our children had grown up. It was an opportunity to be a scholar, to read and to write. Meeting you both had left me with a thirst for knowledge and for a better understanding of the world.

A few years ago the priests started to build a church in Widurok and our world-tree was cut down. Although this greatly pains me, I have taken comfort in knowing its magic lies with you and will continue through the ages.

Until we meet again in the otherworld,

Leofwine

George fiddled with the glass pendant he still wore around his neck. There was something he had to do. He excused himself from the table and went out of the house, down the lane and into the churchyard, where it had all began. He pulled the pendant from his neck and broke it open on a stone. In his palm lay the ash seeds and pieces of bark. He opened his fingers and let them fall out and scatter around the tree stump.

Finally George knew his place in the world and where he belonged. He could be at peace knowing that he would live to see the great world-tree spread its branches again. Nature would be abundant here and in all its glory.

Historical Notes

1) The Anglo-Saxon Chronicles are a collection of annals put together in the ninth century to be given out to various monasteries. Part of the collection was copied from the *Ecclesiastical History of the English People* which was recorded in the previous century by a monk named Bede. Both books have been an invaluable source for the study of this period and original copies can be found in the British Library.

2) *The Old English Rune Poem* is an Anglo-Saxon manuscript that lists twenty-nine runes. The original poem was lost in a fire in 1731, although a copied version remains.

3) The *Lacnunga* is a collection of various Anglo-Saxon medical texts, written mainly in Old English. It is kept at the British Library alongside a collection of medical texts; *Harley 585*. It was probably written down during the first decade of the 1000's and was named 'Lacnunga', meaning remedies, by Oswald Cockayne, the collection's first editor.

4) Translation of Riddle 8 of the *Exeter Book*. The *Exeter Book* (*Codex Exoniensis*is) is the largest known collection of Old English poetry in existence. The manuscript was copied down in the tenth century although it is believed that many of its riddles and poems were in use as early as the seventh

century. It was given to Exeter Cathedral by Bishop Leofric (d.1072) where it is still kept in the Chapter Library.

Wiga is on eorþan wundrum acenned
dryhtum to nytte of dumbum twam
torht atyhted þone on teon wigeð
feond his feonde fer strangne oft
wif hine wrið he him wel hereð
þeowaþ him geþwære gif him þegniað
mægeð mæcgas mid gemete ryhte
fedað hine fægre he him fremum stepeð
life on lissum leanað grimme
þe hine wloncne weorþan læteð

5) Translation of Riddle 19 of the *Exeter Book*

Ðeos lyft byreð lytle wihte
ofer beorghleoþa þa sind blace swiþe
swearte salopade sanges rope
heapum ferað hlude cirmað ·
tredað bearonæssas hwilum burgsalo
niþþa bearna Nemnað hy sylfe

6) The first few translated lines of *The Dream of the Rood. The Dream of the Rood* is one of the earliest Christian poems in Old English literature and is believed to have been composed in the 600's. It was preserved in the 10th Century Vercelli Book, kept in Italy and also found on the Ruthwell Cross, now in Scotland. It is written in alliterative verse in a dream-like style.

Hwætme! Ic swefna cyst secgan wylle,
hwætme gemætte to midre nihte,
syðþan reordberend reste wunedon!
þuhte me þæt ic gesawe syllicre treow
on lyft lædan, leohte bewunden,
beama beorhtost. Eall þæt beacen wæs
begoten mid golde. Gimmas stodon
fægere æt foldan sceatum, swylce þær fife wæron

uppe on þam eaxlegespanne..."

7) Extract from *The Wanderer*. An Anglo-Saxon poem found in the *Exeter Book*.

Swa cwæð eardstapa,
earfeþa gemyndig,
wraþra wælsleahta,
winemæga hryre

8) Old Norse legend of day and night.

9) *The Seafarer*. An Anglo-Saxon poem found in the *Exeter Book*.

Mæg ic be me sylfum soðgied wrecan,
siþas secgan, hu ic geswincdagum
earfoðhwile oft þrowade,
bitre breostceare gebiden hæbbe,
gecunnad in ceole cearselda fela,
atol yþa gewealc, þær mec oft bigeat
nearo nihtwaco æt nacan stefnan,
þonne he be clifum cnossað. Calde geþrungen
wæron mine fet, forste gebunden
caldum clommum, þær þa ceare seofedun
hat ymb heortan; hungor innan slat
merewerges mod....

10) The Waelcyrge are the Anglo-Saxon version of the Valkyrie spirit women. They are often seen with, or as, ravens, who take soldiers that are slain from battle to Valhalla (in Anglo-Saxon possibly Waelheall). It is thought this legend comes from when battlefields are strewn with fallen soldiers and ravens attack the bodies.

11) *The Ruin* is an Anglo-Saxon melancholic poem that envisages the former glory of a Roman ruined city by contrasting its grand past with its present state of decay. It was published during the 8th century in the *Exeter Book* by an unknown author.

Wrætlic is þes wealstan, wyrde gebræcon;
burgstede burston, brosnað enta geweorc.
Hrofas sind gehrorene, hreorge torras,
hrungeat berofen, hrim on lime,
scearde scurbeorge scorene, gedrorene,
ældo undereotone. Eorðgrap hafað
waldend wyrhtan forweorone, geleorene,
heardgripe hrusan, oþ hund cnea
werþeoda gewitan. Oft þæs wag gebad
ræghar ond readfah rice æfter oþrum,
ofstonden under stormum; steap geap gedreas.

12) The nine herb charm is an Old-English charm to cure poisoning and infection, recorded in the *Lacnunga* manuscript. Instructions of the charm include crushing the nine herbs - Mugwort, an unknown herb (possibly Cockspur), Lamb's Cress, Plantain, Chamomile, Nettle, Crab-apple, Thyme and Fennel, and then mixing them with soap and apple juice.

The reader is also directed to sing the charm three times over each of the herbs and into the mouth, ears and wound of the patient before applying the salve. These are the verses printed in the *Lacnunga* that Millie writes down her own version of;

gif ænig attor cume eastan fleogan
oððe ænig norðan cume
oððe ænig westan ofer werðeode.
Crist stod ofer adle ængan cundes.
Ic ana wat ea rinnende
þær þa nygon nædran nean behealdað;
motan ealle weoda nu wyrtum aspringan,
sæs toslupan, eal sealt wæter,
ðonne ic þis attor of ðe geblawe.

13) Tafl was played all over Europe, although the name and rules changed over time and amongst different regions.

14) Based on Norse myth. From *The Prose of Edda Gylfaginning,* Paragraph XLII.

15) The goddess Freo was believed to obtain her wealth from precious metals and gems. It was also believed that she directs the Waelcygre to battle to claim soldiers for Woden.

16) Chich spring is now known as St Osyths Spring, named after Queen Osyth. Osyth was the wife of Prince Saeward's grandson, King Sighere - ruler of East-Seax from 664 to 683.

*

King Saberht ruled the Kingdom of Essex (East-Seax) from 604 to 616. Son of King Sledd of Essex and Ricula, sister of King Althelbert of Kent. It is debated amongst historians whether Saberht and his wife Ethelgoda are buried in the original church building at the site of Westminster Cathedral or at the site of a tomb found in 2003 at Prittlewell on the Essex coast.

Seaxred and Saeward (and possibly Seaxbald) jointly ruled the Kingdom of Essex from their father's death. They did convert Essex back to paganism but were killed in battle by the Gewisse (West Saxons) possibly trying to gain control of Surrey. The recorded dates of their deaths vary according to the source, Bede puts it at 617 but more likely it was 623 or later.

Mellitus was a bishop sent from Italy to England by Pope Gregory 1. He became the first Bishop of London in 604. He was exiled from London in 616 by Seaxred and Saeward and took refuge in Gaul. He returned to England in 617 and lived in Kent where he was made Archbishop of Canterbury. He died in April 624.

King Althelbert was ruler of Kent from about 558 to his

death in 616. He married the daughter of the King of Franks, who had the largest power in Western Europe. This alliance gave Althelbert greater strength and influence.

About the author:

Clare Osborne was raised in the Essex countryside and inherited her father's love of history. She left school to become a teacher in Fiji, then after university, went to live and work in the Canadian Rockies, discovering a passion for snowboarding. If she's not lost in the wilderness she can usually be found glued to her laptop, tapping away at her next work of fiction. *Widurok* is her first novel. *[Author photograph: Wallace Matthew Wainhouse]*